Leylah Attar

X0

Moti on the Water
© 2019 by Leylah Attar

Editing by:
Suanne Laqueur

Proofreading by:
Christine Estevez
Soulla Georgiou

Cover Design ©:
Hang Le

Interior Design and Formatting by:
Champagne Book Design

10 9 8 7 6 5 4 3 2 1

ISBN: 978-1-988054-03-2

MOTI
ON THE
WATER

New York Times Bestselling Author
LEYLAH ATTAR

PITCH73 PUBLISHING

For Soulla,
and
for every
friendship
sparked
by bonding over
the pages
of a book

You are invited

BRIDE'S SIDE

• • • • • • • • • • •

Dolly—*Bride's aunt | Moti's mother*
Fia (Sofia)—*Bride's godmother*
Isabelle—*Bride | Moti's cousin*
Joseph—*Father of the bride | Moti's uncle*
Moti—*Bride's cousin*
Naani—*Bride's grandmother | Rachel & Dolly's mother*
Rachel—*Mother of the bride | Moti's aunt*
Teri—*Maid of Honor*

GROOM'S SIDE:

• • • • • • • • • • •

George—*Father of the groom*
Kassia—*Mother of the groom*
Nikos—*Best Man*
Thomas—*Groom*

OTHER:

• • • • • • • • • • •

Alex—*Chef*
Eddie—*Deckhand*
Hannah—*Chief Steward*
Sandra Bailey—*Captain*
Vasilis—*Alex's father*

MOTI

CHAPTER ONE

I T HAPPENED ON A FRIDAY—THE NIGHT MY LIFE DITCHED ITS GPS (General Personal Sensibility) signal and swerved rudely off track, with me still in the vehicle. If life came with a soundtrack, I might've clued in to what was about to go down, but just like that unsuspecting person in a horror movie—the one who has no idea she's about to get slashed or electrocuted or possessed when she walks into the kitchen for some late-night munchies, I was happily peeling 'Made in China' stickers off the place card holders at my cousin's engagement party. Rewind a few moments and you would've found me holding up Isabelle's billowing organza skirt while she peed. So yeah, I was relatively happy on sticker duty.

Each place card holder was a small wooden frame with a heart-shaped cutout. One side displayed the table number and the other had a photo of Isabelle and Thomas holding up a "She said yes!" sign. Their ecstatic faces were framed by blurry autumn foliage, giving them an added romantic glow. It was a beautiful shot. I was probably the only one creeped out by it. It looked like it had been taken by a bug on a branch, balancing on tiny tripod legs that—

"Moti."

I jumped as Rachel Auntie approached. Growing up in an Indian family, anyone who was mildly close to my parents' age had to be addressed as auntie or uncle. You stuck an 'auntie' or 'uncle' after their name, whether they were family or not. If you didn't know their name, you called them Auntie-ji or Uncle-ji.

Children of immigrants realize early on that their parents' rules have exceptions. For example, when you acknowledge the cashier's name tag with *Thank you, Mildred Auntie,* you can expect horrified looks from both your mother and the cashier. If you're astute, you'll understand certain rules apply only to people who share your cultural heritage. If not, a few sharp twists of your ear will drive the point home. This inherited dualism—like your skin color, and the sound of mustard seeds popping in hot oil—follows you through life. Your parents are from *there,* but they live *here.* You are born *here* but will forever straddle the boundaries between here and there.

Rachel Auntie really *was* my aunt—my mom's younger sister and my cousin Isabelle's mother. As such, she *knew* things.

"Moti, don't you think you should be with Dolly?"

"I'll be over as soon as I'm done with these." I smiled, clutching one of the place card holders behind my back. Hopefully she hadn't seen me sticking confetti on it. Getting the stickers off was impossible. They were glued on with industrial-level shit. So now all the frames were sporting half-ripped 'Made in China' labels which was worse, because now everyone would know not only were we using cheap frames, but that we'd tried to hide they were cheap frames. Obviously, the sensible thing to do was cover up the cover-up by sticking table confetti on the labels.

"Moti, it's a big day for Isabelle. You know we can't have Dolly creating a scene. Stop fiddling around with that and come watch your mother."

"Yes, Rachel Auntie." I plopped the place card holder on the table and followed her.

I was twenty-four years old, but when your elders asked you to do something, you dropped everything and saw it through. A sense of duty was drilled into my DNA. It was my job to look after my mother. If you looked at a family closely enough, you'd see that everyone had a job. There were Bosser-Arounders and Bossed-Arounders. War Makers and Bread Bakers. Promise Keepers and Promise Breakers. When you did something enough times, you got a label so everyone else knew what to expect.

"*God, Moti. Don't go to him for a car loan. He's a Penny Pincher,*" or "*God, Moti. Don't ask her for a loan. She's a Helper-Hitter. She'll help you out and then hit you over the head with it for the rest of your life.*"

Labels made life easier for everyone. I was all about labels and mine read 'Mother Minder', meaning I had to mind my mother, Dolly, at family get-togethers. You see, Dolly liked to play dead. Usually at the most inopportune times.

It started off innocently enough, when our neighbor, Shoo Lin, called me at work one afternoon. Her name was really Shu Lin, or maybe Sue Lin, but in my head, she was Shoo Lin because Dolly was always trying to shoo her out of our apartment. On that particular day, my mother pretended to fall asleep to get Shoo Lin to leave. It was almost time for her favorite Indian soap opera, and she couldn't be bothered to make tea or small talk. Shoo Lin panicked at Dolly's unresponsiveness and called me.

"Moti, you need to come home quick. Your mother... She passed away."

She meant my mother had passed *out*, but things get lost in translation and who could blame her? I dropped everything and arrived in record time, along with the paramedics and all the stay-at-home neighbors on our floor.

I won't lie. My initial reaction to the news of my mother's demise was a jolt of relief. It was like telling the canary the cat was dead.

Hallelujah.

Followed promptly by a tidal wave of guilt.

But then Dolly started coughing, just as the paramedics were getting ready to resuscitate her.

Suddenly she was holding court, enthralling everyone with tales of her 'near-death experience.' Over the next few weeks, she was invited to relate her personal account of heaven, which she did with great detail and animation. The episode fanned her flame for theatrics and crystallized into frequent 'crossing-over' scenarios. Dolly loved the buzz, the attention, the stir it created. No one knew just how many air miles she'd racked up with all her trips to the afterlife, except for Rachel Auntie and me—although I had a feeling Rachel Auntie must have shared with her husband.

Joseph Uncle looked relieved as we approached. "Ah, Moti. You'll keep Dolly and Naani company? The guests have started arriving. Your aunt and I need to go greet them."

"Of course." I took the seat he vacated, between my mother and grandmother.

"Did you see the cake?" Dolly tilted her head toward the multi-tiered construction of purple and white frosting. "It's like they're getting married. Who in their right mind—"

"Ma." I shot her a warning look.

"*Offo!*" Dolly waved my concern away. "Your *naani* isn't even listening. Ever since you created a Facebook account for her, she just tunes out. Look at her. On her phone again. She's as bored as I am. I don't know why they're going to all this troubl—"

"You *know* why."

"So what if the groom's family is paying for the wedding? They're millionaires. Billionaires. Joseph and Rachel didn't have to turn the engagement into a huge affair."

"It's a matter of pride. They can't afford the kind of wedding Isabelle and Thomas want, but they want to contribute *something*."

My cousin and her fiancé were getting married in Greece, where Thomas's family lived. The whole wedding party was going on a two-week cruise of the Greek Isles, courtesy of Thomas and his family.

"It's tacky. This whole setup is tacky." Dolly patted her hair. "If anything, it just highlights the difference between us and them. Weddings have turned into a sham, Moti. It's all about showing off. Thank goodness I don't have to worry about yours any time soon."

Most Indian mothers don't rest until they pair their daughters up with a nice boy, but my mother would be perfectly happy if I never got married. She'd constructed a whole reality for me, with boxed-in edges I could not cross. It wasn't her fault, really. Well, maybe partly. When I was born, she consulted the woman who got her pregnant—not in the literal sense, because that would be my dad—but the woman who gave her the fertility potion that finally got her to conceive. A clairvoyant mystic named Ma Anga. Say it with me and let it echo in the dark recesses of your heart. Ma Anga. See how sinister it sounds? Mahhh Angahhh. My nemesis. Probably a toothless octogenarian now, and someone I'd never meet, given that she lived in a remote village in Goa, India.

The day I was born, Ma Anga plotted my birth chart. From the position of the planets, she predicted my soul mate would have two thumbs on one hand (talk about limiting an already-limited dating pool). I would meet this three-thumbed man by the water (thank God Chicago had an accessible waterfront). But I really shouldn't be hanging around the water because I was going to die in the water (hopefully after I met my soul mate, because that would suck). If Ma Anga stopped there, I'd have been ever so grateful. But no. She saved the best for last: if I ended up marrying someone other than my soul mate, my mother would die within seven days.

Now, technically, I could skip the whole marriage thing, move in with a good old-fashioned non-soul mate and live semi-happily ever after, except my mother wouldn't have that either. A good Indian girl goes straight from her parents' house to her husband's house.

If my life were a game of Monopoly, the rules would sound like this: Do not pass Go. Do not collect two hundred dollars. And do not, whatever you do, collect a boyfriend. Or two. Or three, you slut.

Anyway. I never bought into the idea of soul mates. The notion that the universe owed me this one perfect person who fit me completely, loved me unconditionally, gave me toe-curling orgasms, retained his hair, teeth and erections, *and* put up with my shit through every single phase of life, was a huge burden to put on anyone. Hell, *I'd* run the other way if someone expected all of that from me. Not to say I was a complete cynic. I liked the *idea* of a soul mate, but most days I was lucky if I found a hair tie that was compatible with my big, curly hair. So no, I didn't believe in the stars or destiny or all the stuff my mother tried to impress upon me. I figured I would deal with it when I met someone worth putting up a fight for (although the part about my mother dying sat like a gargoyle on the shelf, giving me the side-eye every time I texted a guy). All I wanted was to live my life and not have Dolly play the martyr every time I went out with a normal guy (you know, a guy with an even set of fingers). You'd think she was going to choke on her chai and keel over before I got in the car with him.

A part of me believed deep down, Dolly was just lonely, and this was her way of holding onto me. My parents got married in Goa and moved to Chicago before I was born. They divorced when I was two. My father was long remarried. I didn't see much of him since he'd moved to Atlanta to be with his new family, but he was always calling and checking up on me. I suspect having me had been Dolly's way of trying to hold onto him. Obviously, it hadn't worked. I wondered why Ma Anga didn't predict *that* when she was soaking toadstools for Dolly's fertility potion.

Ma Anga was also the one who named me Moti. It means pearl in Hindi, but only when you say it with a soft T—with your tongue between your teeth: Mo-thi. When you say it with a hard T, Mo-tee, like most people do, it means fatty or chubby. This slight mispronunciation ruined my childhood. It wasn't the kids in school who teased me. They didn't know their soft Ts from their hard Ts. It was my family—aunts, uncles, cousins, second cousins, and one elderly guy who showed up at every wedding—but no one knew who he was. Of course, it didn't help that I was soft and doughy and jiggled when I ran—which, quite often, was to get away from them.

I might've outrun most of my baby fat, and I was done contemplating a name change, but as I sat between my mother and grandmother—Dolly and Naani—I still felt like apologizing for taking up too much space. Too much air, too much food, too much water. Maybe if I'd been named Isabelle, things would be different. Maybe I'd be able to wear billowing organza skirts and be okay peeing in front of other people. I mean, Isabelle is a statement in itself: She Is A Belle. Don't get me wrong. I was plenty hot—in an Adele-esque way. I could set fire to the rain. Yes. Yes, I totally could. I sat up straighter, pulling my shoulders back.

My grandmother patted my hand under the table. Maybe she caught me watching Isabelle. Maybe she overheard all the times my mother said, "Why can't you be more like your cousin Isabelle, or Monica or Rupa, or [insert name of random brighter, prettier go-getter]?"

"Tumhari baari bhi aayengi. Aur tabh, tum sirf apni dil ki hi soon na," Naani said. *Your turn will come too. And when it does, don't listen to anything but your heart.*

She spoke English but reverted to Hindi when she was dishing out advice. My brain was hardwired to sort her speech accordingly. Everything she said in English went into the temporary cache. Everything she said in Hindi got etched into my subconscious.

Naani leaned in and winked. "Khaas kar ke, uski baaton me mat aana." *Most especially, don't listen to her.*

I laughed. She meant my mother.

"What did you say?" Dolly tuned in, but Naani had already gone back to her phone.

"Oh look. They're here! Come, Naani." I helped her up. "Rachel Auntie wants us all to welcome Thomas and his parents together."

Dolly, Naani and I made our way to the entrance of the banquet hall, where Thomas was struggling to breathe as Joseph Uncle held him in a tight, wiggle-free hug. *You're here, and you're going to marry my daughter! There is no getting out of this now.*

Isabelle cheek-kissed her future in-laws—George and Kassia—while Rachel Auntie beamed as bright as the shimmering beads on her sari.

Growing up, all Isabelle and I heard was, "You have to marry an Indian fellow. Marriage is hard enough without having to gap cultural differences. Make your life easier, and ours too. Marry an Indian fellow."

Indian fellow.

Indian fellow.

What they'd neglected to tell us was the footnote, the loophole, the asterisk: "Marry an Indian fellow unless you land a gazillionaire. Then marry him." Money circumvented a lot of things—opinions, traditions, cultural differences. Of course, the gazillionaire couldn't be a total asshole. And he had to love masala chai, because you can't really bond with someone until you've poured steaming hot masala chai from cup to saucer, swirled it with practiced precision, and slurped it together. That's the way things rolled in my family.

"God, he's a looker," Dolly mumbled under her breath after Isabelle introduced us to Thomas and his parents.

I wasn't sure if she was talking about Thomas or his silver-haired father, who had excused himself to answer his phone. Naani, on the other hand, had more important things on her mind. Like food. She was already zigzagging her way back to the table. She had no problems walking but her balance was off, and she refused to use a cane.

"It's okay. You go." Rachel Auntie traded places with me, standing behind my mom. *I've got your mother. You look after your grandmother.*

It was a blatant switch of our familial roles, but she'd obviously hedged her bets. Between my mother playing dead and my grandmother crashing into the chocolate fountain, the latter was a bigger concern. Much easier to pick Dolly off the ground than clear up a gooey mess of ganache with panache.

"*Beta*, can you get me a glass of water?" asked Naani, sinking into her seat.

"Of course." I scanned the room and noticed pitchers of

water lined up on a table in the back. Picking up the train of my *lehenga*, I made my way toward them. The lady at the store had helped me pair the long embroidered skirt I was wearing with a matching *choli* on top. It was emerald green, with gold embroidery at the border and a scattering of small stones that caught the light.

"So beautiful against that lovely dark hair of yours," she said. "Use some kohl to rim your eyes and you'll knock 'em dead."

"What about this?" I pointed to the patch of skin peeking between the top and skirt.

"That's the style. A bare midriff is sexy! You can always cover it up with your dupatta." She draped the long, sheer scarf around me.

I eyed my reflection. "Can we alter it? Lengthen the top a little?"

She assumed I was too modest to show a little skin, but really I just wanted to be able to wear my Spanx underneath. Nothing stops you from going after that third chicken samosa than being trussed up in a sausage-like encasing.

"Can I get you something?" asked one of the waiters coming out of the kitchen.

"Just helping myself to some water." I smiled as I grabbed a glass and reached for the pitcher.

Okay. Let's freeze this moment for a second.

This moment right here, where I'm reaching for the pitcher.

Because this is the moment where everything starts unraveling.

Are you ready?

Okay. Unfreeze.

My fingers grasped the pitcher the exact moment someone else went for it. Which happens. Someone always goes for the same doughnut I want at work. No biggie.

What *was* a biggie—what made my jaw drop and what warranted this freeze-frame, was the weird little nubbin sticking out of this person's thumb. A dwarf thumb, complete with a miniature nail, like a deviated knob growing off a ginger root.

Polydactyly.

An extra digit in the hand or foot.

More specifically, pre-axial polydactyly.

When that extra digit is a thumb.

Chances of running into a person with this condition: 1 in 1,000. Or was it 1 in 10,000? I should know. I'd googled it enough times, but the only numbers running through my mind at that moment were 1 and 2.

1: Holy

2: Shit

And so I stood there, thumberstruck...er...thunderstruck. It's not every day you get to see an extra thumb in the wild. Trust me. I'd side-eyed many hands—on the bus, at the grocery store, on park benches and, I'm ashamed to say, in the play area at McDonald's (that's mostly dads chasing after their kids, but desperate times call for desperate measures, and who knows—single dad, double thumbs?).

Somewhere between the *Holy* and the *Shit*, my brain was running a background check.

Male hand: check

Age-appropriate: check

Wedding-ring free: check

DING, DING, DING!

No. Wait. Un-check. Wedding ring would be on the other hand.

Dare I look up? I hadn't thought about anything beyond this point, but now that my unicorn was here, I wanted him to be attractive too. To hell with not looking a gift horse in the mouth, because if there was the slightest possibility of me kissing that mouth, then I sure as hell wanted to know what it looked like.

I looked up.

My stomach flipped.

Not just a regular flip but one of those Olympic dive sequences: two-and-a-half somersaults followed by two-and-a-half twists in two-and-a-half seconds. Then my stomach disappeared somewhere in the vicinity of my ovaries, which held up scorecards for the miraculous sequence of human DNA before me.

Ovary 1: "10"

Ovary 2: "01"

Ovary 1: "Seriously?"

Ovary 2: "Hell, yeah! No, wait." (Flips scorecard over.) "10!"

That's when Mr. 10-Out-Of-10 spoke.

"Here." He picked up the pitcher and filled my glass.

My hand fell away from his. I darted a glance at his other hand. No wedding ring.

Yesssssss!

"I'm Nikos," he said, filling his own glass and looking at me.

His eyes were grape green. I know that sounds flat and boring. You want me to say jade green or pine green—the color of the forest after it rains, the color of springtime ferns. But if you knew how much I love food, you'd understand I was awarding him the highest honor. Granted, I could have gone with something more poetic, like fresh asparagus tips, but asparagus makes your pee smell funny.

"Hi, I'm Moti."

What the fuck? Did I just say my own name with a hard T? Hi, I'm Fatty.

"Moti?" he repeated.

"Moti. With a soft T."

"Moti Wither-Softy?"

Good thing I wasn't hiding man parts under my Spanx or I might've taken the *Wither-Softy* part personally. I didn't bother correcting him because I planned to take his last name anyway. I was all about the stars now. And destiny. And soul mates. And all the shit I didn't believe in before.

Nikos's eyes were roving over my body.

Holy crap, it's happening. The planets are aligning. Heavenly cherubs are singing HALLELUJAH.

Thank you, Spanx Gods, and the three sit-ups I did two days ago.

Thank you, rice cakes.

Thank you, steamed vegetables.

"Cheers," Nikos held up his glass and downed it.

I wondered if he tackled sex as ravenously as he drank. I was sure he'd prefer something stronger than water, but Joseph Uncle wasn't about to foot the bill for an open bar. Water, juice, soft drinks, and masala chai. Anything else, you were on your own, buddy.

Nikos wore a blue dress shirt, snug pants, and a black leather belt slung around narrow hips. Not an ounce of extra flab on him—all trim and tight and toned. His hair was slick and luminous, sculpted back with gel and precision. A triangle of sun-kissed skin peeked over his collar. It was February in Chicago. He was obviously from Thomas's side of the family. I watched his throat clench and unclench as he drained his glass. It did weird things to my internal combustion engine.

I took a sip of water to cool down and choked. Why? Because I realized I'd met him by the water. The pitchers of water. Just as Ma Anga predicted. And now I was going to die in the water. Or rather, from choking over a mouthful of water.

Oh God. Please don't let it be so.

"Are you okay?" asked Nikos.

If you've never choked on water in public before, let me tell you, it's the worst thing ever.

No. I take that back. Choking on water in front of someone you're trying to impress is the worst thing ever. Your eyes are tearing, your face is red. You're trying to look cool while spasming all over the place.

I held up one finger and nodded. "Excuse me," I croaked and stumbled away.

I managed to march a few feet before bending over and giving in to a fit of short, loud coughs. Water spilled from my glass as I gasped and coughed and gasped some more. When my breathing got easier, I high-fived myself and straightened. I was going to live.

Take that, Ma Anga.

Refusing to sneak a look over my shoulder and see if Nikos had witnessed my ability to suck water down my windpipe and survive, I made my way back to the table.

"Here you go." I placed the glass before Naani, hoping she wouldn't notice it was only half-full. "Naani, do you see that guy in the back? By all the jugs of water?"

"Who?" She swiveled around and then nodded. "*Achha*, him?"

"Don't make it so obvious," I whispered. "What's he doing? Is he looking this way?"

It's sad when your wing-woman is your grandmother, but I had to find a way to learn more about Nikos before the evening was over. Like was he seeing anyone? A girlfriend? A boyfriend? A parole officer?

"He's wiping the table, Moti."

"What?" I turned around and saw one of the waiters where I had left Nikos.

"Eh?" Naani elbowed me. "You like him?"

"Yes. I mean, no. Not him." My eyes scanned the banquet hall, searching for the sun-kissed Greek god. "You won't believe this. I just met a guy with three—"

"There you are." I felt a sharp tap on my shoulder. It was Isabelle. She leaned in and lowered her voice. "You're supposed to be looking after *me*. That's what a maid of honor is for."

"Sorry, I was just—"

"Never mind. This is a practice run. But honestly, Moti. You can't be taking off on me at the wedding. Come on. We have to get seated." She pulled me up and dragged me away. Halfway to the front of the hall, she slipped and teetered, precariously close to landing on her ass. "What the hell? There's water all over the floor."

Oops. Flashback to me, spilling water as I coughed and sputtered my way back to life.

I *tsked* and shook my head. "Unacceptable. I'll go talk to the event coordinator."

"Later. We need to get on stage right now."

The stage was a raised platform, put up at Isabelle's request. She wanted her table elevated above the guests. I helped her up the makeshift stairs, holding her skirt so it didn't get caught in her heels. Thank God she hadn't fallen earlier because I can't stop myself from laughing when people fall. It's a knee-jerk reaction and I'm very sorry for it afterward, but I'm pretty sure laughing at the bride-to-be would get the maid of honor fired. Not that I'd applied for the position. Isabelle didn't have many friends, and she couldn't be her bossy self with the ones she did. So, the honor had landed on me. Blood is thicker and more boss-aroundable than water because blood takes longer to say, "Screw it. I'm outta here."

Thomas smiled warmly as I arranged Isabelle's skirt and draped it around her chair. He was charming and easy-going, with thick black hair, the same color as his eyes. His parents were seated at the first table, with Rachel Auntie and Joseph Uncle. I caught Rachel Auntie's eye between the pillars of the tiered cake before me. She gave me a discreet thumbs-up; I assumed because Dolly was behaving.

I sat back in my chair and then shot up again. Nikos was weaving through the hall, making his way purposefully toward me.

Holy hell.

Had he felt a connection? Was he being compelled by mysterious forces to seek me out? Was he helpless against the pull that was drawing him nearer and nearer?

God, he was hot. Bold thighs, firm chest. Sleek, sexy, and hopefully single.

Did I call Ma Anga my nemesis? She was a fucking goddess. I was already buying plane tickets for myself, Nikos, and our two kids so I could make the pilgrimage to India and kiss her feet.

My heart was pounding so hard by the time Nikos reached me, I thought I was going to pull a Dolly and pass out at his feet. He took the stairs to the stage, two at a time, and…walked right past me to take the chair next to Thomas.

"Did you meet Nikos?" asked Isabelle. "He's going to be Thomas's best man at the wedding."

My mouth formed a silent O. I was simultaneously deflated and elated—the anti-climax of him *not* singling me out and the realization that he was the best man and I was the maid of honor. Could it get anymore meant-to-be than that?

"Is he related to Thomas?" I asked.

"Childhood friends." Isabelle leaned toward Thomas and flashed a brilliant smile as the photographer took their photo. Nikos had a colossal flower arrangement in front of him and I was hidden behind the cake. Clearly, it would save Isabelle from having to crop us out of the pictures.

A little band of photographers worked its way through the guest tables. Joseph Uncle and Rachel Auntie really went all out. Not many people from the bride's side would be able to attend the wedding in Greece, so the engagement party was in lieu of the ceremony they'd be missing

"Ladies and gentlemen, if I could have your attention, please." Nikos got up and clinked a fork against his glass. "On behalf of Thomas, Isabelle, and their families, I'd like to welcome you here tonight…"

He had a delicious English-isn't-my-first-language accent that told me he could curl his tongue around words and caress them in ways that—

"Moti," Isabelle hissed. "Are you listening?"

"Sorry, what?" I scooted closer.

"My flower is slipping."

I tucked it back in her hair. "So…will Nikos be coming with us on the cruise?"

"Of course. He's part of the wedding party."

"Just him? No wife, no girlfriend?"

"He's not married. And as far as I know, he's not bringing anyone to the wedding either." Isabelle shot me an impatient look. She was too high on engagement fever to put two and two together. Maybe she never saw his thumbs up close to connect the dots.

"Sorry. I just…" I trailed off. This was Isabelle's day. Now was not the time to bring up the best man's extra digits.

Nikos was making a toast. We raised our glasses. I caught a glimpse of his ass, but then Isabelle's up-do obscured it. As any self-respecting woman would, I tilted my chair a smidgen to get a better view. Now the back of Thomas's head was in the way.

Dammit. What does a maid of honor have to do to check out the best man's butt?

I scraped my chair back a few inches.

Next thing I knew, my chair toppled over the edge of the platform with me on it. I gasped as I hit the floor. The sparkling grape juice I'd been holding up to toast Isabelle and Thomas splashed on my face like a cold, rude bitch-slap. Miraculously, no one seemed to notice, given that I was pretty much hidden behind the cake. I might've recovered, gotten off the floor, picked up my chair and, *"Heigh-ho, back to work I go."* But no, I was stuck, my chair wedged in the space between the back of the platform and the wall. Caught at an angle, I stared at the ceiling with my legs sticking straight up toward it, my bum still on the seat. A classic Pilates position—the V-Up. Go ahead. Look it up. I'll wait. It's not like I'm going anywhere.

Isabelle turned around at the thud of my hundred and forty-five-pound frame hitting the floor at a forty-five-degree angle. Then Thomas caught on. He looked startled to see me with my *lehenga* up around my ears, but Isabelle stopped him from getting up. She was smiling at whatever Nikos was saying. Poor Thomas looked confused.

Welcome to the family, bro, I thought. *Appearances are everything. The show must go on. I'll just lie here until I figure out which is going to kill me first. Death by Underwear (my Spanx is killing me) or Death by Embarrassment (please don't let Nikos turn around and see me like this).*

And then it struck me. I'd let Rachel Auntie down. All this

time she'd been concerned about Dolly making a scene and there I was, Master of Disaster.

I blinked at the ceiling. *Why are you so hopeless, Moti?*

After Nikos finished his speech, Isabelle summoned the event coordinator to help me up. Discreetly. Seamlessly. So that, while dinner was being served, Mission Moti was covertly under way behind the stage.

"Thank you." I heaved a sigh of relief once I got dislodged from the chair. My clothes had a huge wet spot, my hair was sticky from grape juice, but I was still holding my glass. I might've goofed big time, but I'd kept the glass from shattering.

"So sorry," I said to Isabelle.

"That won't be necessary," she said, waving away the event coordinator who was propping my chair back on the platform. "I think you should go sit with Naani and Dolly Auntie, Moti."

"I…um… Okay." I grabbed a napkin to hide the wet spot on my clothes.

That's when I realized that I was being fired as Isabelle's maid of honor.

I should've felt relieved. I wouldn't have to worry about throwing Isabelle the perfect bridal shower. Or making goody bags with loofahs, lotions, and scented beads that made me break out in a rash. No more agonizing over how I'd pay for the frothy peach concoction the maid of honor was supposed to wear. Yet, I felt the complete opposite. I'd failed at something yet again.

Aware of the curious eyes on me, I plastered on a smile as I made my way through the guest tables.

"Why is your skirt wet?" asked Dolly. "What happened? Why aren't you sitting with Isabelle?"

"She doesn't want me there."

"You messed up, didn't you, Moti? I knew it. I knew you'd end up doing something silly. And for God's sake, wipe that stupid grin off your face. This is shameful. Disgraceful. How am I going to show my face to everyone?"

"Are you okay, *beta*?" Naani asked, while Dolly rambled on.

I squeezed her hand and nodded.

"So. What did you do?" Dolly asked.

"I…uh…" I opened my purse, pretending to look for something. My hand closed around the thin, wrapped bar of hand soap I'd swiped from the ladies' room. I rubbed it back and forth between my fingers.

"Dolly. Let her be." Naani finished her dinner and pushed her plate away. "Did you eat, Moti?"

"Yes, Naani." What was I going to say? That my food was sitting on Isabelle's table? That I didn't deserve to eat?

I looked away and caught Nikos smiling at me from behind the fronds of a huge fern. Maybe he was laughing because he saw what happened, but that was okay. I laughed when people fell too. And I'd gone for the water the same time *he'd* gone for the water. My face had been hidden by a giant prop on the table. *His* face was hidden by a giant prop on the table. My God, we had so much in common. Could we be any more perfect for each other?

I felt myself grow lighter. I'd just been dislodged from a tight spot—literally and figuratively. Me, falling over backward, could quite possibly have been the best thing to happen to me. And better things were yet to come. Like Nikos falling for me. Just because I was no longer the maid of honor didn't mean I couldn't light a fire under the best man.

My mind cut to a picture of me running barefoot on a beach in Greece—flowy white dress, lasso in hand, a beautiful sunset in the backdrop. Nikos was running up ahead. I threw the rope, cut the slack, and tightened the noose. BOOM. Nikos landed at my feet.

Granted, him being all trussed up wasn't exactly the picture of happily-ever-after, but sometimes a girl just has to go for it and hope for the best—especially when it's the one thing keeping her afloat in the sea of drowning dreams.

I had three months to step up my game.

Three months to Isabelle's wedding.

Two weeks on a family cruise to win over the only man my mother would approve of.

One window of opportunity to break free.

I was ready for this. So, so ready for this.

I put away my purse and smiled back at Three-Thumbed Nikos.

Darling, the stories we're going to tell our children.

CHAPTER TWO

FIRST IMPRESSIONS ARE IMPORTANT, ESPECIALLY THE SECOND TIME around.

I planned meticulously for the next time I saw Nikos, including the speed and direction of the wind, so I'd know which way to face to get that sexy, blown-out, Beyonce-on-stage look. Maybe I was overcompensating for not losing all the weight I wanted to. My clothes were creased from the long flight to Athens, *but* I had the wind situation under control. What I did not anticipate was the yacht.

Holy Mother of Jet-Set Luxury.

I shielded my eyes from the Aegean sun as I looked up. It wasn't just a private, chartered boat but an insanely extravagant mega-yacht with a glistening gold-trimmed superstructure. A line of sweeping portholes suggested an equally impressive interior. In the row of ships moored at the marina, Isabelle and Thomas's love boat cut a sleek, majestic figure. I was going to be on it for two weeks. With Three-Thumbed Nikos.

My ship had come in, quite literally. I should've been swarming the deck, but I had a moment of hesitation—a panic attack knocking at my door. Maybe it was Ma Anga's warning about how I would die in the water. Maybe it was my brain's fear center having a hissy fit because I couldn't swim. Maybe it was the weight of all the expectations I'd piled onto this one trip that were making it hard to breathe. Or maybe I'd simply inherited Dolly's uncanny ability to find drama where none existed.

"Come on, Ma." I took a deep breath and tugged Dolly up

the staircase connecting the yacht to the dock. Yes, an actual teak staircase. No gangway or footbridge to board this baby. Never in my life had I played it so cool while simultaneously freaking out.

A uniformed blond in a white polo shirt and khaki shorts greeted us. "Welcome aboard the Abigail Rose II. You must be Moti and Dolly. I'm Hannah, your Chief Steward. Anything you need, I'm your go-to person." She pronounced my name perfectly. She was competent and confident, the kind of person who'd dive into the water after a flailing passenger while simultaneously giving you makeup advice. I liked her right away.

"We have a barefoot policy on the yacht, so please remove your shoes and deposit them in the basket." Hannah pointed to a jute basket that already had a pile of shoes in it. "Heels can damage the decks and dirty soles leave scuff marks, but you're welcome to wear clean socks or light-soled shoes reserved for indoor use."

I removed my shoes and accepted the cold towel and drink she offered. Dolly sniffed the lightly perfumed towel before dabbing her face and plopping it back on the tray. She was miffed we'd missed the official meet-and-greet with the crew, as well as the extra three nights in Athens that the rest of the wedding party had arrived earlier for. But since I worked for Joseph Uncle and we were both on this cruise at the same time, two weeks off was the best I could do.

When Dolly was pissed, she liked to get everyone around her riled up. Seething over something together is more satisfying than silently fuming in your own corner. On the flight to Athens, she declared I must be suffering some sort of chemical imbalance for not being more upset with Isabelle for firing me as her maid of honor. By the time we were flying over England, the diagnosis changed to *microdeckia* (not playing with a full deck of cards) because I wasn't livid at being replaced by a hired professional (yes, there is such a thing as maids-of-honor-for-hire—guaranteed not to topple off platforms or choke on water at inopportune times).

When she didn't get the response she wanted, Dolly mumbled something about my genetic makeup and babies switched at birth. Then she fell into a deep, blissful sleep (well, blissful for me).

She seemed impressed by the opulence of our surroundings as we followed Hannah through the onyx-floored foyer to the elevator.

"Everyone else is at the safety briefing," Hannah said. "I'll show you to your stateroom and we'll get you up to speed once you've settled in."

"May I have a look at that?" Dolly pointed to the clipboard Hannah was holding. It had a list of all the passengers and their rooms:

AFT DECK:
Cabin One, Owner's Suite: Kassia and George
Thomas's parents.

Since they had chartered the boat, it was only fair that they get the biggest suite.

LOWER DECK
Cabin Two, VIP Suite: Nikos and Thomas
The best man, a.k.a. my future husband.
And the groom.

Cabin Three: Rachel and Joseph
My aunt and uncle.

Cabin Four: Naani and Isabelle
My grandmother and my cousin, the bride.

Even though Isabelle and Thomas were getting married, sharing a room before they tied the knot was a big no-no. Both sets of parents liked to pretend their kids had never slept together. I guess that's fair. You don't want to think about your parents having sex either. Ever.

Cabin Five: Dolly and Moti (pronounced with a soft 't')

I smiled at Rachel Auntie's handwritten note, the reason Hannah pronounced my name correctly.

Cabin Six: Teri and Sofia

Teri was the hired maid of honor. I met her at Isabelle's bridal shower. She was also a professional hair and makeup artist, which worked out great for Isabelle. That left Sofia as the mystery guest Isabelle had been talking about.

Six cabins, twelve passengers, all paired up and ready to rock and roll (hopefully not in a motion-sickness kind of way). It seemed fittingly symbolic—two cabins for the groom's side and four cabins for the bride's side. In other words, Isabelle managed to negotiate double the share. Thomas would do well to heed that ratio when it came to everything else—double the maintenance, double the drama. On the flip side, Thomas managed to hold on to the biggest staterooms for his side of the family, so maybe he wasn't a complete pushover.

"Thank you." Dolly handed the clipboard back to Hannah.

"You're welcome," Hannah replied, as she ushered us into our suite. "One of the deckhands will drop in shortly with your bags. I'll stop by later to help you unpack and give you a quick tour of the yacht. We're waiting on a delivery for Isabelle and one of the passengers, Sofia, is yet to arrive. Once they're here, it's anchors up!" She mini-hopped out of the room like she couldn't contain her enthusiasm.

"Wow." *Help you unpack?* Had I known, I would've rolled my bras up more carefully.

I plopped on the sofa and surveyed the cabin. Sliding doors with a private balcony on one side and an en suite bath on the other. We had two twin beds, a wall-mounted TV, a fridge, snack cabinet, and a double closet. The bathroom was just as spacious, with double vanity sinks, a heated towel rack, shower cubicle, toilet, and a soaking tub. Every amenity had been thought of, including an iPad to control the thermostat and entertainment system.

Dolly lay on her bed and stared at the ceiling. "Moti?"

"Yes, Ma?"

"I'm sorry for what I said to you on the plane earlier."

My heart softened like it always did with the slightest bit of affection from her. "It was a long flight. We were both tired."

"So, this Nikos fellow, with the three thumbs. Is he as rich as Thomas?" She turned on her side and faced me. "Can you imagine? My Moti ending up with someone like him? You can't be your plain, boring self on this trip. Guys like mystery, adventure, someone who's worth the chase. You should take a few tips from Isabelle. She knows how to play her cards right."

All the warmth seeped out of me as my plan to get together with Nikos was twisted into something ugly.

"I'm not interested in him for his money, Ma. I'm interested in him because he's the only one I can be with, without feeling like I'm going against your wishes—"

"Moti!" The door to our cabin flew open and Isabelle swept in. "I'm so glad you're here. My wedding dress needed alterations and the tailor is here with it, but they won't let him into the shipyard. Would you mind collecting it from him? He's waiting on the street. In a silver Toyota Yaris."

I wanted to ask what a Toyota Yaris looked like. Instead, I found myself nodding.

Silver.

I just had to look for a silver car and a man with a big white dress.

How hard could it be, right?

Wrong.

I located the car, but it was parked on the other side of the street. After three close calls, I realized zebra crossings in Greece were nothing more than a bunch of pretty stripes designed to lure you to your final resting place. I was completely invisible to the drivers and motorcyclists. To make matters worse, I'd rushed out without my shoes and my feet were hopping like popcorn on the hot asphalt. On the plus side, my hippity-hoppity dance got me noticed by a driver who slowed down and stared long enough for me to cross.

Getting back to the other side of the street with a voluminous wedding dress was even more difficult. I waited for one of the locals to cross and then used him as a human shield. As I made my way back to the yacht, I caught sight of Nikos standing on one of the outside decks. The afternoon sun glinted off his hair as he leaned against the rail. He looked carefree and relaxed, like hanging out on exclusive boats was something he did every day. Wait. He did. At least according to his social media.

I pushed aside a twinge of insecurity. Maybe I was setting my sights too high? Maybe I really should take some lessons from Isabelle. Three months and a shitload of self-help books don't fix self-esteem issues.

There were puddles everywhere, from people power-washing their boats and dinghies. I skirted a big, muddy one around the marina, carefully holding Isabelle's dress up. My shoulders were starting to ache from the weight, when a guy on a motorbike zoomed past me. I barely had time to register the blur of his yellow helmet before my mouth opened in a silent scream.

Noooooo.

Stop. Now slow it down and play it at 50 percent, in that deep, low pitch.

It's the kind of sound that pairs well with a slow-motion fall in a movie, like when the hero sees someone about to be shot and takes the perpetrator down. In this case, I saw myself about to be shot. By Isabelle. Because this guy, this idiot, this *moron* on a motorbike, left a tsunami of dirty water in his wake.

I gasped the split second before it hit me. I should say *us,* because at this point, Isabelle's dress was a living, breathing thing

I had to protect. With my life. I huddled over, rolling it up and shielding it with my torso.

Take me. Take me instead.

The water hit me like a tail slap from a humpback whale, drenching my clothes, my hair, my face.

Pit, pat, pit, pat. It fell off as I straightened. It took a few seconds before I could bring myself to look at the wedding dress.

Oh, Sweet Mother of All That is Holy and Sweet.

It was still spotless and white beneath the clear plastic bag. The good tailor had the foresight to knot the bag, so it was sealed at both the top and bottom.

I hugged the dress. The tailor. God. Everyone that needed to be hugged, and set off for the boat again.

I'm coming, Abigail Rose II.

Hannah and a couple of the crew members jumped when they saw me—barefoot, drenched, and looking like a zombie rat.

"Are you okay?" Hannah cried. "What happened?"

The other two crew members got busy cleaning up the mess I was dripping all over the floor.

"Can you please dry this off and get it to Isabelle?" I handed Hannah the wet bag with the wedding dress inside it. I would've done it myself, but I couldn't chance Nikos seeing me like this.

I took the elevator down and peered into the hallway when the doors opened.

Yes! All clear.

Tiptoeing to the theme song of The Pink Panther, I was about to step into my suite when I noticed Dolly standing outside one of the other staterooms, her ear pressed to the door.

"What are you doing?"

"Shhh. They're having a big fight."

"Who?"

"Joseph and Rachel and Isabelle. What happened to you? Why are you..." She trailed off as the voices on the other side of the door escalated.

"Stop eavesdropping, Ma."

"It's not eavesdropping if you can hear it out in the hallway. You missed the whole thing. The shit hit the fan. Big time."

I could hear Joseph Uncle and Isabelle shouting. Rachel Auntie was sobbing.

"What's wrong?" I asked.

"We were all hanging out in the salon when Joseph said he had a gift for Thomas's parents. He came back up with a huge heart-shaped box filled with underwear and presented it to George and Kassia. He said it wasn't much, but it was his way of thanking them for the cruise. Isabelle was utterly humiliated. She was livid Joseph didn't check with her first. Apparently, she's been too ashamed to tell Thomas and his parents that her father sells underwear for a living. She said he's a successful entrepreneur and left it at that."

"All my life!" Isabelle was screaming inside. "Laal chadi, pili chadi, neeli chadi."

Red panties, yellow panties, blue panties.

"I'm sick of it. I'm sick of explaining what you do to everyone."

"What's wrong with what I do?" Joseph Uncle said. "Covering your privates is an honorable thing. I'm providing an excellent, humanitarian service, and I make good money doing it. Why should I keep it from anyone? You have no problem walking down the street with bags full of stuff from La Perla. Why is it okay for you but not for me?"

"Because! It's not the cheap, polyester stuff you sell, Dad."

"Let me set you straight. The cheap, polyester stuff put you through college. The cheap, polyester stuff paid for your car. And your hair. Your nails. Your bags. Your shoes. The cheap, polyester stuff keeps a roof over our heads. And you're telling me you're *ashamed*? Now? Because you're all set, and you don't need your father anymore? This is the thanks I get?"

"You should've told me what you planned to do. What are Kassia and George going to do with a bunch of neon thongs? What are they going to think?"

"If you're so concerned about what *they* think, why don't you just leave me out of it? Why bother inviting me? I didn't come here to be humiliated by my daughter. In fact, I'm getting off this boat right now."

"Joseph!" Rachel Auntie spluttered. "You don't mean that."

"I do. If she's so ashamed of me, she can get someone else to walk her down the aisle because I sure as hell won't be doing it."

"You can't!" cried Isabelle. "You can't back out now!"

"Jose—"

"You." Joseph Uncle cut Rachel Auntie off. "This is all *your* fault. Always siding with her, always spoiling her. And now this. She insults me, belittles what I do and you're *still* siding with her."

"I'm not siding with her. I'm just trying to stop a bad situation from getting worse—"

"Get out of my way. Both of you. Where's my bag?"

"Dad. Stop!"

"Joseph." This time there was steel in Rachel Auntie's voice. "Our daughter is getting married. You are *not* getting off this boat and neither am I. I know you're angry, but—"

"I said get out." Joseph Uncle swung the door open. Dolly and I took a guilty jump back. He scowled at us and then glared at Isabelle and Rachel until they left the cabin.

We were all squirming in our skin when he shut the door on our faces. A few awkward beats passed before Rachel Auntie knocked on the door.

"You're not leaving, are you?" she asked, when Joseph Uncle cracked the door open a slit.

"No. But you can go bunk with your darling daughter. I want nothing to do with either of you." The door clicked shut.

A moment later, it opened again. "And get rid of this. I got it for you and Thomas, but it's obviously not wanted." He thrust a clear, plastic, wedding-ring-shaped tube into Isabelle's hands and slammed the door. It looked like an inflatable pool ring, filled with matching His and Hers underwear in black and gold. The 'diamond' part was stuffed with personalized accessories—luggage tags with the couple's initials, a fridge magnet with their photo and wedding date, a handwritten note congratulating them. *With love from Mom and Dad.*

Rachel Auntie started crying again.

"Let's get you some water." Dolly steered her into our stateroom. "Just give him some time. He'll cool off."

"I can't believe this is happening!" Isabelle wailed. I caught a glimpse of Naani as Isabelle walked into their cabin and broke down.

I stood in the empty hallway, my wet hair still plastered to my forehead.

Now what?

I looked right, then left, then right again. All the doors were closed. I could feel them pulsing with their own energy.

Cabin Three: Joseph Uncle (Raging Red)

Cabin Four: Naani and Isabelle (Breakdown Black)

Cabin Five: Dolly and Rachel Auntie (Bawling Blue)

I don't know what the colors are for being insignificant or forgotten, but whatever shades were spilling out of me in that empty hallway were inconspicuous and invisible.

"Moti." The door to Bawling Blue opened and Dolly peeked out. "Can you get Rachel's stuff from her room? She's staying with me. At least until Joseph cools down."

I made a sign of the cross before knocking softly on Raging Red.

No answer.

I knocked again.

"What?!" The door remained closed.

"Uh… Joseph Uncle, it's Moti. Can I get Rachel Auntie's things from your room?"

There was some scuffling. Then Joseph Uncle opened the door and handed me a half-open, hastily stuffed bag. "Tell her she can come in and get the rest when I'm not here."

I carted the bag back to Dolly. "Can I come in and change?"

"Now's not a good time, Moti."

"But where am I supposed to sleep if Rachel Auntie is in our cabin?"

"It's a big yacht. I'm sure they can find something for you. Just go ask."

I trudged back upstairs, looking for Hannah, and found her folding napkins into starched, white rosebuds on the dinner table.

"Sorry to bug you, Hannah. There's been a change in the sleeping arrangements. My aunt and uncle have had a falling out and my aunt's moved into the cabin with my mom, which leaves me without a bed."

"I see." I could feel the ticker tape running in her head. And then it stopped, as if she'd run out of options. "I'm afraid all the staterooms are occupied. I can't set you up in any of the common areas. I think it's best if we handle this discreetly. I'm guessing it's not the kind of thing your uncle and aunt want everyone to know about. We'll have to consult Captain Bailey about this."

"Do you think I could freshen up before I meet the captain?"

"Of course." Hannah looked relieved that being covered in motor oil and grime wasn't part of my onboard fashion statement. "We have a washroom you can use, and I'll get you a change of clothes. Is there anything particular you'd like?"

"Just my jeans. And a white top. They're both in my hand luggage."

"Great. The washroom is just around the corner here…"

The space transitioned seamlessly from indoors to outdoors as we approached one of the decks. It was at this point that I noticed we were heading straight for Thomas and Nikos. I ducked under one of the arches and lost Hannah.

"Moti?" I heard her calling. "Moti?"

I kept my back to the wall and crept around the other side until I was flush against the railing.

There. No chance of them seeing me now.

That was when I happened to glance down into the dark water below.

Argh. My fingers tightened instinctively around the railing and I squeezed my eyes shut, trying to keep the panic at bay.

"Don't do it." It was a male voice—unwelcome and authoritative.

"Do what?" I turned toward it, but the sun was in my eyes, so I couldn't see his face—just a dark silhouette. With a strange looking mini-hat on his head.

"Whatever you're planning to do, it's not worth it." He moved then, and I made out tanned arms, a white shirt, and black pants. And it wasn't a hat. It was a half-ponytail, half man-bun.

My anxiety latched on to it like it was the last life raft on the Titanic. Focusing on something outside of myself always helped. I allowed myself a moment to contemplate this controversial beast.

As far as I was concerned, the only guys who looked good in a man-bun were so insanely masculine, the long hair added a warrior-like vibe. Good, thick hair was vital or it risked looking like an olive. On the other hand, too much texture and it could be mistaken for a small, furry, nesting mammal. A sexy beard or stubble completed the look. Needless to say, man-bunners were always surfing on thin ice with me. But when it worked, it freaking worked. Cue the lusty gazes.

"If you really want to do it, you should go up on one of the higher decks," Mr. Man-bun was saying. "And even then, it's best to wait until we're at sea, not while we're anchored at a marina."

What the hell is he going on about? And then it dawned on me. *He thinks I'm planning to jump off the boat and plunge to my death. Half-ponytailed dingbat.* "It doesn't matter where I jump from. I can't swim."

His body tensed for a moment, the wind ruffling his sun-drenched hair. "In that case, I highly recommend the swimming pool on the sun deck. It's much cleaner than whatever goop is floating down there. Temperature-controlled too. Plus, there's no one up there right now so no chance of anyone diving in to save you."

I gritted my teeth. I didn't know what peeved me off more—his wise-ass comments or the fact that he'd just plagiarized my Beyonce-on-stage, wind-blown look. Outdone by a man who, I bet, had not even bothered looking up the wind forecast.

"Look, Miss, if you don't make a decision soon, I'll have to escort you off the boat myself." Something glinted in his hand as he came closer. A big, sharp butcher knife.

"What the hell? Don't come any closer! I am *not* trying to kill myself and I am *not* a stowaway. I'm a passenger on this yacht, so stop waving that knife at me."

"What kn—" He stopped and looked at it. "Oh, this. I was just getting ready to…" he trailed off and then chuckled. "You're one of our guests?" His brown eyes creased softly at the corners. He looked like he'd spent a lot of time squinting at distant horizons.

"Yes." I sniffed, although I couldn't blame him for assuming otherwise. I looked like I had just crawled out of a well. "Some idiot drove through a puddle and splashed me."

"Well…" He gave me a quick appraisal. "It's not exactly a red-carpet look, but it's not so bad." If his smile wasn't so genuine, I would've resented the dimple that formed on his cheek. When I was little, I prayed for dimples. And now I had them. On my ass. Naturally, people with properly-placed dimples irritated me.

"I'm Alex," he said, tossing the knife in the air. He caught it as it curved around his shoulder, then proceeded to slice and dice an army of invisible ninjas before giving me a slick bow. "Your onboard Executive Chef."

Show-offs irritated me, but half-bunned, half-dimpled guy was giving me major warrior vibes. What I'd initially thought was a white shirt was actually a chef's overcoat. Chefs aren't meant to be all Lean, Mean Cuisine, are they? When I thought of a chef, I pictured someone soft and homely. I hated it when people made me question my beloved stereotypes.

"I'm Moti," I said.

"Ah. No fish heads, snails, tentacles, or anything that looks remotely like it lived or breathed or was capable of having babies. Fillets, boneless cuts, boiled eggs, rice cakes, steamed veggies. No butter, potatoes, pasta, bread, or pastries."

"Impressive." I blinked. He repeated the preference sheet I'd filled out, word for word.

He tilted his head and looked at me. "So, what are you doing out here, Moti?"

"Waiting." My skin flushed under his scrutiny, so I focused on his man-bun and pictured a blue robin's egg hiding in it.

"Waiting for...?"

I tensed as Nikos and Thomas laughed at something.

"Ah." Alex backtracked and peered around the corner. "Which one? The blond or brunette? Wait. Don't tell me. The dark-haired one is the groom. So, it must be the other guy."

"For your information, I'm waiting to see the Captain. And would you please put that knife down?"

"Sorry. Force of habit." Alex grinned. Yep. Just one dimple. "Would you please step away from the railing? I know you said you're not planning to jump, but I just met you and you could be a total nut job, you know?"

"Are you allowed to talk to your passengers like that?"

"Where safety is a concern, yes."

"Said the man wielding a butcher knife."

"A man with a knife is your best bet on the high seas. He can slice open coconuts, scale a fish, fend off aggressive sea gulls and carve your initials on a tree."

"Thanks, but I have a pocketknife."

Alex laughed. "But can a pocketknife hook you up with the Captain?" He winked and made a move, indicating that I should follow. He seemed to sense my hesitation because he paused and looked to me for confirmation. "You said you were waiting to see the Captain?"

"Yes, but not like this."

"Who cares?" He gave a wide-shouldered shrug. "You're a guest on a luxury yacht. It's not your job to impress the Captain or the staff. It's our job to cater to you."

Huh. I hadn't thought of it like that. Probably because I wasn't paying big money for the privilege of being on the boat. But mostly because I was used to walking on eggshells around everyone. I was also tired enough to not care at this point. Not about Nikos. Or the Captain. Or poor Hannah, who was probably still looking for me. It had been go, go, go since I stepped off the plane. The sooner I got my accommodations figured out, the better.

"Please. Lead the way," I said.

We circumvented the elevator and took the stairs to the Bridge deck. Plush chairs surrounded a jacuzzi. As we passed an outdoor dining area, my eyes swept over a lookout house with stunning 360-degree views. Flower arrangements and bowls filled with fruits and nuts punctuated the entire deck.

"Captain Bailey, one of the passengers is here to see you." Alex ushered me into the wheelhouse. It was an impressive command center, decked out with a sleek dashboard, beeping screens, and gadgets galore—the kind of place you'd want to sneak into, just so you could slide into one of the leather chairs and issue commands about traveling at warp speed.

Captain Bailey turned out to be a sandy-haired Canadian in her late fifties—far from the pipe-smoking, salty mariner I was expecting. My stereotypes were being blown to smithereens—left, right, and center.

Alex excused himself once he made introductions, impressing me with the correct pronunciation of my name. Apparently, he listened closely.

"So?" Captain Bailey took off her sunglasses and tucked them in her shirt pocket. They had left permanent grooves on the sides of her nose. If she had any thoughts about my bedraggled state, she kept them to herself. Luckily, my clothes had dried off, so I wasn't sitting in a puddle of humiliation. "What can I do for you, Moti?"

"I'm out of a room." I explained the situation as delicately as I could. "Hannah said there are no extra beds, so I'm hoping we can figure something out."

"Hmmm." Captain Bailey drummed her fingers. She had four gold stripes on her epaulets, indicating some kind of rank, or maybe how many fingers she could drum with. She pulled out a logbook and ran her finger down a page. "We're missing a crew member. He had a family emergency. It leaves us short-handed, but we have a spare bunk in the crew quarters. Until the situation between your uncle and aunt gets resolved, I'll sleep there. You can have the Captain's suite." She smiled and shut the ledger.

"That's very nice of you, but I wouldn't dream of taking your cabin. I'll bunk in the crew quarters."

"I can't assign a passenger to a crew cabin. It's nothing like the stateroom you checked into. Crew accommodations are shared, space is restricted and if you're prone to seasickness, that's where you'll feel it the most—on the lowest deck. Even if you're okay with that, I have to run it by the Principal."

"The Principal?"

"Mr. Papadakis. The groom's father. He's the one who chartered the yacht. It's my responsibility to keep him updated on any changes."

"I was hoping we could keep this between us." *If Principal Papadakis finds out about the feud, Isabelle will have my head. Then I'll be headless and room-less.* "No point in involving everyone in needless drama. Besides, Rachel Auntie and Joseph Uncle could be talking by dinner. They never stay mad at each other for too long."

"You have a point." But Captain Bailey did not look happy about it. "I still think you should take my room. You'll be sharing the crew cabin with a member of the opposite sex."

"How about I try it out for a night? I probably wouldn't be seeing much of my roommate anyway. I'll just be using it to shower and sleep. If it doesn't work out, I'll take you up on the Captain's suite."

For a moment, it seemed like she wasn't going to budge. Then her shoulders relaxed, and she gave me a nod. "Fine. One night. I'll keep it between us, but I want a status report in the morning."

Aye, Aye, Captain.

I signed some consent forms and handed them back with a bright "Thank you!!" (with two exclamation marks, because that's how relieved I was to have the matter resolved).

Captain Bailey escorted me to the crew quarters and showed me to my assigned cabin. In stark contrast to the grandeur of the upper decks, the lower level was a maze of paper-thin walls and fluorescent lighting.

"I'll have someone transfer your bag," Captain Bailey said. "You'll be bunking with Chef Alexandros. I believe you've already met."

I opened my mouth and shut it again. *Chef Alexandros. Alex?*

"Everything okay?" she asked.

"Yes. Yes, everything's fine."

It was only after Captain Bailey left that I walked into the tiny en suite, locked the door, and banged my head against it.

Thud thud thud (but softly because I didn't want to attract any attention).

I lied to Captain Bailey. I had no idea if Rachel Auntie and Joseph Uncle were going to make up any time soon. I had no idea how long I was going to be stuck in the bowels of the ship with a half-bunned, half-dimpled ninja chef. Worse, I was estranged from my future husband-to-be, my plans of midnight trysts in the hall-way (for which I'd spent hours picking out the perfect sexy-but-oh-so-effortless pajamas) put indefinitely on hold.

But that's the way it is with star-crossed lovers. No love story worth its weight in sea salt is ever easy, right?

Right. I straightened and stared at my reflection in the utility mirror. It was lit from above, casting deep shadows. The hollows under my eyes made me look more like something out of a horror story than a romance. The important thing to remember was that the stage was finally set for the most important journey of my life: to seduce the one man Dolly couldn't stop me from being with, the one man she'd have no choice but to accept.

I stepped out of my dirty clothes and got in the shower. I had to tuck in my elbows to fit, but nothing could dampen my resolve. I grinned as I lathered my hair.

It's show time, Moti.

CHAPTER THREE

I MADE MY WAY TO THE SALON—FRESHLY SHOWERED AND UN-ZOMBIFIED. "There you are," Hannah said. "Captain Bailey told me you're bunking in the crew quarters with us. Find everything you need?"

"Yes, thank you." I appreciated her hushed tones even though none of the Papadakis clan was around. "Are we leaving? I heard the engines come on."

"Yes. The last of your wedding party arrived a little while ago. You'll be dining al fresco tonight. One level up. I've set up some appetizers and drinks if you want to grab a spot and watch the sun set before dinner."

"That would be great. Thanks, Hannah." I made my way up and spotted Thomas's parents on the U-shaped seating area. It had been three months since we'd met, so I figured a re-introduction was necessary.

"Hello, I'm Moti."

"Yes, Isabelle's cousin, right?" Thomas's mother held out her hand. "Kassia. And you remember my husband, George."

Principal Papadakis was one of the few men who could carry off a Tom Selleck mustache. He gave me a nod and indicated a spot for me to sit.

"So Moti, what do you do?"

So Fatty, what do you do?

"I work for Isabelle's father. I'm a chartered accountant."

"Ah, not everyone can be a lawyer or doctor or politician. It's not your qualifications that matter. It's how much money you make."

I decided not to be offended. Isabelle mentioned how rattled she'd been the first time she'd met her in-laws. I laughed, but Mama and Papa Papadakis continued to stare at me.

They really expect me to share how much money I make.

Papa Papadakis leaned closer. "Tell me. Why does your family have these names? Isabelle, Rachel, Joseph, Dolly. Only you have a different name. Moti. You're all Indian. Why don't the others have Indian names?"

A stretch of silence followed, during which I mentally retreated to the bowels of the ship, assumed the fetal position, and rocked back and forth while chanting, *Please, make it go away.*

"We're Catholic, so we have Christian names." I fidgeted with the row of bracelets I was wearing. "I was named by a Hindu lady who—"

"George, you're making her uncomfortable." Kassia held out a platter of appetizers for me. "I hope you don't mind all the questions, dear. We're just curious people. Strong opinions, no filters, but the best of intentions."

Papa Papadakis lit a cigarette and took a long, slow inhale, disappointed at having his line of interrogation cut off. The smoke swirled around him—thick and gray like his mustache. Mama Papadakis' expression tightened when his phone went off.

"Sorry, darling. I have to take this." He offered her a reconciliatory kiss on the cheek, but she waved him off.

I popped one of the colorful appetizers into my mouth and sat back. The sun turned everything golden—the roofs of small houses, the foamy crests of waves crashing along the coastline, the underbellies of sea gulls soaring above. It was all picture-perfect, but something else competed for my attention: the flavors bursting in my mouth. I picked up the card on the platter and read: *Roasted Balsamic Cranberries on Brie Crostini.*

Technically, just fruit and cheese on bread. But I'd been off bread the last few months, maybe that's why it tasted so good.

I closed my eyes and popped another morsel into my mouth. "Mmm."

"You sound positively orgasmic."

My eyes flew open, mid-chew. Nikos stood before me in golden, Grecian glory. His cuff links picked up the light from the sunset as he held up his glass in greeting.

Yes! Still with the three thumbs.

"Mind if I sit here?" He didn't wait for an answer as he took the seat next to me, which caused me to swallow the rest of my appetizer whole.

Cranberries? No problem.

Brie? No problem.

Little cube of crostini? Problem.

You have got to be fucking kidding me.

I forced a smile and stood, holding up my index finger.

Stay, Nikos. Stay. I'll be right back.

As soon as I turned the corner, I whipped around the bar area, clutched my throat and proceeded to cough my lungs out. Music piped softly over the speakers as I hacked and wheezed for oxygen. Through sheer willpower, I managed to dislodge the food from my windpipe. I was not having it. Not again. No crumb, no crust, no wretched piece of crostini was going to come between Nikos and me.

"Are you all right?" That deep, annoying voice again.

Alex.

Why couldn't the man let me hide out in peace? Why couldn't someone lock him up in the kitchen? Isn't that where he was supposed to be?

"Yes, fine." I was impressed by the conviction in my tone, considering I was crawling on my hands and knees behind the bar at this point. "Just looking for my earring."

"Need any hel—"

"No. Nope. All good." I coughed. "Found it. See?" I got up and held a tiny, invisible speck before him.

He raised an eyebrow, also known as the universal symbol for skepticism. I'm pretty sure people who can lift one eyebrow spend hours practicing it in front of the mirror, waiting for the opportunity to look all superior and shit: *Oh really? You think you can fool someone who can do THIS?*

I went for the hands-on-hips stance. *Oh yeah? I see your eyebrow cock and I raise you something that makes my arms look like two pot handles.*

I held it until I remembered I was supposed to be holding an earring. "Well then... I best be off."

Alex didn't budge. He moved closer, so close that I felt his warm exhale on my skin. It tripped a network of electric goose bumps and sent my heart racing until I realized that he wasn't overwhelmed by the sudden, irresistible urge to kiss me. He was reaching for something on the bar top.

"Hold still." He wiped my cheek with a napkin. It came away with a dark smudge. He wiped the other cheek and stepped back.

"Oh." My pulse was still high, cheeks flushed, but at least I didn't have raccoon eyes from runny mascara. "I was just..." I pointed to the stained napkin. *I was just choking on a piece of crostini and missed the tears streaming down my face.* But it was humiliating to explain that to someone who'd mastered the eyebrow cock, so I mumbled a thanks and dashed back to Nikos.

Damn.

Competition.

He was talking to Teri, the hired maid of honor. A perky little thing with big eyes that belonged to an anime character. Of course, her hair and makeup were flawless, given that she was a professional hair and makeup artist.

Rachel Auntie and Joseph Uncle were chatting amicably with Thomas's parents.

"Did they make up?" I took the seat next to Dolly.

"Oh, they had a fight too?" A spark of excitement flared in Dolly's eyes as she observed Kassia and George.

"Not them." Although I was pretty sure Thomas's parents

must've had a good chin wag over the unexpected abundance of thongs in their stateroom. "Them."

"Rachel and Joseph? No, they're still not speaking to each other."

Boy, did they know how to put on a show. Joseph Uncle had his arm wrapped around Rachel Auntie and she was resting one hand on his knee. If I hadn't witnessed their blowout myself, I'd think they were the coziest couple on board.

"Where's Naani?" I asked.

"You know how she likes to sleep early. She had dinner served in her cabin. I wish this Sofia person would hurry up. I don't want to fill up on appetizers." Dolly picked up another one from the platter. It looked like avocado mousse, topped with spirals of vibrant beets and carrots. "Delicious," she said.

Weird, because Dolly hated avocado.

"You know she's a photographer?"

"Who?" I asked.

"Sofia." Dolly reached for another appetizer. "I still have to meet her. Apparently, she's the reason we got off to a late start. She had to get some adapters for her equipment."

"Huh." It was more of a response to the way Teri was giggling at whatever Nikos had said.

I shot her a poison-dipped glare—standard protocol when you catch a girl flirting with your man who isn't quite your man yet.

She lifted a hand to brush the hair away from her face and that's when I saw the gold band around her finger. Teri was married.

My poison-dipped glare retracted into a bubble of relief as Nikos caught my eye and shot me a smile.

That's right, baby. Your happiness is sitting right here.

I smiled back and crossed my legs, angling them just so. My varnished toes peeked out from under my maxi dress. I was going for the sexy-but-subtle vibe.

It seemed to work because Nikos excused himself and started coming over.

Oh hey, now. I took a lightning-quick survey as he approached.

No water, crostini, or other hazardous items in my mouth? Check.

Boobs up, tummy in, shoulders back? Check.

Windshield-wiper tongue over teeth. No lipstick or food particles lodged in-between? Check.

I wanted to half-rise, but I kept my cool.

"So sorry to keep everyone waiting." A lady's voice interrupted the epic moment when Nikos and I were about to reconnect.

"Fia." Isabelle got up and embraced the tall, dusky woman. "Everyone, I'd like you to meet my godmother, Sofia. She traveled all the way from India for the wedding."

As Isabelle introduced her to Thomas's parents, Dolly gripped my arm.

"Fia," she said, in a half-horrified, half-glorified whisper. "It's Fia."

"You know her?"

"From when we were kids in India."

"That's great, Ma," I replied. But apparently it wasn't, because Dolly's death grip was cutting off my blood supply and she was acting like a skipper who had just spotted a great white shark circling her boat.

Hannah appeared before the group. "Since we're all here, dinner is served." She sounded a miniature gong for effect.

Dolly let go of my arm.

"Time to eat, Ma."

No response.

I turned to her. "Ma?"

But Dolly wasn't there.

Dolly wasn't to my right, and Dolly wasn't to my left.

Oh shit. I closed my eyes a split second before all hell broke loose.

CHAPTER FOUR

WE LAY HER ON THE COUCH WITH A CUSHION UNDER HER LEGS. "Does she have any medical conditions?"

"Poor thing. It's probably jet lag. The time difference always gets to me."

"Dolly? Can you hear me?"

"Is she diabetic?"

"Any heart problems?"

"Dolly, open your eyes."

"Everybody, just..." My voice rose over everyone else's. "Give her a minute. It happens to her once in a while. She'll be fine." I knelt beside my mother and rubbed her palm.

"Yes, let's not crowd around. Give her some room." Rachel Auntie came through with reinforcements. "Hannah, you can get dinner started. Moti and I will look after Dolly."

After a few reassurances, everyone moved to the dining table, concerned but satisfied that Rachel Auntie and I knew what we were doing.

"I think she's really out this time," I whispered.

Dolly's face was pale and her forehead was dotted with a faint sheen of sweat.

Rachel Auntie wasn't convinced. "Come on, Dolly, that's enough."

"Her hand is limp," I said.

"Let me see."

We exchanged a look. Either Dolly was getting really good at it, or we had a real case of the faints this time.

"What happened?" Rachel Auntie asked.

"Nothing. She started acting weird when she saw Sofia."

"God. Not this again. Dolly." Rachel Auntie pried Dolly's eye open. "Dolly, wake up." As if she'd be able to hear better with one eyeball exposed.

"What's the deal with her and Sofia?" Having a conversation with one of Dolly's eyes bulging at us was weird. I nudged Rachel Auntie's hand away.

"No one knows." Rachel Auntie sighed. "One minute they're best friends. Inseparable. Can't live without each other. And the next, they hate each other's guts."

"Unghhh." Dolly's head turned toward us.

"Oh, thank God." Rachel Auntie kissed the cross around her neck.

"Rachel?" My mother's voice was soft and weak.

"Yes, Dolly. I'm here."

"You fucking cunt."

Rachel Auntie gasped. In all my life, I'd never heard my mother use that word.

"How could you invite Fia to the wedding?" Dolly was coming around fast because she had a tight grip around her sister's lace collar, pulling them nose to nose.

"Ma!" I tried to pry her fingers away.

"You stay out of it," Dolly hissed.

"Everything okay over there?" Thomas's father's voice boomed from the dining table.

"Yes, George. Dolly's come around. She's feeling much better." Rachel Auntie's voice was smooth and cheerful, but in the next instant, it turned into a harsh whisper. "Let go of me, Dolly. What's wrong with you?"

"What's wrong with me? What's wrong with *you*? You know I haven't talked to Fia in ages." A scuffle ensued as Dolly and Rachel slapped each other's hands away. This time, it was Joseph Uncle who interrupted.

"Need any help getting her up?"

"No, no." Dolly chuckled, letting go of Rachel Auntie's neck. "I'm fine. See?" She propped herself up and gave everyone a queenly wave. "Just need a moment, that's all." She waited until everyone went back to their salads.

"I'm. Never. Talking. To. You. Again." She accented each word by jabbing Rachel Auntie in the chest.

Great. Joseph Uncle wasn't talking to Rachel Auntie and Isabelle. And now Rachel Auntie and my mother were going on strike. I stood with my back to the dining table. We were far enough away that no one could hear what was going on, but no way could I shield everyone from what was about to go down between the sisters.

"Dolly, I had no idea you still felt this way." Thankfully, Rachel Auntie's tone was reconciliatory. "It's been years, and besides, it wasn't my call. It was Isabelle's. She needed a photographer for the wedding and with Fia being her godmother, things just fell into place."

"How long has Fia been a photographer?"

"It's what she does. When was the last time you talked to her?"

Dolly shook her head, the fight seeping out of her. "I wish you'd told me."

Her vulnerability caught me off-guard—a sad softness I rarely saw. At some point in my life, I'd started thinking of my mother as Dolly. I still called her *Ma*, but she was always Dolly in my head. When I thought of the word *mother*, I thought of someone you could go to when you were hurt or hungry or sad or lonely. Someone who loved, nurtured, and cared about you. I didn't know what Dolly expected of me, but I never seemed to make her happy. Something was broken in our relationship and I couldn't figure out how to fix it. I wanted her to be somebody else, and she wanted me to be somebody else.

I sat and picked up a pack of playing cards from the side

table. Still in their box, they were crisp, clean, and in perfect order.

As Dolly and Rachel Auntie made up in hushed tones, I shuffled the deck and picked a card.

Queen of Diamonds.

I returned it to the deck and picked another card.

Three of Spades.

Better. The Three of Spades was exactly what I needed, given the shit-shoveling day I was having:

1) Getting splashed by some moron on a NASA-fueled motorbike.

2) Losing my room.

3) Choking in front of Nikos. Again.

4) Having Dolly faint. For real.

Wait. That was four. But I liked three. Three was odd. Three was the number haunting my life. Three was the number of thumbs I looked for. Three was *me.*

I slipped the Three of Spades into my dress pocket.

"Are you feeling well enough to eat?" Hannah asked Dolly. "Or should I have the chef prepare something light for you?"

"I'm fine. I'll have what everyone else is having." Dolly rose and smoothed her hair. "Come, Rachel." She held her hand out and they walked to the table as if they hadn't just been clawing at each other like wildcats.

Family. I smiled and followed, taking the only empty seat remaining—across from Fia. Whatever the animosity between her and Dolly, it didn't extend to me because Fia smiled warmly and introduced herself.

"Pan-fried Barbounia and Naxian potatoes on a bed of wilted greens," Hannah said, as she placed a gold-rimmed plate before Thomas's mother.

I had no idea what Barbounia was—it sounded like a harpoon-wielding pirate who shouldn't be allowed on board. But the way Kassia beamed, I couldn't wait for mine.

"Is mine gluten-free?" Isabelle asked.

"It certainly is," Hannah replied, serving the rest of the table.

"I asked for organic," said Nikos.

"All your preferences have been taken into account," Hannah said. "Enjoy."

I was looking forward to my first real meal of the day. Prepared to order by an executive chef. On a private yacht. If the appetizers were anything to go by, I was in for a real treat. My anticipation turned into disbelief, then shock, then downright despair as everyone started digging in. I stared at the beautifully presented dish before me and gagged. Three small, red-skinned fish, their tails pinched together stared back at me. Atop a pyramid of three potatoes. Three was turning out to be the theme for the evening.

"Hannah?" I called. "Could I have a word with the chef, please?"

"He's busy preparing the next course, but I can relay your message."

"Maybe I can send a note?" It seemed like the more diplomatic thing to do.

"Sure." Hannah handed me a pen and notepad. The table seemed eerily quiet. I looked up, expecting all eyes on me, but they were all focused on their dinner.

No fish heads, sheep heads or any heads, I wrote. *Or tails. Could you please substitute something else? I also requested no potatoes.*

Hannah left with my note, and I wondered what could've gone wrong. Alex had reeled off my likes and dislikes as if he knew them inside out. Isabelle had her gluten-free meal. Nikos was enjoying his organic stuff. How could Alex have forgotten my preferences in the span of a few short hours? I could just shut my trap and eat the greens, but this was not a onetime thing. The only meals I was going to get for the next two weeks would be prepared by Alex. If he thought I was acting spoiled and entitled, so be it. Besides, having my dinner stare back at me was giving me the creeps.

I turned the plate around so the barbounia looked at Fia instead. She'd put aside her fork and was eating the rosy fish with her hands. Thomas's father was doing the same. Rachel Auntie was *licking* her fingers. Nikos had his eyes closed. His lips glistened as he chewed. Teri stared at the line of his throat while sucking on a cleanly picked line of thin, delicate fish bones. Thomas stroked Isabelle's wrist absently, a sated, glazed look in his eyes.

What the hell is going on? I glanced at Dolly. Given her recent agitated state, I was sure she hadn't succumbed to whatever weird spell everyone else seemed to be under.

"Chef Alexandros asked me to give you this." Hannah handed me a piece of paper before I could appraise Dolly.

I unfolded the note and read:

This morning, as the sun rose over the water I saw fishermen pull a net full of barbounia from the sea—red and pink with flashes of gold. I thought, What better meal to serve on the first night than this fine, fresh delicacy? They are sweet from their diet of minuscule shrimp, with an earthy, buttery texture. I prepared them with a simple dusting of flour—fried crispy on the outside, juicy on the inside, and still smelling of the sea. A dash of salt and a squeeze of lemon are all they need. I thought about serving yours headless, without the bones, but it would take away from the experience. And it would be a shame if you didn't taste the potatoes at least once while you're in Greece. They are sourced from a small farm in Naxos. I know food. I know how to cook it. I know how to serve it. Try it. If you don't like it, I have rice cakes.

Great. A chef with an attitude. He hadn't forgotten my requests. He'd chosen to ignore them.

I crumpled up the note and thanked Hannah.

"Everything okay?" she asked.

"Fine." I managed to muster up a smile.

Not only was I stuck with Alex's culinary whims, I was also stuck as his roommate. It didn't help that everyone around me was intent on licking their plates clean. So much ooh-ing and aah-ing, you'd think they were at an orgy. I picked up my fork and speared a potato with an eye roll.

It's just dinner, folks. Fried fish and a bunch of...

Potatoes. Naxian. From the island of Naxos. Maybe that's why they were melting in my mouth like sweet, sweet heaven. I tasted herbs, olive oil, the kick of something tart and the grit of coarsely ground salt and pepper. So simple yet so divine. Curse Chef Alexandros for reminding me how much I loved potatoes. I speared the wilted greens next. They were wilted. They'd already given up. They *had* to taste like shit, right? Wrong. They complemented the potatoes perfectly with their earthy texture and dusky bitterness.

I fought the urge to close my eyes and savor each bite. No way was I falling under Chef Alexandros' spell. His magic was turning us all into putty and I didn't like it. I didn't like it one bit. I might've finished everything on my plate, but I didn't touch the fish-that-still-looked-like-fish. I was sending a message, clear as a marine flare on a dark, empty night.

You can serve it, Chef Alexandros, but I don't have to eat it.

I would've loved to see the look on his face when Hannah took my plate back to the kitchen.

Return to sender.

CHAPTER FIVE

I WENT UP TO THE SKY DECK AFTER EVERYONE RETIRED FOR THE NIGHT. I wasn't ready to say goodnight to the stars. Away from the city lights, they were bright and dazzling. I lay on my back, marveling at how something as simple as looking at the night sky could fill you up.

There was a splash as someone dived into the pool. It was lit from the inside and glowed with blue-green luminescence.

So much decadence. A pool, on a boat, on the sea.

I wondered how they kept the water from sloshing all over the place when the seas got choppy. A big-ass drain? A cover? My thoughts were interrupted by the dark figure slicing through the water in quick, sure strokes.

Nikos.

I should've been pleased to see him—alone, under the stars, on a warm June night. Instead, I felt a flash of annoyance. I liked my alone time. My brain had switched from conversation mode to solitude. I lay silent under the cocoon of my dark shawl, hoping he wouldn't notice the mummified lump on the outdoor sofa.

It was a black lump on a white couch.

He noticed.

He swam up to the edge of the pool, rested his elbows on the rounded lip, and eyeballed me.

I would've un-mummified myself, but I might've ended up rolling off the couch like a log, so I remained in corpse pose.

"I'm almost afraid to talk to you." He tilted his head and smiled. "Every time I say something to you, you take off."

"Well…" I unraveled myself slowly, hoping he wouldn't notice all the fidgeting going on under my shawl. I would *die* if he thought I'd been out here touching myself. "If it's any consolation, it's not you. It's me."

I forget how to breathe around you and suck all kinds of things down my throat.

"That's usually a line reserved for when you're breaking up with someone." He flashed his perfectly aligned teeth. "I don't think I've ever been shut down before I could even begin."

No. Why would you? Look at you.

Shirtless Nikos. Moonlit Nikos. Water-slicked Nikos.

"Come join me," he said. "The water's perfect."

Okay. A moment here, please.

A man with three thumbs was flirting with me.

Let that sink in.

The probability of this miraculous moment happening in my lifetime was mind-boggling.

But I couldn't sidle up to him because I was terrified of drowning. Ever since I could remember, Dolly had banned me from the water. No swimming pools, no oceans, no baths, no puddles.

Oh Dolly. I know you were trying to protect me. I know you were afraid, but if someone tells you your child is going to die in the water—and you believe them—what's the best thing you can do for both of you? You get her swimming lessons. You teach her how to swim. That's what.

"I didn't bring a swimsuit," I said, finally free of my shawl and sitting up.

"So, go get it. I'll wait right here." He winked.

Score 1 for Moti. Subject has indicated his interest.

"It's not in my room. I didn't pack a swimsuit for the trip."

"So, get in without one."

Score 2 for Moti. Subject is in active pursuit.

I walked over to the pool and raised the hem of my dress. The higher it went, the higher Nikos's brows lifted. We got to my thighs until I stopped and sat next to him, my feet dangling in the water.

"Tease." Nikos grinned. His half-submerged body beckoned under wavy lines of water. "We'll have to get you a bikini. We're going to be anchored in all kinds of secluded coves and nooks. Trust me, you don't want to miss it."

I wasn't sure if *it* meant swimming with Nikos or nooky with Nikos. Maybe *it* was his way of referring to *it*—you know, his thingamajig.

Trust me, you don't want to miss it.

"I have a pretty little bluff picked out for next week. Perfect for diving. Get yourself a swimsuit by then."

I should've told Nikos I didn't swim, that just sitting with my feet in the pool was stretching it. Diving off a pretty little bluff and hurtling to my death was really not my thing. I should've told him, but I didn't. Because Nikos raised my hand to his lips and kissed it, as if to seal the deal.

"You and I are going to have a lot of fun on this trip," he said.

Considering the only other single passengers on the boat were my grandmother, my mother, and my mother's estranged friend, the pickings were slim for Nikos. Still, I had to rise to the challenge. Guys wanted adventurous, outgoing, *fun* girls, not mummified lumps staring at stars.

"It's a date," I said. Maybe I could keep him occupied enough to forget about diving off cliffs. Or maybe he could dive off a cliff and I could clap so hard, he'd want to do it again, and forget about me getting in the water. At some point I'd have to explain things to him—the real reason I didn't know how to swim, which meant Ma Anga would come up, and then the thumbs and... Oh God, this was going to be so awkward.

I'd dug myself into enough of a hole for the night.

"I'm going to turn in," I said. "Goodnight."

Nikos pouted when I swung my legs out of the water. "So soon?"

"It's been a long day." I laughed and picked up my discarded shawl. He didn't know the half of it. "See you tomorrow." I congratulated myself for pulling off a graceful exit. No stumbling or slipping and more importantly, no choking.

Score 3 for Moti.

Life was looking good until I got to the crew deck. It was a little past eleven. Apart from a few crew members who were on night duty, everyone else was in bed. That meant Alex would be in the cabin. I opened the door slowly, with the kind of caution reserved for public washroom stalls—you know, where you're praying you don't end up locking eyes with someone sitting inside. He wasn't there. Both bunk beds were empty and the bathroom was dark.

I washed my face and brushed my teeth in lightning mode. As an only child, I wasn't comfortable sharing my space with anyone, let alone a stranger. An arrogant, eyebrow-cocking stranger who wanted to feed me fish with eyes.

I slipped into a T-shirt and shorts. No point wasting my sexy-but-effortless-but-itchy ensemble on Alex. It looked like the bottom bunk was mine, because a breakfast card with my name was on the pillow.

Please tick your preference and hang outside on your doorknob.

The choice was staggering—everything from cinnamon mascarpone pancakes, to blueberry French toast, to savory pies, to a blank section for custom requests. I picked the omelet, indicated egg-whites only, my time preference, and stuck it on the door.

I had just turned the lights off when Alex arrived. He shut the door behind him and leaned against it, taking a deep breath. Then he started dropping his clothes—his T-shirt, pants, God knows what else. Thankfully, it was too dark to see…until he turned the light on in the en suite. There he stood, bare-bottomed as the day he was born, tan lines stark against his skin, splashing water on his face. He undid his hair and turned around, his thick hair tumbling around his shoulders, naked silhouette outlined against the frame of the bathroom door.

I squeezed my eyes and pulled the covers up to my chin. As if *I* was the one that needed covering up. He let out a string of Greek curses when he saw me. I heard some thudding and hopping as he retrieved his underwear. Or his pants. Hopefully, both.

"What are you doing h—"

"How dare you—"

Our sentences collided, and I got the distinct impression I'd caught him off-guard. He'd been expecting an empty room.

"Didn't they tell you I was going to be here?" I blinked, the covers still clutched to my nose.

"Had I known, I would've turned on *all* the lights and given you a proper show."

We glared at each other. He had a very nice butt. Okay, nice wasn't the word. He had a spectacular butt—round and firm. Unlike mine, it was smooth and dimple-less, which made me glare at him harder.

"Why are you here?" he asked, arms folded across his chest. Pants on, shirt still on the floor.

"It's not out of choice. Trust me."

"How long?"

"I don't know. Depends. Captain Bailey said it was okay until things get sorted out."

He continued focusing his laser gaze on me, as if I'd vaporize if he persisted long enough. "This is what you wanted to talk to her about?"

I nodded.

He sighed and raked his fingers through his hair. "Hannah was saying something, but I had my earphones on. It might've been this." He motioned to my bunk bed. "I saw the breakfast card on the door, but I figured it was one of the crew fooling around and putting in an order."

It seemed safe to come up for air, so I let the covers slide off my face.

"The top bunk is bigger," he said, picking up his T-shirt. "You'll be more comfortable there."

"I like being on the bottom. You get on top."

"Yes, ma'am." He chuckled, and I felt my color rise as the double meaning sank in.

This time, he shut the bathroom door as he got ready for bed. It was only after he climbed into the top bunk that I finally relaxed. Slipping my hand under the pillow, I felt the cool, smooth surface of a playing card.

Goodnight, Three of Spades.

Without a window, the room was pitch dark. We had anchored, so the ship was quiet, but it wasn't completely still. I could feel it bobbing and swaying on the water. It was a gentle, soothing motion, but I wasn't used to it. I drifted in and out of sleep, strange dreams floating through my head. Around dawn, my stomach chimed in. The three small potatoes I had for dinner weren't cutting it. My tummy was reminding me that it was dinner time in Chicago.

I ignored it.

It growled.

I flipped to my side.

It growled louder.

Some people will tell you that hunger is a sensation. Lies. Hunger is the mother of all emotions. Angry? Check how long it's been since you last ate. Tired? You probably didn't have enough to eat. Bored? You're eating the same thing—same place, same time. Pretty much every disaster in human history can be traced back to the lack of a burrito.

I tiptoed out of the cabin and made my way to the kitchen— or to use the proper term—the galley. Why you can't call a kitchen a kitchen on a boat beats me. I was hoping to ask one of the night crew for a snack, but no one was around. There was a plate on the counter, under a glass dome. I walked over and uncovered it, feeling a little guilty. What if it was the Captain's snack? Or whoever was keeping watch? Maybe just a nibble? Surely, they wouldn't miss a nibble.

I picked up the half-folded piece of paper propped against the plate, and recognized the bold, upright strokes from the note Alex had sent me at dinner:

Caramelized pineapple.

I soused out all the eyes.
Have it with a drizzle of honey from Kythira, where the air turns purple with thyme. You'll hear the song of bees ravishing its wild herbs and blossoms.
Some Greek yogurt to balance the flavors, and crushed maple walnuts for texture.

PS: Baby pineapples are the most adorable fruit you'll ever see. Don't worry. This was a full-grown adult.

I glanced at the note, then at the plate. Alex had clearly left it out for me. A peace offering for the fish fiasco? Had he received my message, loud and clear? Or had he anticipated I'd get hungry again? Either way, the dollop of yogurt looked like a white flag. It was a simple, unassembled dish—two sticky-sweet slices of pineapple in the center, the rest arranged artfully around a white plate.

I swirled my finger in the coppery, viscous honey and sucked it. It was bright and aromatic—the sweetness almost savory, unlike the honey I was used to. The aftertaste was undeniably pleasurable—like the buzz of a long-awaited kiss. Gratifying and zingy.

I ate the honey slowly with my fingers, suspended in its matrix like a bee caught in a vat of amber nectar.

Peace offering, my ass. Alex set a trap, and I fell into it.

I dipped my finger in the yogurt and sampled it with the tip of my tongue. It danced a tangy, velvet tango with the honey. How odd that a few licks of honey and yogurt managed to silence my stomach. I wasn't ravenous for food anymore. I was ravenous for taste.

Picking up the pineapple with sticky fingers, I bit into it and savored the chewy caramel crust around its edges. Something hot and spicy jolted my taste buds. I opened my eyes and noticed flakes of chili clinging to the pineapple. It was like someone had just pulled an unexpectedly erotic move on me. I'd never had a food orgasm before, but standing in the galley that night, with moonbeams streaming through the window, my taste buds quivered in a state of heightened arousal. A few more bites and I slammed both palms on the counter while my mouth silently screamed, *Yes. Yesss. YESSS.*

I hadn't even gotten to Alex's nuts. His maple walnuts, that is. But I was sated and full and happy and loopy. I stumbled back to my cabin and fell into the most restful sleep I'd had in months.

CHAPTER SIX

I WOKE UP TO A HIGH, GREEN ISLAND WITH PICTURESQUE BAYS AND FRUIT
trees running down to the sea. Kea—the first of the Cyclades
islands on our itinerary. Southeast of Athens, the Cyclades were a
cluster of islands scattered across the azure waters of the Aegean Sea.

Even though the sun was barely warm, the yacht buzzed with
the excitement of the first day of a trip. Deckhands were launch-
ing the tender—a small boat designed to ferry crew and passengers
between the ship and ports of call. A crew member was clearing
plates from the table. Another was mixing drinks at the bar.

Already? What Time O'Clock did I wake up?

I was halfway through my breakfast when Nikos slid into the
chair beside me. His green eyes took on the sparkling hues of the
sea.

"Kalimera, glikia mou," he said.

Good morning, something. I would have to look up *glikia mou*
on the English/Greek translation app I downloaded.

"Kalimera, Nikos." I raised my coffee in a morning salute.

"We're going diving today. Some spectacular shipwrecks in
the area. They have wet suits on board. Isabelle, Thomas, and Teri
are getting fitted. You up for it?"

Dammit. The no-swimsuit excuse wasn't going to cut it. "I've
never gone diving before."

*Diving is bullshit. You finally learn to swim, then you want to stay
submerged. What kind of nonsense hobby is this, Nikos?*

But we weren't married yet, so I filed it under *Future Projects
With Future Husband.*

"Come anyway. You can do some snorkeling. One of the deckhands is taking us out in the boat. Captain Bailey said he's a professional scuba diving instructor. Maybe he can give you a lesson while we're out there."

Maybe he can roll me up in bubble wrap instead, because that's the only way you'll get me to a diving site in the middle of the sea.

"I'm going to sit this one out. I'm still a little jet-lagged."

"Sorry to interrupt." Captain Bailey's shadow cast over our table. "Could I have a word with you, Moti?"

"Sounds like you're in trouble with the big boss." Nikos winked at me and took his cue. "If you change your mind, come find me. You're going to be bored as hell with no one but oldies to keep you company today. No disrespect, Captain Bailey."

"None taken," she replied, as Nikos blew us a kiss and took off. "So how did you manage in the crew quarters last night?"

An image of Alex's bare butt flashed before my eyes. "Fine. Not bad at all."

"I talked to your mother. The situation with your uncle and aunt hasn't changed."

Great. Another night in the cramped bowels of the ship.

"I don't mind taking the same bunk again. I mean, it's just to sleep." I flashed Captain Bailey a convincing smile and realized I actually meant it. I'd slept surprisingly well after my midnight snack.

"Fine." Captain Bailey nodded. "Come see me if you need anything."

"Well..." I gazed at the clusters of white houses set into the surrounding hillsides. "I was hoping to check out the island. Is there anyone who can take me ashore?"

"Chef Alexandros will be leaving soon. He's picking up some supplies for dinner, so you'll be on your own while he's at the market. Unless one of the other guests want to join you."

"I'm okay going solo, but I'll see if anyone else wants to join."

"You have half an hour."

I watched Nikos, Isabelle, Thomas, and Teri take off on the small boat, until they were tiny specks against the horizon. I'd lost a full day with Nikos, but better safe than dead. It was nice to soak up the sun and scenery while I had breakfast. I always enjoyed eating outside—al fresco. I liked the expression al fresco. It sounded like a multi-national conglomerate of fresh air, run by a benevolent man named Al. One of my co-workers told me Italians sometimes used the term to mean that someone was 'in the chill,' a.k.a in prison.

I certainly wasn't eating like I was in prison. My breakfast came exactly as I'd requested and it was delicious. Alex was behaving, or maybe he just wanted to avoid having to make extra snacks for me. I gobbled up the last bite and made my way to the salon.

Joseph Uncle and Thomas's father, George, were playing cards. Naani chatted with Fia, while Dolly and Rachel Auntie went over wedding stuff with Thomas's mother.

"Kalimera," Kassia said when she saw me. "Did you have breakfast? You need to eat more. Look at you. All skin and bones."

I'm pretty sure she would've said the same thing to a sumo wrestler at the peak of his bulking diet.

"Kalimera, Kassia. Kalimera, everyone." I dropped a kiss on Naani's cheek. "I'm headed to the island if anyone wants to join me."

"Poh," said George. "Nothing but bees and mule tracks out there. Wait until we get to Hydra, where I was born. Then you will see what a *real* island looks like."

I laughed. "I look forward to it." Thomas's parents had an opinion about everything.

"I would love to join you, Moti," said Fia. "I'll go grab my camera."

Dolly harrumphed from her corner, still pissed she had to share the same planet as her. Fia shot her a venomous parting look. The air hissed between them.

"This is wrong." George threw his playing cards on the table. "We're ruined."

It took me a minute to realize he was referring to the game he was playing with Joseph Uncle, and not what had gone wrong between Dolly and Fia in a galaxy far, far away.

"We're missing a card." Joseph Uncle spread out his cards, and the two men peered over them.

"The Three of Spades," George said.

Oh shit.

"Hannah, where is the Three of Spades?" He turned to one of the crew hands, who was definitely not Hannah.

"I'll get you a new pack." She darted out of the salon.

"Can you believe this?" George moaned to Kassia.

"Ti na kanoume tora?" She shrugged. "What are we going to do now?"

Not satisfied by her level of sympathy, George turned to Joseph Uncle. "Thousands and thousands of Euros, and this is what we get. A used pack of cards."

"I'll see you all later," I said. A trail of guilt followed as I left the room. Swiping a card from that deck had been one of the impulses I often got. I took random, insignificant things—stuff I thought no one would miss. I'd miscalculated this time, and the crew was being blamed for it.

I turned the corner, looking dejectedly at my toes, and ran smack into Alex.

"Whoa, easy." He steadied me, then rubbed his chest where I'd head-butted him. "I thought we made up." He was referring to the stupor-inducing midnight snack he'd left for me. I flushed as I recalled licking dribbles of honey off my fingers.

"Yeah, that was pretty...good. Thanks." I hid my hands behind my back, as if he'd be able to replay the scene if he saw them.

"The Captain said you're joining me ashore."

"Yes. And Fia is coming too."

"She's already on the boat. I was coming to get you."

Our boat wasn't as fancy as the one Nikos had taken, but a rigid inflatable dinghy that wobbled when I got on. I clutched my seat, cursing my short-sightedness. I'd pictured floating on a beautiful castle for two weeks, completely ignoring that I'd have to get on and off it. Now the only thing between me and the bottomless pit of the sea was a piece of puffed-up plastic.

"Here." Alex handed me a life vest. He seemed to remember things I told him in passing, like the fact that I couldn't swim. On the other hand, it could just be a standard safety protocol.

No. Fia isn't wearing one. Maybe I just look like the one most likely to tip over.

"Let's go, Eddie." Alex gave the guy at the wheel a thumbs-up. His dark hair whipped wildly as we took off. No man-bun today. No chef's coat either. He wore a T-shirt, shorts, and leather sandals—nothing that screamed for attention, but when you threw in his coarse stubble and unruly locks...

I put on my sunglasses, because that's the polite way to ogle hot people. You have to look casual and a bit bored. I angled my face away when he settled next to Fia, dropping a tote full of net shopping bags by his feet.

It didn't take us long to get to the sandy beach lining the bay. Windmills and churches dotted the hills around us. Alex helped Fia out first, grabbing her camera and lenses. Then he held his hand out for me. My heart leaped the same time I did. I'm pretty sure it had to do with the fear of falling into the water and not from the way he grabbed me—warm and strong—as he pulled me on to the pier.

"I have to get back to the yacht in time to make lunch," he said. "Eddie's needed onboard, so he'll be back in two hours. If you'd like to stay longer, he can swing by again later." Both men looked at me and Fia for confirmation.

"That's more than enough time for me," Fia said. "I just want to take in the sights and shoot a couple of frames. Unless you want to stay longer, Moti?"

"No. Two hours is perfect."

"Great." Eddie started maneuvering the dinghy back out to

sea. "I'll pick you guys up by the pier. Enjoy the island." He waved as he took off.

"You ladies know where you're heading?" Alex asked as we walked down the pier. He gave us a few pointers—highlights of places we might want to see—and then took off for the market. We heard him greet a line of locals having their morning coffee outside the stores and cafes. He told them to get their lazy asses to work. They reacted with wild gestures, some good-natured cursing and hearty guffaws.

Fia and I took the bus to the main village, admiring the rugged slopes, the almond groves, and homes of rust-colored stone. The village itself was a labyrinth of winding streets, terracotta rooftops, and cobbled steps. Courtyards filled with herbs and geraniums. Mulberry trees sheltered taverna tables and the odd bougainvillea waved brightly.

We walked under an archway of flowers, took the tiny steps off an alley, and ended up on the rooftops. The village lay before us, dotted with fountains and little churches. Fia clicked her camera with Oscar-night-like frenzy.

"A couple of frames, huh?" I said.

She laughed as she reviewed an image on her screen. "I can't stop."

I leaned back against the wall and watched her. Although she'd grown up with Dolly and Rachel Auntie, she was different. Dolly would've freaked at the thought of jumping on a local bus. Rachel Auntie would've gotten on the bus, then glared at all the passengers, because surely one of them was going to pounce on her gold chain. Both of them would nag me for not getting a taxi instead. But Fia... She didn't nag. She didn't drag. She didn't fill up silences with endless chatter. She had a relaxed sense of freedom—a lightness that came from not caring if the world saw you or not. Her riot of silver hair added a touch of defiance. She was trim and toned and looked fantastic for her age. I got the impression it was something she did for herself—because she respected her body and made it a priority.

I thought back to the last three months—my quest to lose weight, so I'd feel good enough and confident enough when I saw Nikos again. I could take a few lessons from this lady.

"So, what happened between you and my mother?"

She said nothing for a moment, peering into the viewfinder of her camera as if recalling the landscape of another time. Then she turned around and gave me a half-shrug.

"Life," she said.

"Was it a guy?" Besties fight. It's a given. The jealous fight a.k.a "I introduced you to my friend and now you're spending more time with her." The "I saw that dress first" fight. The time your bestie hits you where it hurts, then plays the "I'm telling you the harsh truth because I love you" card. Sometimes your bestie hates the guy you're dating and uses every dirty trick in the book to sabotage your relationship. But the "You hooked up with my dude" fight trumps all. The dude in question could be a crush who has no clue you exist, but as long as your bestie knows it, she's bound by the Code of Bestie Ethics. The only exception is when you both fawn over the same unattainable celebrities. Mutual fangirling is a powerful bonding experience, but when it crosses over to a real-life crush, the gloves come off. Next thing you know, you're posting pictures of each other that you both swore you deleted.

Fia fiddled with the dials on her camera. She clicked a photo of me beneath the tumble of roses growing over the walls. "You could say that." She took a few more shots, nodded at the screen and added, "It was most definitely a guy."

People's pasts were fascinating. Scratch the surface deep enough and you'd unearth all kinds of dusty stories. "Was he worth it?"

"I don't know." Fia shrugged. "You should ask Dolly." She slid the camera strap over her shoulder, cross-body style. "It's all water under the bridge, at least for me. The important thing is being able to look yourself in the eye."

Okayyy. So apparently it was Dolly who overstepped her turf. With whom? My father? Someone before my father?

We returned to the port on foot instead of taking the bus again. Following one of the trails Alex told us about, we wandered down the hillside to the cheerful, grinning mascot of Kea—a giant stone lion. Legend had it that Kea was once inhabited by water nymphs whose beauty, along with their idyllic green island, provoked the jealousy of the Gods. As this was a recipe for tragedy in ancient Greece, a kerfuffle of epic proportions followed. The Gods sent a lion to chase the nymphs away and destroy the island. All the water disappeared and the plants and trees began to die. A temple was built in honor of the most powerful God—Zeus, who was quite chuffed with this turn of events and sent rain, restoring the island's beauty. As a bonus, he restrained the lion and left him carved in stone. In another account, the nymphs were real bitches and wreaked havoc on the island, until the lion appeared and chased them away. Either way, the lion sat, smiling cheekily over ancient mysteries as we trekked by on our way to the harbor.

The cafes had their tables set outside for lunch. People sat under wide umbrellas, sharing ouzo and *mezedes*. We stopped at a shop for souvenirs. It sold everything from cheese and beer to sarongs, snorkeling gear, and furniture. At the back of the store, was a rack full of oddities: curtain fabric with the hooks still attached, a fishing net that looked like it was gnawed through by a rodent, rope flower baskets, a brand-new wedding dress, and two ladies' swimsuits.

"You throw nothing out on an island," said Fia, brushing past me to check out the ceramics. "Things are difficult to come by and equally difficult to get rid of."

I pulled out one of the swimsuits and held it against me. It was a one-piece with thin stripes running vertically—an important detail when you're trying to look lean and long (as opposed to horizontal stripes that made me look like a round-bottomed flask). The back was a U-shaped dip. The price tag was faded, its edges starting to yellow. It looked like the suit had been hanging on the rack a long, long time, but it had clean, classic lines and was exactly my size.

Come join me. The water's perfect. Nikos had beckoned from the pool. And then he'd said something about secluded coves and nooks.

I saw myself wearing the swimsuit, laughing and cavorting on a white pebble beach with him. My three-thumbed unicorn.

The important thing is being able to look yourself in the eye. Fia's words came back to me.

I hovered over the swimsuit. Was I being fair to Nikos? Did I like him for *him* or his extra thumb? Was I being fair to myself? I didn't swim. I was terrified of the water, yet I was contemplating this purchase because it would help me get closer to Nikos. The suit would paint the picture of a fun-loving girl, who had the same fun-loving goals that he did, which included (shudder) diving off a cliff.

If Ma Anga was right and Nikos really was my soul mate, it would just happen, right? Without me trying to mold myself into someone else. I placed the swimsuit back on the rack and walked away.

Fia and I took a table outside one of the fish tavernas. She chugged down a cold beer while I enjoyed an ice-cream. It was barely noon, but the pavements sizzled with hazy heat.

"Is that Alex?" Fia pointed the heel of her bottle toward the beach.

We watched as he dropped his bags and shrugged out of his clothes. He wore a pair of swim shorts underneath, obviously prepared for impromptu dips in the sea. He started running bare-chested—Baywatch-style—toward the water.

Such a show-off.

Slicing through the waves until his head was a small, dark blob, he disappeared under the surface for an alarming and ridiculously show-offy stretch of time. Doused in seawater and glistening from head to toe, he came back out, emulating an iconic James Bond scene where Daniel Craig saunters out of the water in tight trunks—rugged and sun-soaked against the backdrop of sparkling water.

It was weird witnessing a hunk-in-trunks moment with Fia. She slid her sunglasses down her nose and observed him over the rim. Obviously, she hadn't been listening to my inner dialogue when I said it's best to ogle hot people from *behind* the shade of dark lenses.

"What's he doing?" she asked.

Hmmm, maybe she really was observing and not ogling.

Alex sat cross-legged on the beach, half in the water, and half out. The waves lapped around him as he twisted and turned something in his hand.

We left the taverna and walked to the sandy shore of the harbor. Fia slipped out of her sandals and waded over to Alex. I stood by the pier, keeping an eye out for our pickup.

"Moti!" Fia waved, calling me over.

I stepped into the water gingerly. It came up to my calves—not enough to sweep me away, but people could drown in an inch of this shit, so it was a valiant move on my part. Holding up the hem of my dress, I walked to where Fia watched Alex with great interest.

"Look," she said. "It's a starfish."

Alex was extricating a tiny, lobster-red starfish from the cords of a discarded fishing net. Its bumpy spines radiated from the center in perfect symmetry—a fiery star fallen from the heavens into Poseidon's realm.

"Is it alive?" I asked. Starfish breathe through little tubes that run over their entire body. To survive, they need to be completely submerged in water.

"It's hard to tell." Alex untangled another arm from the netting. The pattern of sun-filtered waves danced on the back of his hands through the water. He kept the starfish under the surface and worked it gently through the knots. "Let's see, shall we?" he said when it was finally free.

I held my breath as he rested the starfish on the seabed. Tips of broken shells peeked through the sand. The three of us peered over the motionless starfish as seaweed swirled around our legs.

Come on. Come on.

It was suddenly imperative the little starfish move. The whole day distilled down to that one moment and that one vibrant sea star in the water. Waves broke around us with lacey froth on the shore. A cloud drifted across the sky like the brilliant white sail of a ship.

The starfish moved. At first it looked like it was just being rocked by the waves. Then its arm extended, feeling the sand with the wiggly feet on its underside. It had thousands of soft, rippling tubes that moved with coordinated grace, gripping and releasing the sand, propelling the starfish forward in wavelike motions.

"Ha!" Fia high-fived Alex. He grinned like a proud daddy as his baby disappeared into the sea.

"Eddie will be here soon," he said. "We should make our way to the pier."

"Be there in a minute," I said. The starfish was gone, but I stood rooted to the spot, not ready to leave.

As Fia and Alex walked to the meeting point, I dropped the hem of my dress and let it float around my knees. The water felt warm—tiny bubbles of foam breaking against my skin. The tiny sea star had jump-started something in me. Maybe I identified with it because starfish don't swim either. And yet it had reached for the water. The sea was its home.

Oh, to be so sure of your place in the sun. Or the sea. Or the sky.

I turned as a kid shrieked in delight behind me. He had a spade and bucket in his hands. The waves splashed him, and he splashed back, throwing spades full of sand at them. His cap shadowed his face, baring just the tip of a sun-warmed nose and the curve of his smile.

I want to be like that, I thought.

Like him.

Like the starfish.

No worries, no fears.

I closed my eyes and breathed in the salty smell of the sea. The waves came and went, the sound pulsating to the rhythm of my breath. I rose over it—floating weightlessly, aimlessly—as gritty particles of sand washed away from my feet.

"I want to learn how to swim!" I yelled, and then laughed at the startled expression on the little boy's face. "I want to learn how to swim for *me.*"

I ran past him, past Fia, past Alex, all the way back to the souvenir shop on the quay.

"Hi." I was breathless as I held up my purchase for the cashier. The wet hem of my dress made little puddles on the floor. "I'd like to buy this swimsuit, please."

CHAPTER SEVEN

B UYING A SWIMSUIT WAS ONE THING. GETTING IN THE WATER WAS another.

I figured I'd wait until no one was around before dipping my feet in the pool. Learning to swim on my own wasn't happening. It would be just another Greek tragedy. I could picture Ma Anga crowing, *'I told you so!'* the moment they dragged my limp body out of the pool. All I wanted to do was to make friends with the water—touch it, feel it, say hello. Like a first date. Not that I'm touchy-feely on the first date, except for that one time with Jay—I got turned on because he said he could make a prosthetic thumb I could stick on any guy I wanted to introduce to Dolly.

Jay turned out to be a liar, but providence had now graced me with someone who didn't need a prosthetic thumb to win Dolly's approval. Nikos was naturally endowed. And he'd just climbed aboard the Abigail Rose II like a boss, holding...an octopus.

"Look what I caught." He waved the floppy sea creature at us. "And there are more in the boat."

Apparently, spearing octopuses was a thing. Nikos and Thomas had returned from their diving trip with dinner for everyone. They showed off their catch, relaying stories of their hunting skills.

Isabelle looked a bit green and marched off to her cabin with her attendant in tow. "Teri, I need your help. I have octopus ink all over me."

Hannah stepped aside as they brushed past her. "I'll let the chef know you'll be having octopus for dinner."

Fia and I exchanged a look. We were both thinking of Alex hauling bags of brown-paper wrapped meat and herbs and vegetables into the dinghy.

"I can't wait to make dinner for you tonight," he said. "You're going to love this." He waved a feathery herb in our faces, his enthusiasm infectious. "Wild fennel. So sweet and fragrant."

I felt a pang of sympathy for Alex as I made my way to the cabin. He was probably used to juggling passengers' wishes, but being a yacht chef was not an easy gig. He was responsible for every meal served onboard. He cooked for both the clients and crew—breakfast, lunch, dinner, dessert, snacks—while keeping track of dietary restrictions and requests. He went to bed after midnight and was up hours before me. And, he'd still managed to leave a little treat on the kitchen counter for me. Maybe I needed to cut him some slack.

The bathroom door opened and out strolled Alex, interrupting my thoughts.

"What's this?" He dangled my bra on the tip of his finger.

"God, you startled me. I didn't know you were here."

He continued to advance, his infuriating eyebrow cock in place.

"It's a bra." I swatted his finger out of my face.

"What's it doing in there?" He motioned toward the en suite.

"Brushing its teeth. What do you *think* it's doing?" I huffed. "I washed it and hung it up to dry."

"This boat has a whole crew to cater to your needs. You do not wash. You do not dry. And for crying out loud, you do not ambush me with random, falling objects." He shook the double-cupped garment at me. "I get in the shower and this thing bitch-slapped me in the face. Just hand your laundry to the crew and everything will be looked after. Katalaves?"

"No. No katala..." Whatever he said. "I don't like anyone touching my underwear."

His eyebrow quirked higher.

God, how was I feeling sorry for this guy a little while ago?

He looked like he was about to say something, but then his expression changed. Obviously, the crew had rules of conduct when it came to fraternizing with passengers. Alex had been about to flirt with me. I was pretty sure of it.

"How about we pick a designated spot for your bra?" He walked back into the bathroom, found a hook and hung it by the strap. Then, he patted it in a *there, there* gesture, as if to appease me, but we both knew what he was really doing. Touching my underwear.

Before I could protest, Alex gave me a smart salute and sauntered out the door.

I walked up to my bra, tight lipped, with every intention of staying mad. Something tugged at the corners of my mouth. Could it be? Was I...smiling?

Dammit, I was smiling.

"Well, well," I said to my bra, untwisting the strap so it hung straight. "At least one of us is getting some action."

I showered and changed for my dinner date with Naani. Chasing a three-thumbed unicorn is fun and thrilling in a nerve-wracking way, but a girl's got to make time for her grandma. Naani took her evening meals early, so I joined her at the table Hannah set up for us, away from everyone else.

"Isn't this romantic?" Naani chuckled.

"Just you, me, and the sea." I flipped my freshly shampooed hair to the side.

We were on the way to Syros, the next island on the itinerary. The sea stretched around the yacht in sun-flecked ripples toward a dusky horizon. A salty breeze whipped the waves into little white crests.

When Hannah presented us with the menu, Naani waved it away.

"Let the chef surprise us," she said. Leaning closer, she whispered, "His food did strange things to me last night. Your Naani felt like a young filly."

"You too?" I laughed as I nibbled one of the appetizers. "He left me a late-night snack and I felt like my bones turned to honey."

Hannah returned with two steaming platters. "Chef Alexandros has prepared *revithia* for you tonight—chickpea stew." It was topped with feta cheese and accompanied by olives and slices of crusty bread. "Enjoy."

Naani was vegetarian by choice, and I had requested the same meal (because hello? The alternative was octopus—courtesy of Nikos and Thomas—and I didn't do suckers or tentacles), but we were both deflated as we stared at our dinner. Everything looked and smelled delicious, but let's face it. Chickpeas? They were beige. And bland. And humble. And boring. Naani had cans full of them in her pantry. We silently and unanimously expected something more exotic. Well, exotic to us. Where was the *spanakopita*? The *skordalia*? The *saganaki*? All the things that sounded like they'd hiss and sizzle on your tongue?

"Hey." Naani speared a chickpea on the prong of her fork. "What do they call it when you kill a chickpea?" She chewed it slowly while I waited for the punchline. "A hummuside. Get it?" She chuckled. "Homicide, hummus-cide."

"That's awful, Naani. Really, *really* bad. What makes it worse is that it was a pea-meditated hummuside."

We laughed at our terrible puns, but with the second bite of our dinner, we grew quiet. Something was different about Alex's chickpeas. They were drunk and voluptuous, like they'd simmered in dark wine for hours, turning fat and round and luscious. They had a rustic, appealing sweetness that was hard to pin down.

"Did he use sugar?" I asked.

"No. Not sugar." Naani shook her head. "Dates, maybe? Or prunes?"

We ate some more and tried to dissect what we were tasting.

"Chocolate," I said.

"Close. But it's more earthy."

I eyed Naani as she used the crusty bread to soak up the last bits of gravy clinging to her bowl. Bread was a no-no for me, but it was exactly what the rest of my dish was begging for. I caved in and did the same.

Potatoes on Day 1. Bread on Day 2. Alex is breaking down my objections, one by one—like a referee in my lifelong fight against food.

When Hannah stopped by the table, we were sitting back in our chairs, whipped into a state of submission by the humble chickpea. Alex didn't serve big portions, but what he served was infinitely satisfying.

"I would like to have a word with the chef," Naani said.

"I'll let him know," Hannah said, collecting our plates.

"Young man," said Naani, when Alex appeared at our table. "I've been cooking my whole life, but I've never been able to get chickpeas to taste like this. They were absolutely divine." She pinched her fingers, brought them to her lips and smacked them.

"Thank you." He gave Naani a little bow.

"What's your secret?"

Yes, Alex. Tell us. What's the secret to making a shapeless chef's coat look so cool?

"Onions. Lots and lots of onions."

"Onions?"

"The right kind of onions. Equal parts sharp and sweet. You slice them real thin. Then you add them to a pan of hot olive oil. Turn down the heat and let them do their thing. You'll be tempted to lift the lid and check on them. Don't. Wait until they tell you they are ready, until they start smelling like cinnamon and sugar. Then you stir, until they are rich and thick and chocolaty."

"Ahhh. So that's what I was tasting." Naani absorbed this nugget of culinary treasure. "But I didn't see any onions in the stew."

"They disintegrate once you add water and more heat. Throw in your cooked chickpeas, some rosemary and a few more glugs of olive oil. You can add whatever else you like, but that's the base for my *revithia*. I let it bake in the oven until all the flavors meld."

"Moti," Naani turned to me with great solemnity. "You must marry this man. We have to take him home with us."

"*You* marry him." I laughed. Alex looked amused, but not the eyebrow-cocking kind of amusement, which he reserved for my bras and awkward mishaps.

"Young man, what's your name?"

"Alexandros Veronis, but please call me Alex."

"Alex, I am too old for you, but your eggplant fritters last night? They took me back to my younger days, to my first love. Did I ever tell you about him, Moti?"

I shook my head.

"Prem Prakash Pyarelal. He sold vegetables in the market with his father. My mother took me with her all the time, because he always slipped something extra into our bag when he saw me. Whenever his father caught him, he got smacked in the head, but it didn't stop him. He told me I had the most elegant fingers he'd ever seen. He used to leave food outside our door. Random things...two *rotis* and a block of jaggery, half a *ladoo* wrapped in foil, a carrot that was half orange, half purple. I remember stuffing two pillows under my blanket one night and sneaking out to meet him. We had a picnic under the moon. He fed me eggplant fritters. It was the most scandalous thing I'd ever done. He was Hindu. I was Christian. My parents had a fit when they found out. It was a small town. Someone saw me with him. Reputations were at stake. I was married within a fortnight and whisked off to the city. I never saw him again. And you know...

we never kissed. We barely spoke. He smiled, and I smiled and most of the time, we sat on a bench and stared at the grass. The whole time, I was so happy, I thought my heart would burst.

"Last night, eating those fritters, I remembered how thrilling it all was. The secret looks, the butterflies in my stomach, the half-empty bottle of perfume he slipped into my hands. I wish I did more scandalous things, but my time has passed. Now, this one here..." Naani placed her hand over mine. "She has her whole life ahead, but you know what she's doing? She's angling for that guy over there." Naani pointed to Nikos, seated behind the pane of glass separating us from the salon. "Why? Because he has three thumbs." She slapped her thigh and hooted. "Because that's the only man her mother will have as her son-in-law. I think it's high time she gave everyone the—"

"Naani!" I glared at her.

"They want an extra digit? Here." Naani stuck her middle finger out. "Ehhh?" She held it up toward the salon, where everyone remained oblivious to her salute. She waved it at the sea, the sky, the whole world. "You don't need a man with three thumbs, Moti. Just one with magic in his hands. One who will hold your heart as if it's the most precious thing in the world. See this man here, standing right in front of you? He can transform onions into chocolate. If that's not magic, I don't know what is. We'll have to do something about his hair, but—"

"I'm so sorry." I apologized to Alex, while simultaneously trying to contain Naani's rebel finger. I wasn't really sorry. I was embarrassed that Alex knew about my quest for Mr. Three Thumbs, so I was cringe-shushing Naani's finger. "She *did* say your food does strange things to her."

It's your fault, Alex. Your cooking is messing with our brains.

"Come, Naani. I'll see you to your cabin."

We left Alex on the deck, with a strange expression on his face. He was probably thinking, *Wait, what's wrong with my hair?*

"This is what I should've done a long time ago." Naani was

not going down without a fight. "This is what I wanted to do all those years I was married to your Naana. Tell him to piss off, and everyone else along with it."

She held her veiny hand up high, the offensive gesture still in place. I draped my shawl over it, but now it looked like I was carefully escorting a giant, tented erection to her cabin.

CHAPTER EIGHT

B Y THE TIME I SAID GOODNIGHT TO NAANI AND MADE MY WAY UP TO the sky deck, the sun had set. Birds were flying home against a pomegranate sky. Bits of conversation drifted up from the lower deck, where everyone was finishing up dinner. I cocooned myself up in my shawl again, lay on the leather sectional, and stared at the sky. It was becoming my favorite thing to do. I didn't get to see stars often enough at home. One by one they appeared, as darkness swept across the heavens.

How far must they be that I don't feel them burning? Do they feel each other's warmth, or do they spend eternity being cool and blue and distant? Shining and looking pretty.

"Mind if I join you?" It was Joseph Uncle, a cup of coffee in one hand and dessert in another.

I sat up and made room for him. He balanced his coffee on the armrest and offered me his cake.

"It's good," he said, when I declined. He had a forkful and stared at the horizon. "Do you miss having your father around, Moti?"

Joseph Uncle had never broached the subject before. Something was obviously on his mind. "I don't remember having him around," I said. "I was two when he left. I know I can go to him if I need anything, but we've never been close. Do I miss having a father figure I can turn to every day? Of course. But I have you to boss me around at work." I laughed, but his expression remained gloomy. "Are you okay? Did you and Rachel Auntie make up?"

"Rachel is ashamed of me, Moti. And so is Isabelle. All this time, I didn't even know. I didn't know what they really thought of me." He had another bite and kept his eyes on the silhouette of the distant shore. I'd never seen Joseph Uncle so sad.

"It's not like that," I said. "The wedding is stressing everyone out."

"Rachel and I were different, you know? We married for love. In that day, in that time and place, we were an exception. Your father and Dolly? They were introduced by their families. Rachel and I held our breath as they got to know each other, because it was customary for the older sibling to get married before the younger one. I had to wait until Dolly tied the knot before I could ask for Rachel's hand in marriage. Our wedding was the happiest day of my life. When Isabelle was born, our world was complete. I started seeing myself through their eyes. I thought I was a good husband, a good father. But now, I feel like I've been an embarrassment all along. One they've been putting up with because I'm also their meal ticket."

"That's not true. Rachel Auntie could have married that newspaper mogul her father had lined up for her. But she chose you. She fought for you. And she has her own things going on. I know you think of them as hobbies, but she feels good when she's contributing financially too. Are you really going to let a box of underwear get in the way of the big picture?"

"It was a pretty big box," he said, finishing his cake.

"I'm sure it was." I chuckled, wishing I'd seen the look on George and Kassia's faces when he'd presented it. I understood why Joseph Uncle saw nothing wrong with it. He took pride in what he did. If he were a baker, he would've given them a basket full of loaves. But he sold underwear—crotchless, seamless, G-string, V-string, leather, lace, and the elephant-faced ones with a hollow trunk to hold a man's ding dong. Thongs were his thing, so he didn't understand why it would embarrass his wife and daughter.

"You need to stop taking it so seriously and go make up with Rachel Auntie and Isabelle," I said.

"No. Not this time. This time they crossed the line. Let them come to me." He drained his coffee and got up. His ego-wounded frame disappeared as the elevator doors shut behind him.

A moment later, they re-opened and Nikos strutted out—blue jeans, black shirt, slicked-back hair. Something shifted in my belly. *Yes!*

Yes, to butterflies in my stomach. Although it could also be the chickpeas. I always had trouble digesting those.

"There you are." He slid next to me—aftershave and smooth confidence. "Missed you at dinner, glikia mou."

"I ate early with my grandmother."

"Yes, I saw the two of you out on the deck. Do you mind?" He held up a cigarette.

I watched as he lit it and took a drag, blowing the smoke into the air slowly. His lips formed a small O, like the aftermath of a kiss you don't want to end. He tapped the glowing tip of his cigarette on the ashtray and caught me staring at his double thumb.

"It's ugly, yes?" He stretched his hand out, turning his wrist to examine it.

"It's different, but I don't think it's ugly." *It's holy. It's holy-fuck-I'm-sitting-next-to-a-guy-with-three-thumbs.* "In fact, when I was born, a fortune-teller told my mother that my soul mate would have an extra thumb."

Nikos stared at me for a moment, his O transforming into an *Oh-my-God-I'm-sitting-next-to-a-girl-who-will-boil-my-pet-rabbit-if-her-horoscope-says-so.* Then his face cracked and he burst out laughing. "That's a good one." He pointed his cigarette at me. The wispy smoke did exactly what I wanted to do—curling up and dying.

I mean, I finally got it out there, even if Nikos had taken it as a joke. It was a bit like Joseph Uncle's big box of underwear. It's funny to everyone else, but it means something to you.

"Something else I need to tell you." I might as well put it *all* out there. "I bought a swimsuit today, but I can't go diving or snorkeling because I can't swim."

"Can you kiss?" Nikos stubbed his cigarette out and leaned closer. I could smell the tobacco on his breath. "Because swimming is…" He shrugged indifference. "But kissing. Kissing is important."

My throat went dry as his face filled the frame of my vision.

Please let it be epic and beautiful and memorable. I know it's not a rain kiss, or a chase-through-the-airport kiss, or a top-of-the-Empire-State-Building kiss. But it's the kiss I've been waiting for since the moment I ran into Nikos and his extra appendage. And it's happening. It's happening right now.

My eyelids fluttered shut and I raised my lips to meet his.

"Nikos!" We flew apart at Isabelle's voice. "What are you doing?" Her eyes darted between Nikos and me. "Did you forget about our meeting?"

"That's tonight?" Nikos pinched the bridge of his nose. He extricated himself and got up sheepishly under Isabelle's icy glare. "Give me a minute," he said to her. "I'll be right there."

Isabelle hovered for a few beats. Then she got in the elevator and punched her floor.

"Sorry, glikia mou." Nikos sounded remorseful over our almost-kiss. "I have to go. Isabelle and Thomas are going over wedding stuff with Teri and me. They want to make sure the best man and maid of honor know what they're doing. But I'm all yours tomorrow night. We'll be in Mykonos. Put on your dancing shoes because I'm taking you clubbing."

I sat back with a happy grin after he left.

Yes! Dancing with Nikos in Mykonos—the bronzed, throbbing, party animal in the heart of the Cyclades.

It was clear Nikos was open to having some fun on the high seas but was a relationship on his horizon? The forever-kind that I was looking for? And even if it was, how would we handle a long-distance relationship in the interim?

Ugh. I pulled the brakes on my train-wreck of thoughts. It

was the kind of self-sabotaging most women do to themselves. We race *way* ahead. We want to cover all the possibilities. We want to jump in, but we also want to protect ourselves. Men? They're just grateful if we show them our boobs. And who knows? Maybe I wouldn't think Nikos was so hot after I got to know him. I mean, I admired his muscles, but his bulgy biceps made his arms stick out like twin parentheses, like he was perpetually carrying carpet rolls under them. After a while, that could get annoying.

Forget the muscles. Think about the thumbs. The THUMBS.

My brain went back and forth until I drifted off under the stars.

When I woke, the moon was high in the sky. I stretched and re-draped my shawl around me. Time to get to bed. Since Joseph Uncle and Rachel Auntie were still on the outs, that meant another night in Alex's cabin. Hopefully, he was already asleep.

I was halfway to the elevator when I stepped on a pool noodle. I returned it to the big bunker that stored all the pool toys and gadgets. A volleyball net, inflatable pool loungers, yoga mats, and even a remote-controlled snack float. My fingers closed around a ping-pong ball. It was light and round—a sphere of air on my palm. It would never drown, it would always float back up to the top. I rolled it back and forth between my fingers before putting it in my pocket. No one would miss it. A whole bag of ping-pong balls lay on top of a foam collar—the kind you put around your neck to keep your head above the surface. I picked up the collar and gazed at the pool. It was glassy and quiet under the light of the moon. Blue-green lights glowed under its rim.

Should I? Shouldn't I?

I had tried on the swimsuit after my shower and left it on under my clothes, so the moment was perfect. With no one around, I wouldn't be making a fool of myself either. Still, I was filled with all kinds of dread.

Go ahead. Make friends with it.

Or stand there like a loser all your life, Moti.

I hated that voice. The inner niggling that made me feel like shit.

I slipped out of my dress and positioned the neck float around me, gripping it tight.

All right. Let's do this.

Standing by the edge of the stairs, I took a deep breath and lowered myself onto the first step. The water felt warm around my ankles. I lifted my foot and drew a figure eight. Ripples danced across the surface of the pool.

It's not so bad.

I took the next step. This time the water rose to my knees.

Okay. Good enough. Let's just wave and say hello to the rest of the pool from here.

I sat on the step and let the water flow around my navel. It was a total Instagram moment, sitting in the pool with the sea around me and the night sky above. Except the stiff blue float around my neck was ruining the coolness factor.

I dipped lower, sliding my butt onto the next step and gasped. The water lapped around my shoulders now, a little too close to my nose and mouth.

Turns out swimming is ten times worse than an ex who won't go away. Normally when you don't like something, you move away from it. Or, with that persistent ex, you slap a restraining order. But there's no restraining water. It's fluid and it comes at you from all directions—no shape, no form, nothing you can shove or knee or pepper-spray to defend yourself. So, this thing between Mr. Pool and me? I didn't see it happening. Still, like a bad date, I decided to grin and bear it. Well, not grin. Because my lips were clenched tight. Not a drop of water was getting through.

"Go back up one step." I jumped at the sound of Alex's voice.

"Dammit, Alex. I could have drowned!" I glared at him as I stood in waist-deep water. "How long have you been there?" I was pretty sure he allowed himself a smile because it took a couple of beats before he came out of the shadows.

"You were sleeping when I got here. I didn't want to disturb you, so I did what I usually do."

"Which is?"

"I come up here at the end of my shift to unwind, to look at the lights." He pointed to the glimmer of distant places on the shore. "And you? I assume, are trying to swim?" He squatted beside the pool and motioned to my neck float.

I didn't feel like explaining myself to a guy who had nicer hair than me. "I'm fine. I'm just mucking around."

"I can see that, but I'm not comfortable leaving you in the water alone, so you either listen to me or you get out of the pool."

My jaw stiffened as I considered his options. "I'm not going anywhere."

"Fine. Then do as I say. Go back up one step."

Fireworks flew between us.

"Fine." I plopped myself on the step and folded my arms across my chest. Water swirled around my shoulders.

"Moti." His tone caught me off-guard. It was softer, less bossy. "There are some skills in life that are essential. Learning to survive in water is one of them. Swimming is important."

Earlier, Nikos had dismissed the skill with a shrug and said kissing was more important.

One night, two men, two different opinions. I agreed with them both. Kissing *and* swimming were both important. If you couldn't swim, you died. If you couldn't kiss, you died (at least, in the dating world, because it substantially reduced the probability of your genes mingling with someone else's).

Alex sensed my resistance slipping away and started coaching me. "Start slow. Scoop up some water and splash it on your face. Good. This time hold your breath when you do it. See? It's not getting in your nose or mouth. It's just like when you're in the shower. Now, take that float off and hand it to me."

"This?" I gripped the foam collar around my neck. "But—"

"Do you trust me?" Alex held his hand out, waiting for it.

I looked from his eyes to his hands to the water.

Human vs. an element of nature.

"Not really," I said. "I mean, you're a great swimmer, and you saved that starfish, but—"

"Wrong question," said Alex. "What I mean is, do you *really* want to learn to swim?"

"Yes." I held onto my foam collar. Vampires wore high collars. Evil queens wore high collars. I needed an air of villainy if I was going to win this battle.

"Let go, Moti." Alex's hand was still outstretched.

I unhooked my safety net from around my neck and handed it to him.

"Thank you. Now just move your hands in the water. Feel it glide against your skin. That's all."

His words soothed the knot in my stomach. My core loosened. My breath started coming easier.

"It's nice," I said, adapting to the feel of water around me. My arms swished from side to side. The movement felt smooth and graceful. "I feel...lighter."

"Good. Now crouch down until your lips are just above the surface. Keep your mouth closed. Yes. Like that. Now do it again, but see if you can get your mouth under the water this time. Just take little dips. You're doing great. Can you go lower? Hold your breath and immerse your nose."

I followed his instructions but came back up sputtering, shaking my head like a wet dog. "Water went in my ears." The feeling of something moving around in my ear canal made me shudder.

Alex laughed as I pulled on my earlobes. "I think that's enough for one night."

I exited the pool and took the towel he held out for me. As he laid it around my shoulders, his fingers brushed against my skin. The rush of air that escaped me caught me off-guard. What the hell?

"Thank you for..." I tilted my head toward the pool.

Alex shrugged and returned my neck float as I dried off. "Just make sure I don't catch you in there by yourself."

The first time he saw me, I was drenched in shipyard waste from head to toe. Then he found me crawling under the bar, choking on a crumb of crostini. As far as Alex was concerned, I was a disaster waiting to happen. No telling what catastrophe I could spin if I decided to test the waters on my own. And he didn't even know about Ma Anga's dire prediction.

I'm going to get it, I thought, throwing a backward glance at the pool as we left. *I'm going to learn. And before this trip is over, I'm going to swim in the sea.*

CHAPTER NINE

T RAITOROUS, *LYING, DOUBLE-CROSSING, DECEITFUL, DEVIOUS*...
I punched the words into my pillow as I tried to fall asleep. My insults did nothing to shut my stomach up. As far as it was concerned, my early dinner with Naani was a distant memory. Been there, digested that. No matter how much I tossed and turned, the beast refused to be silenced.

I tiptoed to the galley for the second night in a row. And for the second night in a row, a covered plate waited on the counter. I picked up the note—the handwriting familiar now.

Amygdalota (almond cookies)

Almond trees grow all over the Greek islands, but you don't always find almonds in the market because gathering and shelling them is costly and time-consuming. I stole these from a friend's orchard in Kea. There were just enough to make a small batch—scented with rose water and flavored with tangerine peel. Chewy, flourless, unbaked. I usually let them set for a few days, but they taste infinitely more vulnerable like this. They are traditionally served at weddings and baptisms, but rebel chefs sometimes pass them off as a midnight snack.

I laughed at the last part. Was I the only one who crept up here in the middle of the night, or did he leave these out to appease any hungry guests?

My stomach didn't care. Half a dozen of the exquisite, white cookies were on the plate, each shaped like a tiny pear, with a clove bud piercing the tip. A dusting of powdered sugar made them look like they were covered in soft snow. It was almost a shame to ruin such a perfect arrangement, but I picked one up and bit into the tender morsel.

The rawness of it took me by surprise. Warm and sweet—the softness of a newborn babe, the brightness of citrus, the soul of roses. As Alex's carefully molded creation came apart in my mouth, a fragment of bittersweet nostalgia surfaced through my awareness. I was a child again—pure and sure, before the world started chewing at my edges. Had Dolly cradled me then? Had she rocked me to sleep? Had she loved me then?

I put the rest of the cookie in my mouth, the rounded bottom half, and held it in the nest of my tongue. I wanted to keep it there, carry it safe in my mouth, but it grew smaller and smaller, dissolving bit by bit until it was all gone. My eyes spilled over, two fat tears rolling down my cheeks.

I pushed the plate away, discarding the clove I was still holding. Alex's cooking was doing things to me. Strange, weird things. All my yearnings and burnings were eating and growing and taking form. His food was giving flesh to my feelings. Alex held the prism to the transcendental, and I filtered through in bands of rainbow emotions. Last night, pineapple and honey aroused me. Tonight, humble almond cookies made me want to curl up in my mother's arms.

I wasn't the only one succumbing to Alex's food-spells. Dolly fainted upon seeing Fia, right after she devoured a plate of appetizers. Naani consumed a bowl of chickpea-and-onion stew and gave the whole world the finger. Joseph Uncle cradled his cake and poured his heart out in a way he'd never done before, starving for Rachel Auntie and Isabelle's respect, ravenous for appreciation.

I put the cover back on the cookies and saved Alex's note. His food spoke to us. It whispered to our deepest desires and stoked our deepest fears. Maybe it was my imagination, and maybe it wasn't. Either way, I was determined to get to the bottom of it. At the same time, I couldn't let Alex distract me from winning Niko's heart. Time was ticking away, and Nikos was my *only* chance to win Dolly's approval. If I failed...

No. Failure was not an option. My whole life was at stake. The thought of crawling back to Chicago and having Dolly's disappointment shadow me around, day in and day out, filled me with dread: *He was right there, Moti. And you couldn't even do that right.*

Well, Ma, guess what? I thought. *I have a date with him tomorrow night. And I can't wait to see your reaction when I tell you about it.*

CHAPTER TEN

"**A** NIGHT OUT WITH NIKOS?" ISABELLE SHRIEKED. IT WAS MORNING on the island of Syros, and we were boarding a private bus. Thomas and his parents wanted to give us a tour of the island before we departed for Mykonos.

"Shh. Keep it down." I was hoping it was a happy shriek, the kind that Dolly made when I told her I was going dancing with Nikos.

"Are you *nuts*?" Isabelle nudged me to the back of the bus. "He'll eat you alive and have your bones for breakfast."

Okay, so it wasn't a happy shriek. For as long as I could remember, everyone around me was on a seesaw. If you tried to make one person happy, it sent the other one off-balance. Up down, up down, we went.

"I knew something was going on between you two when I came looking for him last night." Isabelle spit-whispered in my ear as we took our seats. "Did he kiss you?"

"No, but he would have if you hadn't interrupted."

"Well, it's a good thing I interrupted." If Isabelle's forehead wasn't paralyzed by Botox, it would've furrowed. I could only go by the tone of her voice, which was disconcerting. You don't realize how much you rely on visual cues until they go missing.

I wondered if you could pick different levels when you went in for Botox:

Level 1: High School Reunion. "Doctor, just give me enough to look better than whoever Dylan Jackson is bringing to the event. Because Dylan Jackson has to pay for dumping me, and the sound of his jaw hitting the floor will do nicely, thank you."

Level 2: The Shining. Reserved for when I have kids. First, get them to watch the movie. Then, a little Botox to get my brows up to Jack Nicholson's maniacal level. Next, I poke my head through the door like he did and grin at them. "Who's in charge now, you little shits?"

Level 3: Poker Face. Max me out, so no one can tell what I'm thinking. Tsunami rolling over me or Chris Hemsworth at my door? Same beatific expression.

"Look," Isabelle said. "All this stuff Dolly Auntie keeps going on about... You don't believe in all that bullshit, do you? Nikos having an extra thumb is just a coincidence. Dolly Auntie isn't going to drop dead if you marry someone else."

"Who's marrying someone else?" Dolly slid next to Rachel Auntie on the seat in front of us. "What are you two buzzing about?"

"Nothing," Isabelle and I chimed at the same time. It was a childhood code. One of us could be burying the other in the garden, but if an adult showed up, we played nice until they left.

"What's wrong with Nikos?" I whispered when Dolly and Rachel Auntie started talking to Teri.

"Nothing," Isabelle said. "He's hot, rich, and fabulous. He'll show you a good time. A *great* time. But don't go planning a future with him. He's not about to settle down."

"Isn't that what Joseph Uncle said to you about Thomas?"

"Yes. So?"

"So here you are, getting married."

"It's not everything it's cracked up to be, Moti. Every girl thinks that she'll be the one to tame the player, that she's the one he'll change for. If you had any idea how much *I've* had to change for Thomas..." She looked away and stared out the window.

"All set!" The tour guide clapped as we left the port of Ermoupoli. Pink, white, and ocher buildings cascaded over the hilltops, many crowned by a dazzling church.

I reached for Isabelle's hand and gave it a squeeze. "Is everything okay with you and Thomas?"

She turned to me and smiled. "It is now. I just have to figure out a way to tell Mom and Dad I've converted to the Greek
Orthodox faith."

"You *what*?" My family was mildly Roman Catholic. Mildly,
meaning we picked what we liked and ignored the rest. Basically,
we were going to hell, with a mild chance of heaven.

"You heard me. Thomas's parents weren't ready to accept me
until I converted. It's important *all* their family is Greek Orthodox,
including any children Thomas and I have. And Thomas... Well,
it was just easier to go along with it. Although sometimes I wish
Thomas stood up for me. Mostly though, I wish I stood up for myself." Isabelle shrugged and looked out the window again, dabbing
the corner of her eye.

"Hey, give Joseph Uncle and Rachel Auntie some credit," I
said. "The only thing that matters to them is that you're happy.
They'll handle the news just fine."

"They can't even handle themselves." Isabelle sniffed. "They're
still not talking to each other."

Joseph Uncle's head bounced a few seats ahead. He was con-
versing with Thomas and Nikos.

"He won't even walk me down the aisle," said Isabelle. "This
whole wedding is turning out to be a nightmare." Isabelle honked
her nose, blowing loudly into a tissue. Fortunately, the loud Greek
music playing over the speakers drowned out her snot rocket.

"You want?" She unwrapped two triangles of pastry from her
bag and offered one to me.

"What is it?" I asked, trying to keep the relief out of my voice.
For a second, I'd thought she was passing me her tissue. I'm all for
family supporting family, but I wasn't about to sympathy-sob into
Isabelle's snotty Kleenex.

"I don't know, but it's so good." She closed her eyes as she
tried to pin down the flavor. "Pumpkin and fennel, I think. I saved
a couple from breakfast."

I grabbed her hand. "Don't eat it, Isabelle."

"What's wrong with you?" Isabelle pulled her pastry back.

It's powerful stuff. A few bites and you'll be honking your nose again, like an angry goose on the loose.

I glanced from her to the little parcel of magic that Alex had baked into golden, flaky layers of phyllo.

No, Moti.

No.

Steady now.

Don't. Do. It.

"Gimme that." I snatched the other one.

We licked our fingers and let the crumbs fall on our laps as the bus lumbered up the hills surrounding the shimmering harbor.

Our first stop was a museum in the beautiful Venetian settlement of Ano Syros. As we filed out of the bus, Dolly and Fia bumped each other. They recoiled like they'd touched flaming booger balls and retreated to mutually exclusive trajectories.

Joseph Uncle stood in front of the ticket office making mental calculations. When he first arrived in Chicago from Goa, he would convert everything from U.S. dollars to Indian rupees. Thirty years later, he was still doing it—a habit that always had him shaking his head and trying to bargain. Once, he took Naani to the surgeon and tried to get her a discount.

If one thing had been drilled into me early on, it was to never pay full price without putting up a respectable objection. Every time I bought a coffee at Starbucks, I heard my ancestors chanting, *Shame, shame, shame.*

"Why would anyone pay to look at a bunch of old things?" Joseph Uncle scowled at the exhibit poster.

"Exactly. See?" George elbowed Kassia. "I'm not the only who one thinks that way."

Joseph Uncle and Thomas's father beamed at each other. They'd just found a rare kinship—their dislike for having to part with money. Underwear salesman or billionaire, their atitude about money was the same. Rachel Auntie and Kassia shot each other a sympathetic look.

George's phone rang.

He glanced at the number, then at Kassia. "You guys go on ahead. I'll catch up as soon as I'm done."

"Really, George? Even when we're on a holiday?" Hand on her hip, Kassia waited for an answer, but George was already looking for some place private to take the call.

"A billionaire's lifestyle. Tethered to his phone." Joseph Uncle chuckled, but Kassia shook her head.

"He knows better." She watched him disappear around the building and sighed. "Well, I guess we'll just go on without him."

We walked through the narrow, winding lanes to a lookout point at the top of the hill. Nikos singled me out the moment Isabelle left my side.

"I like your hair up like his." He slid his finger down my nape and an electric jolt shot all the way up to my ponytail. "I can't wait to be alone with you tonight." His voice was low and husky. For my ears only. And from my ears to my brain, where it fried things up good.

While everyone was ooh-ing and aah-ing over the breathtaking views of the island from the top of the hill, I was suffering from the temporary decline in cognitive function that follows an encounter with a really hot guy. It happens to the best of us. Why? Because this is where your evolutionary instinct kicks you to the curb, jumps in the driver's seat, and goes chasing after the potential to elevate your gene pool. There's a science to swooning, compounded by providence dropping a sexy, three-thumbed man into my life.

The rest of the day turned into a blur as I mentally flipped through my luggage for the perfect outfit to induce a mutual swoon. My trip wardrobe was nothing like my Chicago wardrobe. It was a projected wardrobe built around projected scenarios:

Sunset in Santorini or having a drink over the caldera with Nikos: maxi skirt with a thigh-high side slit and a T-shirt to keep it from looking like I was trying too hard.

Yeah, baby.

Lounging by the pool: floppy hat, Jackie O sunglasses, high-waisted shorts, cropped top.

Try to resist me now.

Chance make-out session with Nikos: wide-necked top slipped seductively off one shoulder. Lacy, push-up bra. A swipe of highlighter on the boobs.

Uh-huh. Shine on, girls.

Unfortunately, I'd failed to anticipate a dancing scenario. It had been a while since I'd gone clubbing. Anytime I stayed out past eleven, I braced myself for an escalating stream of texts from Dolly. My mother was a highly evolved worrier. Not only did she cover all the worst-case scenarios, she also had dreams to back them up. Dead relatives were always showing up in her dreams with messages for me. I might have bought it, except the only things dead people wanted me to do were the things Dolly wanted me to do.

They certainly weren't chiming in with tips on what I should wear for my night out with Nikos.

In the end, I opted for a curve-hugging black dress and metallic booties. The only accessory I needed was sex-bomb hair—amped up, but shiny and soft.

Getting ready in the tiny en suite was a challenge. The lighting was horrendous, and I kept bumping my elbows as I tried to blow-dry my hair. I turned on my phone, searched for a track, and kicked up the volume.

Elvis Presley, "It's Now or Never."

Because this was it—my make-it or break-it opportunity with Nikos.

I flipped my head upside down, spritzed on some spray, and

tossed it back up. My hairbrush became a microphone as I sang along with Elvis.

Switching out the hairbrush for my lipstick, I swiped on a shimmery layer and pouted. The siren in the mirror pouted back at me. She curled her eyelashes and applied mascara, her mouth open (because it's impossible *not* to make that face when you have a mascara wand in your hand). Damn, she looked fine.

Elvis and I crooned our devotion to her, our lips curling in tribute.

I pumped up my boobies and backed away from the mirror, giving my reflection two *pew-pew* finger-gun salutes. When the chorus hit, I closed my eyes and swiveled my body around the door frame like it was a pole. My hips gyrated against it for good measure. Then I stood wide-stanced, bending my body at the waist, ass to the ceiling, and performed a saucy hair flip. Dark, sex-bomb tresses fell around my face as the song concluded. My breasts rose and fell in self-congratulatory exhilaration.

It was at this point that I realized I had an audience. Exhilaration turned into trepidation, which turned into indignation when I saw who it was.

"What are you doing here?" My arms crossed instinctively over my chest, as if Alex caught me naked.

"I…uh…" He scratched his chin, like he'd forgotten how to string words into sentences.

"You what?"

His infuriating dimple took over. "That was hot."

I took a step toward him. My intention was to walk past him and out the door—maybe get a face transplant while I was at it. I was tired of the permanent cringe that altered my face whenever I was around Alex.

He must've thought I was about to cause him bodily harm, because he stepped aside and held his palms up. "Captain Bailey's given me the night off. Kassia's cousin in Mykonos has invited all the passengers to her place for dinner. We'll be dropping anchor in a little while. I thought I'd freshen up before heading out. I didn't realize that you'd be…uh…making out with Elvis." He gestured to the door frame I'd been gyrating against.

"Oh no." I sat down on my bed. If we were all expected at Kassia's cousin's place, Nikos and I would have to cancel our plans.

"Don't look so dejected." Alex tossed his chef's coat on the top bunk and shot me a cheeky grin. "We still have many nights together. You just have to put up with someone else's cooking tonight." His T-shirt hugged him in all the right places. Too bad his ego ruined the effect by bulging out in six stupid lumps where his tummy was supposed to be.

Hannah rapped on the door. "Sorry to disturb. Dolly is asking for you, Moti. She said Nikos is looking for you."

"Thanks, Hannah. I'll be up in a minute." As far as Thomas's side of the wedding party was concerned, I was still sharing the suite with my mother. Nikos must've dropped in, hoping to find me. I slipped my phone into my evening bag and was about to leave when I caught Alex's look.

"You and Nikos?" he said. "I thought your grandmother was joking about the whole…" He wiggled his thumbs at me.

"It's written in the stars." I got up, forgetting there was another bed on top of mine. My noggin hit the steel frame and I yelped, pretty sure it would leave a nice, egg-sized lump.

"This is all your fault." I glared at Alex, rubbing my scalp.

My life was chapter after chapter of awkward, embarrassing scenes, but did this jerk have to stand there, witnessing them all?

Double jerk, I thought when his laughter followed me out of the room.

CHAPTER ELEVEN

A S IT TURNED OUT, NIKOS AND I DIDN'T HAVE TO CANCEL OUR date. Clubs in Mykonos didn't start coming alive until after midnight. While everyone waited for the tender to take them back to the yacht after dinner, Nikos called for a limo.

Naani pulled me aside while he was on the phone. "Have fun, *beta*. You need to get out there and taste life. But not all in one bite, if you know what I mean."

I giggled and gave her a peck on the cheek. "I'll be good."

"Good-schmood. You'll know the minute you kiss him."

"Teri!" Isabelle yelled for her maid of honor.

"Look." Naani pointed to the Christmas tree dashing toward us. Teri's arms were laden with gifts from Thomas's relatives in Mykonos. "That would've been you. Aren't you glad things worked out the way they did?"

"Wait." Isabelle intercepted Teri and threaded another gift bag through her arms. "Oh, there's the boat. Let's go, Naani. Dolly, watch your step." She rounded everyone up before cornering me. "You're going to be okay, right? No offense, but all your dates have been pretty mild so far. This is the big leagues. Nikos is intense. Smooth but intense. I've seen the way he looks at you. Like a hungry wolf. Just say the word and I'll throw a tantrum to get you back on the boat."

"Oh my God, stop, will you? Maybe I *want* a hungry wolf." I pushed her toward the boat. "Goodnight."

Then it was just Nikos and me. You know the feeling when you've thought about something forever and it finally happens, and you want to say something witty or funny or cool, but you also really, really want to puke, so you keep your mouth shut because you don't know which will come out? Yeah. That.

Nikos had a whole different way of dealing with nerves. He morphed into an octopus the minute we got into the limo—one hand around my shoulder, the other on my thigh, a third wrapping around my waist. All the while, he was on the phone with the club, arranging a private booth.

We pulled into an alley behind the club and were ushered in through the back entrance.

Two burly bouncers escorted us through a dimly lit hallway.

"We get a lot of celebrities dropping in," Nikos said. "The back entrance keeps them happy."

"We?" I raised my voice over the music. The whole place reverberated with a pulsating beat.

"My family and I. We own the club. And a few others in Athens, Rhodes, Corfu…" He waved his hand, like he was talking about apples and oranges scattered under the trees.

So, Nikos is a nightclub owner, I thought, as he guided me into a reserved section overlooking the dance floor. *This is what happens when the person you're stalking on social media keeps some parts of his public life private. You get bits and pieces, never the whole picture. So inconsiderate, Nikos.*

Retro music blared around us—Boom, boom, boom. Let's go back to my room—while a guy in an LED suit shot streams of cool, white mist into the crowd with a smoke gun.

Nightclubs weren't really my thing. A lot of people packed really close, squirming, moving, drinking, and making out. And let's face it—clubs had nothing good to eat.

But maybe I'd been doing nightclubs wrong all this time. Maybe I needed to do them with Nikos, because an impeccably clad hostess placed a platter of *mezedes* before us—cheeses, dips, cured meats, olives, pickles, salted fish. She returned with a carafe, two shot glasses and a bowl of ice.

Nikos dropped a couple of ice cubes into the glasses and poured a clear liquid from the carafe over them.

"Cheers." He held up his glass.

I raised mine cautiously. "What is it?"

Apart from the occasional cocktail on vacation and a bottle of Ny-Quil that I downed while dying with the flu, I wasn't much of a drinker.

"This is tsipouro."

"Sip what?"

"Tsipouro. It's made from grape residue. This batch is from a Greek monastery."

"Ah." I smiled.

Grapes, meaning wine.

And monks, meaning blessed wine.

I followed Nikos's lead and downed my drink.

Holy Mother of All Fucking Firewater.

"Oh-hwah!" I thumped my chest to jump-start my lungs.

"What?" Nikos held his hand up to his ear.

My throat had just swallowed an entire colony of red ants. My eyes watered as I set the record for repeatedly choking in front of the same person.

Nikos finally clued in. "Are you all right?"

I fanned my face and nodded as the pungent spirit receded into the pit of my stomach. *How can something that looks like water taste like hell?*

"Would you like something…?"

"Sweeter," I said.

A Coke. Lemonade. Kool-Aid. Anything to wash out the taste of Crap-In-A-Carafe. Sorry, monks.

Nikos called the hostess over. "Make her one of these…" He held up my empty glass. "But with saffron syrup and something fruity."

I was okay with the fruity part and the saffron syrup sounded nice, but I wasn't convinced anything would make the crap taste less crappy.

"So?" Nikos cozied up to me. The top two buttons of his shirt were undone and when he put his arm around my shoulder, the gap widened, giving me a glimpse of smooth, bronzed skin. "What do you think?" He waved his other hand, showing off his domain.

It was a wickedly indulgent setting—soaring ceilings, an open terrace overlooking the garden, a glimmering cocktail bar with pearlescent finishes. Sleek panels wrapped around our booth, creating an intimate multi-sensory make-out oasis for two. Or three. Whatever your heart desired. Food, music, drinks, possibilities.

"Thank you," I said, when the hostess returned with my drink. I took a sip, thankful that it didn't taste nearly as awful now.

"You have to eat something with that." Nikos fed me an olive and licked the glistening residue off his finger. He took another shot from the carafe and leaned closer.

"I like these." He played with my earrings. "And I *really* like these." His finger traced my lips.

I jumped when he touched me and tried to cover it up by lunging for my drink.

Nikos surmised I wasn't ready to lock lips with him and asked if I wanted to dance. As we made our way downstairs, he was stopped several times—friends, staff, men in expensive suits, women who weighed me up and down—all wanting a word with him. Drinks were offered, shots were downed. Vodka, tequila, rum, gin, whiskey.

"Sorry," Nikos said to me. "I haven't been around much this season."

Just as we were about to hit the dance floor, one of the bouncers pulled him aside. "Olympia Aravani just arrived with her entourage. Party of six."

"Olympia Aravani? The model?" Nikos's hand dropped from around my waist. "Escort her upstairs. Booth 4. Find Dina. Tell her to get the bubbly going—six bottles of Perrier-Jouët. Caviar, truffles. She knows the drill. I'll be there in a minute."

Nikos adjusted his collars after the man left. "Wow. Olympia Aravani. It's your lucky night, glikia mou." He held his arm out for me to take.

"Wow." I'd never heard of her Olympia Aravani, but she was obviously a big deal. No Crap-in-a-Carafe for her. And if the height of Nikos's collar was any indication of her effect on men, she was also beautiful.

When we got upstairs, the stunning model and her friends were lounging in one of the private balconies. It was easy to pick her out. The attitude. The sequin-encrusted hoodie. Perfect, pore-less skin. I disliked her immediately, because Nikos forgot all about me the minute introductions were made.

I sat next to one of Olympia's friends—a greasy-haired guy whose eyes sparkled a little too brightly. The growing stub of ash at the end of his cigarette fascinated me. I wondered how long it could grow before it fell off.

Now.

Now.

Now?

By some miracle, it held fast. When it finally dropped, I grinned with a sense of personal satisfaction and took another sip of the fancy champagne that was going around.

Cheers. I raised my glass to the powdery ash on the floor.

"Hey." Cigarette Man thought I was saluting him. "I'm Kostas."

"Moti." We were the only ones not having a Wi-Fi party on our phones. Nikos was sidled up next to Olympia, laughing at something on her screen. Two of her girlfriends were taking self-ies at angles that would have challenged Pythagoras himself, and the couple was filming their make-out session.

"You want to dance?" Kostas stubbed his cigarette out and got up.

"Sure." Anything was better than watching your soul mate cozy up to a sequined celebrity. It's not like I didn't already have the inner dialog going. You know the one. It makes you feel like everyone else is way ahead of you, more accomplished, more fun, more interesting, more with it. I didn't need to measure myself up against Olympia Aravani. She had Nikos's attention at the drop of her name. My name and I were forever quibbling over pronunciation.

The room whirled as I followed Kostas downstairs. I grabbed the railing and slid down the stairs. It struck me that the club's moving walkways and hallways might actually be stationary, that I was the one zigzagging like a loose cannon in a pinball machine—an image that made me giggle uncontrollably. Apparently, I was really happy when I drank.

Kostas claimed some space for us on the dance floor. As if on cue, the bass dropped, the synthesizer kicked in, and the whole place exploded with lights and lasers. Swirls of acid green and hot pinks swept around us in psychedelic flashes.

Kostas scooped me up and started grinding against me, his hands on my butt cheeks. I was drunk, but I could still hear my internal alarm bells going off.

"Hey. Stop it." I untangled myself from his clutches and teetered away.

I'd barely taken a few steps when Kostas grabbed my waist and started rubbing his junk against my backside.

Trapped in a pulsing, screaming nightmare of lights and sound and rough hands, panic rose in my throat. Bodies thronged around me, but nobody could hear me. And worse, nobody cared.

"Let her go, dickhead." Someone gripped my wrist and pulled me away from Kostas.

"Mind your own business." Kostas shoved the guy in the chest. "She was asking for it."

"Touch her again and I'll rip your face off." Through the blinding strobes of white light, I caught glimpses of the other figure moving toward Kostas until they were nose to nose. Everything looked like it was happening in slow motion.

It wasn't until he turned to face me that I realized it was Alex.

"Let's go." He grabbed my hand and started steering me through the crowd.

"Hey, asshole." Kostas yanked him back and threw a punch. Alex ducked. The punch landed on someone else's head.

"What the fuck?" The girl's boyfriend launched himself at Kostas. They tumbled and landed on another group of dancers. More yelling and screaming. More fists getting involved.

Alex pulled me away from the circle of expanding chaos. "Where the hell is Nikos and why aren't you with him?"

"He's up there." I pointed to the balconies overlooking the dance floor. "With Olympia Aravani." I figured dropping her name would soften the smoldering expression on Alex's face. I was wrong. All at once, I felt like shit. Cold sweat glistened over my lip and waves of heat coursed through my body. My body was starting to quiver with the aftershocks of alcohol, the sensory overload of lights and music, and my encounter with Kostas. Everything was going foggy.

"What are you doing here?" I asked.

"I drop in to see Eleni whenever I'm in town." He motioned to the pretty bartender behind the counter.

"A girl in every port, huh?"

"She's my cousin."

That made me feel worse. Like I'd just accused him of incest. "I'm so sorry," I wailed. "I'm a horrible huban meing." I slumped against him. Apparently, I was miserable when I drank.

"Let's get you to Nikos, okay?" Alex started leading me toward the stairs.

The club was getting louder and rowdier. Someone flung a bottle into the crowd. It hit the wall and shattered into tiny shards. Security guards jumped in and started breaking up the brawl.

"Alex." I paused halfway up the stairs. "There's something I have to tell you."

He stopped, and we stared at each other.

"I think…" My throat clenched, but I couldn't stop the warm feeling rising in my chest. "I think…"

And then I puked all over Alex's shoes.

"I think I'm going to be sick," I said, wiping the dribble off my mouth. My heart pounded loudly, echoing in my ears. I took a step back and thought, *Oh, hell. Hell, no.*

I'd always imagined fainting with Victorian-like delicacy, a lace handkerchief pressed to my forehead. Instead, I went down like a sack of turnips. Alex caught me, swearing through the inky space rapidly claiming my vision. Scooping me up, he made his way back down through the crowd. "Eleni! Let Nikos know I'm taking his date back to the yacht."

A lot of jostling, the feeling of being cradled through a stampede, and then everything receded into blissful darkness.

CHAPTER TWELVE

C HURCH BELLS WERE CHIMING WHEN I WOKE. NO, WAIT. IT WAS my teeth. And my bones. Every time the blood rushed through my veins, it hit my nerves like a hammer striking a bell. I moaned and retreated under the covers. I had a vague recollection of loud music, red sequins, cigarette ash…

Oh shit.

Kostas.

I sat up and immediately regretted it. My head throbbed with the worst hangover in history. *My* history. I swung my feet over the edge of the bed and cast a bleary glance around the room. Alex was gone. His bunk bed was made up, neat and tight. The absence of windows made it difficult to guess what time it was.

I crawled into the bathroom and turned on the light, cringing at my reflection. My eyes were a lattice of blood-red vessels. Mascara clumped my lashes together when I blinked. My bra strap had slid down my shoulder, and I was still wearing the dress from last night. I thanked Alex silently for not helping me into something more comfortable while I was passed out.

My first hangover, I thought. *Not a fan.* It felt like all the bad decisions I ever made were having a reunion in my head.

I showered and slipped into a T-shirt and shorts. After unsuccessfully googling *hangover cures* (because I kept typing *hangover curse*), I made my way upstairs, heavy limbed and deflated over my disastrous date with Nikos. When the elevator doors opened, I shrank back from the sun like a vampire. Thank God for sunglasses. I slipped them on and tried again.

The boat was oddly quiet. No one in the salon. No one on the deck. No guests. No crew members. My first thought was everyone had abandoned me after my night of debauchery. I was Roman Catholic, raised in an Indian family. Guilt and the fear of punishment were my childhood companions. We still played see-saw—I liked to test how far I could go without tipping them over. Mostly, they kicked my butt around the playground of life.

After failing to locate someone who could point me in the direction of the nearest aspirin, I stumbled into the galley. Alex was working with his back turned to me, earbuds in place, oblivious to my inspection. You look at a man differently after he's rescued you. You either resent him, because you're an independent woman and he made you feel like you needed rescuing. Or you romanticize him, because you're an independent woman and he made you feel like you needed rescuing. Hopefully, you don't puke on his shoes in either of those scenarios.

I was leaning more toward romanticizing him, conjuring up the scene in *The Bodyguard*, where Kevin Costner carries Whitney Houston out of the club, booting and throat-chopping everyone out of the way. Though I doubted Kevin Costner's spanakopita rose as spectacularly as Alex's. Alex pulled a tray of the little pies out of the oven. His mitts were shaped like sharks, with teeth facing out, so it looked like they were taking a bite off what they were holding.

He pulled off his earbuds when he saw me. "It's alive."

"It feels like death." I plopped down on the nearest stool.

"It needs water." He poured me a glass and slid it my way.

I didn't stop until I had drained all of it. My mouth felt like someone had rubbed it with sandpaper.

"You want some masala chai?" Alex put loose black tea and milk in a saucepan. Then he started adding spices—cloves, cinnamon, cardamom, ginger. Since when did cardamom pods crack open so *loudly*?

"You know how to make masala chai?" I asked.

"When I was training at the CIA, my mentor was Indian. He taught me masala chai. Also, mango pickle, *chaat papri*, *chevda*, *parath*—"

"The CIA? You trained at the CIA?"

Alex refilled my water and held it out like a bribe. "You can't share that information. It's top secret. I'm working undercover as we speak."

"You're working undercover?" I was repeating everything he said, but I couldn't help it. To say I was gobsmacked would be putting it mildly. I chugged down another glass of water. "What kind of undercover assignment?"

"Well…" Alex leaned closer, elbows on the counter. "The Papadakis family—Thomas and his parents? They're involved in all kinds of shady stuff. We've been trying to bust them for years. They're all coming for the wedding—a Who's Who of Greek Mafia. No better time to round them up. All the kingpins, including Nikos."

"Nikos?" My three-thumbed ticket to happily-ever-after was in the *mob*? "What does he have to do with it?"

"Nikos funnels all the dirty money through his clubs."

"What? That's just… Wait, does Isabelle know?" The pounding in my head got louder. "I have to tell her."

"You can't tell anyone. You'll jeopardize the whole operation."

Alex poured the masala chai in a mug, pulled out a stool, and regarded me with his cinnamon eyes. I held my head in my hands to keep it from toppling over with the weight of all the things I just learned. It also explained why Alex said my name with all the right inflections. His mentor at the CIA had been Indian.

"Moti?" Alex pushed the sugar bowl toward me.

I didn't answer. I didn't want to know.

"In the culinary world, CIA stands for the Culinary Institute of America."

It took a moment for his statement to sink in. The bastard played me. He not only let me think he was talking about *the* CIA, he ran with it, spinning a wild, crazy story that I'd fallen for like an idiot.

Slowly, I lifted my head.

"Uh-oh. It's pissed." He stood and backed away. "Perhaps it would like some *spanakopita?*" Piling some pies on a plate, he sat it at the edge of the counter and slid it toward me with a pair of tongs. Granted, I might have been foaming at the mouth like a rabid dog, but what kind of person pulls a prank like that on someone in the throes of a major hangover?

I bit into the pie instead of murdering him. Revenge is a dish best served with zero alcohol in your system. My time would come. For now, I was relieved Isabelle wasn't marrying into the Greek Mafia.

"Where is everyone?" I asked after I finished my tea. Alex made a mean cup of masala chai. It rivaled Naani's, but I wasn't about to tell him that.

"We're anchored off Naxos. The captain found a nice spot this morning. Perfect for a beach picnic. Everyone's out there." He paused and looked up from his chopping board. "Everyone except Nikos."

"He's sleeping in?" Probably recovering from Olympia Aravani.

"Nikos had to sort out some stuff with the authorities after the brawl at the nightclub last night. We had to leave Mykonos without him."

"The brawl at the nightclub…" *Oh God.* The one I started. I was the reason Nikos wasn't back on the yacht. "How bad was it?"

"Pretty bad. It snow-balled after we left. Things got damaged. People were hurt. Someone informed the media Olympia Aravani was there, then all hell broke loose. The police came. Nikos has a pretty big mess on his hands."

It was worse than I thought. I should never have agreed to dance with Kostas. "Will Nikos be back in time for the wedding?"

"Captain Bailey said he'll probably be joining us in a couple of days. He's waiting on a loan from his crime lords to get the repairs going."

"Wiseass." I flung a shark mitt at him. Then picked up the other one and threw that too. Alex laughed as they bounced off his chest.

I should've been more upset over Nikos's absence, but I found myself smiling. I liked the sound of Alex's laughter.

As he turned back to the stove, I realized how much stress I'd put myself under. Ever since Isabelle's engagement, I'd been chasing a goal. The stakes were high, because winning Nikos over also meant winning Dolly over. But now, with Nikos temporarily out of the picture, I could kick back and enjoy the cruise—no pressure, no agenda and hopefully, no Nikos-induced choking.

CHAPTER THIRTEEN

"**M**OTI."

Ugh. I burrowed deeper into the covers, ignoring the annoying, persistent call.

Afternoon naps were a luxury, and even more precious when you were trying to sleep away a hangover.

"Moti." This time, Isabelle shook me awake.

"What?!" I squinted at her.

"I have a fabulous idea. Are you listening?" My eyes closed. She shook me again. "I'm sleeping with Thomas tonight."

"Congratulations. I thought you'd already been there and done that."

"I don't mean it like that, silly. I mean, with Nikos gone, I can spend the night in Thomas's room, and you can take my spot in the cabin upstairs."

I blinked and rolled over to face her. "That *does* sound like a good idea. There's just one thing."

"Naani," we both said in unison. No way was she going to let Isabelle and Thomas spend the night together before the wedding.

"She's always had a soft spot for you, Moti," Isabelle said. "If anyone can convince her not to tell Mom and Dad, it's you. You've got to help me. You've *got* to."

In the absence of siblings, Isabelle and I always turned to each other. It wasn't always a fair arrangement because she was always the one who needed an alibi or scapegoat or someone to pin the tail on. But I intended to collect one day. Maybe when I was a grizzled old lady who got evicted for having too many feline friends.

We approached Naani with our proposition and were immediately shut down.

"No."

"But—"

"Isabelle, you're staying right here with me. Moti, you're sleeping with the chef."

I opened my mouth, then let it go. *That's not what she means.*

"Bu—"

"No buts. From either of you. Joseph is upset enough with you and Rachel, Isabelle. If he finds out about this, Lord help us all. You girls know you can come to me with anything, but I won't have any part of this."

"But—"

"Out. Both of you." And just like that, Naani shut us down and went back to her laptop.

"Always typing away on that thing. Or her phone." Isabelle sighed, her mouth set in a semi-pout. "I shouldn't have asked for your help, Moti. I should've snuck out and slipped back into my bed in the morning." She shook her head and retreated, as if this had been a failure on my part.

"Moti." The door to Naani's stateroom opened. Her hand snaked around my wrist. "I'm glad you're still here. Can you help me with this?" She handed me a jar of Vicks VapoRub and pointed to her ankle.

For as long as I can remember, Naani smelled of Vicks VapoRub and honeysuckle. Honeysuckle was the first scent she bought upon moving to America, courtesy of a neighbor who was an Avon sales rep. I imagined it reminded her of new beginnings, or perhaps, the garden she had left behind in India. The Vicks VapoRub, on the other hand, was a sacred tradition passed on by her mother. Cough? Cold? Headache? Broken leg? Broken heart? Got run over by a truck? Slap on the Vicks. On your chest, your temples, around the rim of your nostrils. Hell, put a gob on a cotton ball and stick it in your ear. Maybe it was a placebo effect but having Naani rub the camphorated ointment on me really did make me feel better. My entire childhood revolved around trips to the doctor postponed by Vicks, except for the one time when it failed to suck pneumonia out of my feet (Naani maintained it must have been a bad batch).

I rubbed the salve over Naani's translucent skin, the veins running beneath it like a network of blue-green tunnels. The reversal of roles was a comforting ritual, tied to the smell of childhood nostalgia. Sitting cross-legged on the floor, with Naani's foot on my lap, I felt a sense of peace—the kind that comes and sits on your shoulder when you least expect it.

"How was your date with Nikos?" she asked.

"Not so great." I switched to her other ankle. "I don't know, Naani. Maybe I'm not meant to find love. No, not love. Reciprocal love. Both hearts have to catch fire at the same time, you know? Otherwise, it just hurts."

"Is that what you're feeling with Nikos? Hurt?"

"I don't know if I'm invested enough at this point to feel hurt, but I feel *something*. And what I really want to feel is sparks, electricity, kisses that make everything disappear. Am I ever going to find that, Naani?"

"Ha. The luxury you kids have."

"What do you mean?"

"When I was young, it was never about finding love. Love was something you cultivated. Your parents picked your life partner. Romance never entered the equation until then. People didn't marry people. Families married families. Your father liked his father, or his grandmother played cards with your grandmother. That was how it started. Marriage was a garden that grew slowly. You only got one patch, so you worked hard at it. You planted the seeds, you watered them, you waited for things to bloom— love, respect, intimacy, connection. But things are different now. Everyone expects fruits and flowers right off the bat. When those are done, it gets plain and boring. Then it's time to move on to the next patch. Relationships are more disposable now. So many people, so many choices. I look at you, I look at Isabelle, and I see both the blessing and curse that freedom brings you—so much potential for happiness, so much pressure to realize it. And then, with you, there's the thumb…" Naani stuck her gnarly digit in my face and wiggled it.

We laughed because her thumb was impossibly knobby, but also at the absurdity of the situation. I lifted her feet off my lap and placed them on the floor. Retrieving her slippers, I held them out for her.

"Your grandfather wasn't an easy man to live with." She slipped her foot into the slipper and paused, reflecting on distant memories. "He was controlling, hot-tempered, critical. At times, downright cruel. I wish I could tell you I grew to love him, but no matter how hard I tried, I could never find the door to his heart. I felt like a failure. My friends' arranged marriages were working out just fine. Thriving. It wasn't until much later that I realized some people are never satisfied, no matter what you do. When I think back, I feel sorry for him. He could never figure out how to be happy…" She put on the other slipper and trailed off.

I'd never known my maternal grandfather. He passed away before I was born. We had a picture of him on the mantle, but Dolly never talked about him. Nobody did. I waited for Naani to finish her story.

"And?" I prompted.

"And what?" She reached for her laptop and reclined against the headboard.

"The moral of the story? You were making a point?"

Naani scoffed. "What? Just because I'm old? Sometimes, I just go off on a tangent." She screwed the lid back on the Vicks VapoRub and shooed me out. "Get the curtains before you go, *beta*. The sun is glaring off my screen."

I suppressed a giggle. Naani was addicted to the internet, and oblivious to the expressions she made as she sampled the world through her screen. As I slid the blackout panels across the window, my eyes fell on the tray in the sitting area. Two slim champagne glasses sat on top. They reminded me of bubbles... Rising, always rising to the top. Happy bubbles, fizzy bubbles, sparkly, golden bubbles. I slipped one of the glasses into my handbag and shut the door behind me.

My phone pinged with a new notification. Nikos Manolas had sent me a friend request on Facebook.

Nikos, inviting me into his inner circle after realizing it's me, not Olympia Aravani who belongs there? Yes!

Nikos, going through security footage and realizing I'm the one responsible for sparking chaos at his nightclub? No!

My finger hovered over the button for a few seconds before I accepted.

His message came through almost immediately: *Sorry about last night. Promise to make it up to you. Just checking in to make sure you made it back okay.*

My shoulders relaxed.

Sorry about the mess you're dealing with, I typed back.

It happens. The business I'm in. Sorting through it as we speak. Hope to get back to you soon, glikia mou. Winky Face. Followed by Winky Face With Tongue Hanging Out.

Ugh. Emojis. The flirt-bombs of online dating. Interpret them wrong and they could explode in your face. Ignore them and you could miss something substantial. Was there a sexual connotation to the tongue hanging out? What exactly was Nikos trying to say?

I'm hyperventilating because I think you're so hot?

I want to lick you playfully?

I started replying, backtracked, then started over again. Five minutes later, I settled on the perfect response: a single Winky Face. By then, Nikos had signed off, but I was one click away from accessing his profile. All the answers to my questions about him just waiting to be discovered.

Instead, I googled CIA.

Central Intelligence Agency: *The CIA collects, evaluates, and disseminates vital information on economic, military, political, scientific, and other developments abroad to safeguard the national security of the United States federal government.*

Canadian Institute of Actuaries: *The CIA is the national organization of the actuarial profession, dedicated to serving the public through the provision of actuarial services and advice of the highest quality.*

Culinary Institute of America: *The CIA is the world's top culinary school. We offer Bachelor's degrees in applied food studies, culinary science, food business management, hospitality management, and more.*

Bingo.

I smiled. Alex really was trained at the CIA.

CHAPTER FOURTEEN

WHEN I MADE MY WAY TO THE SKY DECK THAT NIGHT, ALEX WAS already there, gazing at the horizon. We were anchored off the shores of Naxos for the night. Between my hangover and my nap, I'd missed the chance to see the beautiful island.

I padded up beside him and rested my elbows on the railing. He said nothing, but his posture made a slight shift—the kind of reaction when someone's presence affects you. We stood there in comfortable silence.

The sky was freckled with stars. Silhouettes of churches and Venetian castles stood against the moon-bleached valleys and mountains.

"Somewhere out there are farms that grow potatoes," I said, remembering the scrumptious Naxian potatoes Alex served on the first night of the cruise.

Alex chuckled.

"What?" I prodded.

"I see the moon. Galaxies above us. The sea below us. Over there, I see the rain." He pointed to a distant spot on the horizon. "I think of wet cobblestones, pigeons roosting under a statue in the plaza, a man hurrying home to his family—coffee in one hand, a wet umbrella in the other. You?" He angled his body toward me. "You think of potatoes."

"So?"

"So." He laughed. "I like it. I like that I can never tell what I'm going to get with you. I like that you're weird and quirky, and you see things I don't."

"Thanks." I gave him the side-eye. "I think."

We went back to gazing at the sea and the sky, and the trail of yellow lampposts that lined the roads like golden orbs in the night.

"Do you come up here every night?" I asked.

"Most nights, yes. I like to look at the lights. Somewhere out there is a mother who has fallen asleep next to her child. And there, in a smoky jazz bar, a couple on their first date—nervous, excited, still to kiss. Over there…" He pointed to one of the lights still burning in the hillside. "A man is leaving his wife in the morning. Next door, someone is putting together a crib for a new baby. You know what they have in common?"

I turned and caught his profile, his hair brushed away from his brow and tied loosely around his nape.

"What?" I asked. In another life, he could have been an admiral, a poet, a pirate.

"Food." His gaze scanned the island. "They all pass each other in the same markets—the same bakers, the same winemakers. They gather in the town square for mezes and ice-cream, or just to watch the world go by. At weddings, they eat lamb. At funerals, they eat *koliva*. Food binds them together. You see it no matter where you go. Friends, families, strangers—sharing a meal. Whether it's in someone's kitchen, a Michelin-starred restaurant in France, or a street stall in Vietnam.

"Every time you share a meal with someone, you bring your history, your country, your region, your religion, your tribe, your grandmother with you. You sit with your past, your opinions, your love, your curiosity, your resentments, your hospitality. Food is where we all intersect. Everywhere you go, anywhere you go.

"For now, I'm just circling. Learning the language of food. But someday, I want to be one of those lights—somewhere by the water, where people can eat and share and connect. I want to be a link in a story that's as old as time."

I sighed. "That's a beautiful dream."

"And you? What is it that you want?"

What did I dream of? To be loved. To be happy. But wasn't that what everyone wanted? My dream felt ordinary next to Alex's.

"I'd be happy if I could swim," I said.

He looked at me, as if he were considering what my cheek would feel like, resting on his palm. "That's not a big thing to ask of the world."

I turned away, unprepared for the tenderness of his words. "It is when you're afraid."

I swallowed the lump in my throat. It wasn't just swimming I was afraid of. Despite Ma Anga's prophecy, I wasn't afraid of dying. I was afraid of dying without living.

This time, the silence made me uneasy because Alex wasn't looking at the lights. He was still looking at me.

"Maybe you'd consider a trade-off?" he said. "I'll teach you how to swim. One lesson every night. In exchange, you help me in the kitchen. An hour or two every day. My sous-chef, the guy who was to bunk with me, had to skip this charter, and I could use an extra pair of hands. What do you say?"

I considered his proposition. Apart from the scheduled activities, I had plenty of free time.

A voice much like Dolly's chimed in: *Time you're supposed to use getting to know Nikos.*

But he's not around, and I promised myself that I would learn to swim.

"Deal," I said to Alex.

"Great." He pushed himself off the railing. "Let's get started."

"What? Now?"

"You have ten more nights to learn in the luxury of your own private pool. After that…" He shrugged.

"You're right." I ticked off the dates. We were already on night number four. "I don't have my swimsuit on though."

"You don't need it." Alex dragged two swim mattresses out from the bunker and placed them side by side. "Come lie down."

I stretched out beside him and we stared up at the sky.

"Um, what are we doing?" *Maybe taking swimming lessons from a chef isn't such a great idea.*

"We're learning to float."

"How exactly are we learning to float?" *Yep, definitely a bad idea. A chef's sole purpose is to ply you with food. The more you eat, the more you sink.*

Alex chuckled. "Did you ever watch *The Karate Kid?*"

"Yes."

"You remember the part where Daniel thinks Mr. Miyagi will teach him karate, but he makes him do all the chores instead? Wash the car, sand the floor, paint the fence."

"Wax on, wax off." I made the hand motions that went with the famous line.

"That's what we're doing. Stargazing. Looking up at the sky. Shoulders back, head up, arms and legs easy, letting the mattress support our weight. That's how you do the back float."

Hmmm. Maybe Alex knows what he's doing, after all.

I relaxed and let myself open up to his instructions.

"Extend your arms like an airplane wing and point your belly button to the stars. That's it. Chin up. And breathe. Imagine yourself floating down a river, being carried like a feather on the water. Softly, effortlessly."

With my eyes on the constellations and the sea lapping around us, it was easy to give in to the sensation. I was suspended between the sea and the sky. Peaceful, serene, secure.

Moments ticked by before Alex spoke again. "Are we floating yet?"

"It's nice." A smile broke through my voice.

"Learn the feeling. Tomorrow, we do it in the water." He got up and held out his hand.

"You really think I'll be able to do it?" I asked, as he pulled me up.

"Easy as pie."

"I suck at pie."

"Well, I excel at pie," he said. "At least you're learning from the best."

Later that night, when we were both in our bunk beds, I found myself talking to him in the dark.

"Alex?"

"I'm listening…"

"How many lessons before you learned to swim?"

"Lessons?" His laugh was loud and throaty. "I was thrown into the sea, clinging to my Pappou's neck."

"Your Pappou?"

"My grandfather."

"And you kept going? You kept getting into the water with him?"

"It was either that or suffer a few hard whacks of the pando-fla—his hard, leathery slipper."

I giggled at the thought of it landing on little Alex's butt, which immediately took me to grown-up Alex's very round, very firm butt. Yeehaw.

"You laugh? Where is your sense of outrage?"

"Please." I cuddled deeper into the covers. "My mother used to come after me with a wooden spoon."

"Because you wouldn't go swimming?"

"Because all my American friends got an allowance, so I demanded one too. I got it then for the first time, and it came out whenever I rolled my eyes or muttered something under my breath."

"Hm."

"Hm, what?"

"I have a lot of wooden spoons. I'll have you swimming in no time."

I kicked the bottom of his bed. "You wouldn't dare abuse your sous-chef. I'll report you to the CIA."

Alex laughed, and in that moment, I felt buoyant—like a bubble was growing inside me. Maybe if I just allowed myself to be, I'd get carried to the top, and there, like a champagne bubble, I'd break through the surface with a bright pop.

CHAPTER FIFTEEN

"THIS WASN'T A FAIR EXCHANGE." I USED MY WRIST TO NUDGE MY hair out of my face. One hand held a knife, the other an onion.

Alex placed a basket of green-topped carrots before me, adding to the chaos on the counter. "You're looking a little red in the face. Having trouble keeping up? We have a special meditation chamber if you need to cool off."

"Oh yeah?" I looked up.

He unlatched the walk-in refrigerator and held the door open for me. A cool blast of air hit the back of my neck.

"This was *not* a fair exchange," I repeated, and went back to sniffling over the diced onions. "You get to stargaze and I get stuck cutting and chopping and peeling." I gestured to the vegetables around me.

"You're free to leave any time you want. In fact, if Captain Bailey finds out you're in here prepping meals with me, she'll have my head."

"I'm surprised she's not after you already. Aren't you supposed to be wearing a hairnet?" I pointed to his half-bun. I wasn't really concerned about food hygiene. I just wanted to throw a hairnet on Alex. Anything to flatten, constrain, and keep his magnetic appeal from crawling under my skin.

Working in close quarters with Alex was playing havoc on me. The scent of his shower gel when he opened the hot oven. The brush of his skin as he reached over to grab a pan. His movements were smooth and precise, like a conductor orchestrating a symphony, keeping time and track of all the parts that went into feeding everyone on the yacht. He had a bulletin board crammed with paper clippings, handwritten menus, prep lists, names of passengers and their preferences, names of crew members, highlights of food allergies and special diets.

"Yes." Alex heaped grated tomatoes on barley rusks and plated them with a sprinkling of herbs and cheese.

"Yes, what?"

Alex zoned in and out when he was working. One moment he'd be talking to me and the next, he'd get so focused on what he was doing, he'd tune everything else out. When he was alone, he put on his earbuds and listened to an eclectic mix of Greek songs and 80's music. When I was in the kitchen, he streamed his playlist through speakers.

"Yes, I should be wearing a hairnet."

He gave no explanation for why he wasn't. If Captain Bailey ever called him out on it, she'd probably get a rebellious hair flip.

I moved on to the carrots. I was preparing what Alex called a mirepoix—a mixture of onions, carrots, and celery—used as a base for soups, sauces, stocks, and stews. I felt pretty good about my slicing and dicing, given that Dolly always lamented my lack of kitchen skills. Maybe I should take a video for her.

Look Ma, I'm getting domesticated.

On second thought, no. She'd probably upload it to a matchmaking site:

Looking For A Nice Indian Boy With Three Thumbs.

"Hey." Alex rapped his knuckles on the counter. "No daydreaming when you're working."

"Oh please. What's the worst that can happen? I'll end up dicing the potatoes instead of the carrots?"

"A girl lost her finger on a boat one time. In a galley just like this. On a chopping board just like that."

"That's horrible." I shuddered. "What did you do?"

"I didn't say I was there. I'm just saying be careful."

I made a face but paid more attention to what I was doing. As I slid the first batch of carrots off the cutting board, I noticed an hourglass by the sink. It hung in a white frame on rubber feet and was filled with bright, yellow sand. I flipped it over and watched the tiny grains empty into the bottom chamber. Something about watching the cheerful pile dwindling away was both sad and lovely. It was a little like the hopes I'd pinned on this trip, pivoting my life around these fourteen days on the water. But the days were slipping away and nothing had changed.

I glanced at Alex. He was seasoning something on the stove. My fingers closed around the hourglass, stopping the rest of the sand from emptying out. It was small and slender, and fit perfectly inside my pocket.

I picked up the knife and went back to dicing the next batch of carrots.

"Three minutes," said Alex, without looking up from the pan.

"Sorry?"

"The hourglass takes three minutes to empty." He rested his wooden spoon on the rim of the pan and turned around. "I use it to time poached eggs."

"I..." My protest was crushed by the uncomfortable sensation that goes with betraying someone. "I—"

"I see you, Moti." He rested his hands on either side of me, trapping me against the counter.

I stood frozen to the spot, my heart thumping in my chest.

"I see you." He unclenched the knife from my hand, bits of carrot peel still sticking to its edge, and dropped it in the sink. "I've seen the bag you have, stashed under your bed. A light bulb, coffee stirrers, a playing card, a pen, a ping-pong ball... I didn't know what to make of it, but I see it now." His hand slid into my pocket and he pulled out the hourglass. It caught the sun between us and sent glints of light into his eyes, warming up the cinnamon specks.

Something in me twisted as he held my gaze. It slid into my core and latched on to my trembling gut. No one had ever caught me stealing before. No one had confronted me over it. I bit down on my lip to steady myself and stand still. I bit until salty blood filled my mouth, but I still felt naked and vulnerable. I waited for Alex's gaze to cloud with judgment, disgust, accusation.

Instead, he slipped the hourglass back in my pocket.

"I…" I wanted to apologize, to explain, but how could I? I didn't understand it myself.

"You're hungry," he said. "People don't take things unless they're hungry. For food, for love, for a buzz, for attention. For whatever they feel is missing." He touched my bottom lip with his thumb, prompting me to free it from the clamp of my teeth. "Don't beat yourself up over it."

Then, as if nothing had happened, he picked up his spoon and went back to stirring.

I stood hunched over the sink a few minutes, light-headed, feeling like my skin had been ripped off, leaving me with nothing to hide behind. Then I picked up my knife. The mechanical slicing and dicing soothed me. I was almost done when Alex spoke again.

"Eddie is getting ready to take everyone ashore." He nodded toward the window, where the deckhand was lowering the small boat into the water. "You should get going. You don't want to miss Paros. Naousa is one of the prettiest villages in the Cyclades."

I nodded and untied my apron. Washing my hands, I felt the weight of the hourglass in my pocket. Part of me wanted to put it back, but the other wanted to keep it hidden. Who wants a reminder of their shame on the counter?

"Try this before you go." He held out his spoon, his other hand hovering beneath it to catch any spills. Steam rose from the vibrant yellow broth.

"What is it?"

"Avgolemono soup. Well, my version of it." He lifted it to my lips.

I closed my eyes, savoring tangy lemon, shredded chicken, rice, spice. Simple, light, and comforting.

When I opened my eyes, my gaze was level with Alex's chin. His mouth was a soup spoon away—soft and pink, nestled in the angular planes of his stubble. A familiar feeling shot through my veins. The urge to take. The urge to steal. But this time, a kiss.

I wanted to feel Alex's lips on mine.

The realization made me jolt back.

Raspy vocals streamed through the speakers: *Sign your name across my heart...*

No. No.

This was going very wrong. I wasn't supposed to feel this way for Alex. I was supposed to feel this way for Nikos. People wait their whole lives for a sign and I had a clear-cut sign Nikos was the one for me. And Dolly was watching and waiting to see if I messed up, if I fell short of her expectations once again.

I backed out of the kitchen, clutching the hourglass in my pocket.

When was I going to stop taking things that weren't meant for me?

CHAPTER SIXTEEN

WE WALKED DOWN THE NARROW, COBBLESTONE STREETS OF Naousa in pairs:

Joseph Uncle and George (fathers of the bride and groom).

Kassia and Fia (mother of the groom and the bride's godmother).

Rachel Auntie and Dolly (mother of the bride and my mother).

Teri and me (the hired maid of honor and the fired maid of honor).

Isabelle and Thomas (the bride and groom) had chosen to skip the onshore excursion, preferring to spend time alone before the big day. Naani also stayed onboard, partly to keep an eye on them, and partly because her unbalanced gait made her a hazard on narrow streets. Naani's chaperoning duties, however, were redundant. Before we left, Isabelle pulled me aside for a top-secret mission: to buy a pregnancy test and smuggle it back without anyone finding out.

"Take Teri with you," she said. "You guys can come up with an excuse and branch off together."

As the group meandered down the streets of Naousa, Teri and I kept our eyes peeled for a pharmacy. This was Greece, home of Hippocrates, the father of Western medicine. How hard could it be to find a pharmacy?

There were cute boutiques selling handmade jewelry and leather shoes. There were restaurants overlooking the water, with rows of octopus drying across their fronts. White-washed homes greeted us at every turn. Bougainvillea tumbled over the walls. Music streamed out of ouzeries.

No pharmacy.

Teri and I exchanged a look. She was catlike—silent and stealthy, which unsettled me, because it was a trait I attributed to serial killers. I preferred hanging out with people whose footsteps I could hear. Maybe we'd find a place that sold pregnancy kits *and* bells. Or clogs.

We seized the opportunity to break away when the group stopped to sample spoon sweets at a bakery. "Teri and I are going to head over that way." I pointed in the opposite direction. "How about we meet you back here in an hour?"

"It's not safe to wander off on your own," Dolly said, but George waved us off.

"Go, but don't be late," he said.

We hadn't gone too far when Teri stopped. "I need to use the bathroom. You think they'll let me?" She pointed to the taverna before us.

"Maybe we should buy something." You can't just use the facilities and skip out. Our neighbor, Shoo Lin, had a sign at the entrance of her restaurant: *You no fee, you no pee.*

I got us a table while Teri went to the bathroom. I ordered one of the mezes the waiter recommended—a creamy fava bean puree, topped with bite-sized pieces of chicken, simmered in wine and bay leaves.

"So good." Teri dug in when she returned.

"Delicious," I agreed.

We finished it in record time and signaled for the bill.

"I think it's the way they grill the octopus that makes it so good," Teri said.

"What?" I blinked.

"The charcoal. It gives it a whole different flavor."

"Before that." I gestured, rewinding with my hands. "Did you say octopus? I thought it was chicken."

"Definitely octopus."

"I just had octopus?" It didn't taste like octopus, or rather, what I imagined octopus would taste like. "I didn't see any suckers."

"It was chopped up pretty fine. My husband *loves* octopus. Haven't you had it before?" Teri followed as I made a beeline for the door.

I just ate octopus.

Gross.

And then, as I walked past all the tentacles draped over the railing of the terrace, I felt guilty for calling them gross. *Sorry,* I apologized to each cephalopod. *Sorry for calling you names and eating you.* Which was weird, because I didn't apologize to cows or chickens or fish, and I ate them too. Maybe because I'd grown up eating them, and now my circle of carnivorous tendencies had expanded to yet another species. *Sorry. Sorry. Sorry.*

We passed a waiter, sweeping mounds of squashed figs off the street. Teri tugged at my sleeve. "Over there." She pointed to a rusty sign—a green cross against a white background.

A pharmacy.

Yes!

It was dimly lit, with merchandise stacked neatly on wooden shelves, but everything was arranged randomly—as if space had been made for it as it had come in.

"Oh, my husband would *love* those." Teri pointed toward the back of the store and took off, abandoning me in our quest to locate a pregnancy test for Isabelle.

I glanced at my watch. It would be easier to ask one of the store clerks but asking for a pregnancy test was a bit like asking for condoms. You always threw in a couple of unnecessary things to distract the cashier or the person in line behind you, so it didn't seem like you came in *just* for the condoms. *I'm about to have sex, everyone!* Asking for a pregnancy test declared, *I had sex, everyone!* It's even worse when you're in a foreign place, without a ring on your finger, and you're hoping there's no ancient by-law that would get you stoned in the village square.

I smiled at the cashier—a stout woman with grizzled skin and kind eyes, as I rounded one of the aisles. There, against the wall, was a selection of condoms.

My eyes darted around. The pregnancy tests had to be near. Or maybe not. I had to think like the storekeeper. Maybe the pregnancy tests were with under-eye creams, because dark circles would follow sleepless nights, once the baby was born. *Just please, please don't let the pregnancy tests be locked up in one of those glass case cabinets.*

I walked down the entire section with no luck. Another glance at my watch told me we were running out of time. Isabelle's pregnancy test would have to wait until we got to the next port, then she could go get it herself.

Just as I made up my mind to leave, I saw a couple of pregnancy tests hanging from a hook, next to other things that needed to be hung from hooks. Thermometers. Walking canes. Nail clippers.

Of course. I was finally starting to get it. I grabbed one of the kits and started heading for the checkout. On the way, I grabbed some chewing gum and a lip balm.

"Teri." I leaned away from the counter to catch her eye as the cashier rang me up. "We have to go."

"Coming," she said.

I turned to pay the cashier and knocked my purchases over. The pregnancy test went flying across the floor. It stopped at someone's foot, by the entrance of the store.

"Sorry," I said, as I bent to retrieve it. "It just—" I came to an abrupt halt when I saw who it was.

Joseph Uncle. And behind him Rachel Auntie. And Fia. And George. And Kassia.

All staring at me and the pregnancy test in my hand.

"What's the holdup?" Dolly stuck her head out behind the group. "Moti? Oh good, we were just about to head back to…"

Her face warped in a five-step, slow motion reaction. First, she blinked. Then her eyes rounded, eyebrows stretching up, up, to the heavens. Her mouth fell open slowly, as if catching up to the information her eyeballs were sending. Then, her chest swelled. This was the point that determined it all. She was either going to turn into a fire-breathing dragon or flip over like a fainting goat.

"Is that what I think it is?" Her eyes narrowed.

Shit. It's going to be Day of the Dragon.

It didn't help that the box in my hand had the universal pregnancy test logo emblazoned on the front—a bold blue plus and minus sign. Denying what it was, was useless. Explaining it would mean ratting Isabelle out. Confirming it would unleash a Greek tragedy of epic proportions on the stone-paved streets of Naousa. So, I stood, not blinking or breathing, like I'd been turned to stone.

"What does it matter?" Fia stepped between the Dragon-Formerly-Known-As-Dolly and me. "That's Moti's business, not yours."

Dolly's fiery gaze landed full blast on Fia. Instead of backing down, Fia got up in her face. I'm pretty sure they would have chest-butted, if Dolly's bosom wasn't so soft and cushiony.

"This is between my daughter and me." Dolly's voice burned with dangerous intensity. "Why don't you mind your own business?"

"It *is* my business. You know why? Because you never had the guts to live life on your own terms, so don't go pushing your failures and resentments on your daughter. The least you can do is stand aside and let her do her own thing."

There was a collective gasp from the rest of the group and Dolly's mouth fell open. Fia had just verbally bitch-slapped my mother. The hair on the back of my neck stood. This was not good. Not good at all. I had to find a way to avert the oncoming disaster.

Think, Moti. Think.

"Ah, you found it." Teri came up from behind and snatched the pregnancy test from my hand. "Thank you. My husband *loves* kids. He can't wait for us to have a little one. Wish me luck!" She flashed her teeth at everyone, breaking up the battle.

The fact I wasn't having a baby (or sex, for that matter) should've appeased Dolly, but the tension remained high between her and Fia on the way back to the yacht. I couldn't make out what they were saying, only a lot of muttering. The rest of us sat on the other side of the tender, excluded from their bubble of mutual spite.

As we came up to the Abigail Rose II, I caught sight of Alex on the swim platform. He was buying seafood from a fisherman who had brought his boat up to the yacht. My heart stumbled as his gaze settled on me. I expected judgment and disdain after he caught me stealing, but his eyes warmed as we approached. What was this feeling that curled up tight in my stomach? It wasn't just attraction, making me squeeze my knuckles around my bag. It was something else—the kind of thing that grabs your attention and says, *Wait. There's something here…*

The fisherman took off, grinning at us, his vessel many pounds lighter, judging by all the catch he'd managed to offload.

Alex moved the buckets out of the way and helped us off, one by one, until the only people left on the tender were Dolly, Fia, and Eddie—the deckhand who drove us back to the yacht.

I was following Teri into the salon when I heard a loud splash. Swinging around, I caught sight of Dolly flailing in the water, her blouse swelling around her like a purple puffer fish.

"Oh, my God." I bolted toward the railing.

Dolly knew how to swim, and she was only a few feet from the swim platform, but she was sputtering and struggling. Fia held her hand out, but Dolly refused to take it. My heart sank as she went under. She came up for air with a great, big gulp, dismissed Fia's help, and went down again. Eddie dove in and dragged her, face up, to the platform. I leaned over and helped her in. She crawled into the yacht on all fours, her clothes plastered to her body, bosom heaving like she just ran a marathon.

"Are you okay?" I asked, pushing the hair away from her face. Everyone gathered around, waiting for her response. "Ma?"

She turned to her side slowly, her head resting on my lap, and pointed at Fia. "She pushed me."

"What?" Fia's brows knitted together. "I did no such thing."

"Liar." Dolly coughed and wheezed. "You shoved me so hard, I toppled off."

"I *poked* you in the chest. With *one* finger."

"You shoved me. You said, 'Stay away from me', and then you shoved me."

Fia stared at her. "You're unbelievable." She shook her head and walked away.

"You see that?" Dolly said. "She doesn't care. She pushes me and then…" She gave in to a series of wet, hacking coughs. "She just takes off."

"Let's get you inside, Dolly," Rachel Auntie said. "Joseph, help me get her to her room."

Rachel Auntie and Joseph Uncle were still on the outs, but they were a team. When push came to shove, they worked together.

As everyone followed them inside, I noticed Alex. He'd been standing there the whole time, and not once offered to help. He picked up his buckets, the corded muscles of his forearms straining under their weight. He must've caught the question in my eyes, because he shrugged before hauling the pails inside.

CHAPTER SEVENTEEN

"WHY DIDN'T YOU HELP DOLLY WHEN SHE FELL IN THE water?" I was in the middle of my second swimming lesson with Alex. The water came up to my chest—the deepest I dared to venture into the pool without freaking out.

"Why do you call your mother Dolly?" Alex leaned against the side of the pool, his wet hair glinting in the moonlight.

"You didn't answer my question."

"You didn't answer mine either, but fair enough." He grinned. "I didn't help Dolly because she didn't need saving. No one pushed her into the water. I helped Fia off, turned around to get your mother, and saw her jump into the water. Eddie was busy securing the boat, and Fia was nowhere near her. So, when she started screaming and hollering, I didn't care to engage."

I sighed. "Dolly can be a bit of a—"

"A drama queen? An attention seeker?"

Normally, I was all about labels. Sorting, tagging, and organizing appealed to the accountant part of my brain, but I was also fiercely protective. I didn't care for anyone else sticking labels on my family.

"Dolly has her reasons," I said. I'd never been able to fully decode her, but I knew aging was not my mother's forte. She refused to fade away or go unnoticed. She attacked things that made her feel she was being swept under the rug. One time she stole a shoe with a security tag attached to it—one shoe, two sizes too big for her. The alarms went off as we exited the store.

Security was called and we found ourselves in the manager's office. All the while, Dolly acted frail, confused, and apologetic.

"My memory isn't what it used to be," she said, clinging to me as if they were about to drag her away to the death chamber.

"What was that about?" I asked, when they let us go.

"I didn't like the way the saleslady ignored me."

"When?"

"She asked if you wanted to have a closer look at the watch. Why you? Why not me?"

I didn't dwell on it. I was just relieved no one had asked to see *my* bag. We were both flawed in curious, inexplicable ways.

"Ready for more?" Alex waded closer.

So far, I'd learned that flutter kicks were another name for making splashing noises with your feet while clinging tightly to the edge of the pool. And that if you pushed off the wall with your feet, you could glide through the water in a pseudo-stroke. Also, if I had to do it over again, I'd never choose Alex for a swim instructor. Trying to breathe, swim, and coordinate my movements was a challenge in itself. It didn't help when my brain kept taking a detour over his slick skin and thinking about how it would feel—

"Moti? Are you listening?"

"Of course, I'm listening."

Alex crossed his arms. "Well?"

"Well, what?"

"The back float. Remember what we were practicing last night? Shoulders back, head up, looking at the sky." He demonstrated, then gave me a nod. "Your turn."

Doing the back float on a swim mattress was completely different from doing it in the water, but I followed Alex's instructions and did spectacularly well. I shot him a proud look.

"Uh, yeah, that's great." Alex's face loomed between me and the stars. "Let's try it with your feet *off* the floor. It's a back float. You're not doing the limbo or dodging bullets in *The Matrix*."

I rolled my eyes and stood in chest-deep water. "I liked that movie. And that scene."

"Back float." Alex was not falling for my distraction tactics. "This time, I'll support your back."

"I think I'll be okay on my own." Up to this point, there'd been no physical contact between Alex and me. The thought of his hands on my body made my toes curl against the glossy tiles.

"Like this?" I eased into the float, but the moment I lifted my feet off the floor, my face disappeared under the water. "This is bullshit." I spluttered, glaring at the pool for trying to drown me.

"Like this." A small gasp escaped me as Alex lifted my body. My arms wrapped instinctively around his neck as he lowered me into the water—one hand supporting my head, the other my back.

"Mi fovase," he said. "Don't be afraid."

Our eyes locked, his lashes dark and wet from the water. An electric blue current buzzed between us. His skin against mine. The hard, heavy beating of our hearts. My lips throbbed as his gaze wandered over them, the sensation as red-hot as a caress.

When he lay me on my back, my body offered no resistance.

"How does that feel?" he asked, carrying me through the water.

It feels like I'm trusting you with all of my weight. All of my insecurities. All of me.

Speaking would break the spell, so I nodded.

Moments passed before Alex spoke again. "Arch your back. Chin up. Lift your chest. Arms out, palms toward the sky. That's it. Just let your legs hang."

"You won't let go?"

"Not unless you tell me to."

I took a deep breath and let my arms float at my sides. My legs stretched out in a V, toes pointing skyward as I lay on my back. Tilting my head up, I gazed at the night sky and focused on a flickering star. A hot, swirling ball of gas, billions of miles away, but I saw a starfish, its five points mirroring my body, floating in the heavens, as I was floating down below. I was a million tiny feelers, moving through life.

In that moment, I felt like Alex was untangling me from all the cords holding me down. He was uncovering my soft, vulnerable underside, feeding the tips of my nerve endings with touch and taste and emotions I'd never experienced before.

"I think I can do it," I said. "I think I'm ready."

"You sure?" It sounded like he didn't want to let go.

He released me slowly, first my head and when I was holding steady, my back.

I held my breath.

And floated.

It was glorious.

For all of three milliseconds, I floated.

Then I turned into a flailing inflatable-arms-tube-man. One of those giant twenty-foot air dancers, waving madly outside used-car sales lots to get your attention.

I clawed my way back to the surface and latched on to the nearest solid object around me. Alex. I clung to him like a panda bear clinging to the last patch of bamboo on the planet. My legs wrapped around his waist and I buried my face in his neck.

Bad water. Bad, bad water.

This was replaced by louder alarm bells.

Naked chest. Naked, naked chest.

And my boobs were squished right up against it.

It dawned on me we were in the shallow end. I was clinging to him in tummy-deep water. At this point, I could slide down his body—down, down, down, and hopefully disappear through the pool drain. However, Alex had instinctively caught me when I'd jumped on him. His arms were clamped around my body—more specifically, he was holding me up by my butt. The longer the moment stretched, the more I could feel things…stir. It wasn't possible for me to glide down his body without hitting a speed bump. I kept my face hidden in Alex's neck and pretended to ignore his erection. And let me tell you, this thing felt like it could knock a drink off a table. Maybe if I held still enough, it would go away. Meanwhile, my brain was memorizing every detail for archival purposes, so it could replay them (along with a parade of all of life's spectacularly awkward moments) at 3 a.m., when these tapes usually played in my head.

A deep rumbling started in Alex's belly.

Holy hell. The speed bump is about to launch into the stratosphere.

But it turned into loud, throaty laughter.

"What?" If I were his penis, I'd be mortified for showing up uninvited to a pool party.

"You're allowed to breathe, you know." His infuriating dimple made an appearance. "I apologize. Wholeheartedly. It was never my intention to make you uncomfortable. What I won't apologize for is the fact that I find you wildly attractive, Moti. From the moment I saw you—your hands gripping the railing like a bird about to take its first flight. When you showed up in my cabin, I didn't know how I was going to handle being so close to you. Then that dance I walked in on? I haven't been able to get it out of my head. And now, with your body wrapped around mine. You have no idea what you feel like in my arms right now. But I get it. I know it's Nikos you're interested in."

My brain was still trying to process *wildly attractive.*

I held a certain image of myself, and it didn't always coincide with the mirror, let alone Alex's words. A lot of times, the image wasn't kind. Childhood taunts echoed in my head.

MoTi! MoTi! Fatty! Chubby!

I'd talked a big game on this trip. I figured I'd go after Nikos, he'd realize we had a connection, we'd fall in love, and live happily ever after. In reality, I felt inadequate around Nikos, I had to keep trying to be sexy, smart, fun, interesting. But with Alex, I was all those things effortlessly. No facade, no pretenses.

And yet, all the signs pointed to Nikos, from the moment I had been born. My natal chart said so, Ma Anga said so, Dolly said so. It was as if the Greek gods had orchestrated a cosmic game, put me in the center of it, and placed bets on what I would do.

This is who you're supposed to be with, said Zeus and Hera, holding up a marble bust of Nikos. These two head honchos of Greek mythology threw their son off the top of Mount Olympus because they didn't like the way he looked. You didn't want to incur their wrath.

Aphrodite, Goddess of love, clapped her hands. *Ah, but what you really want to do right now is kiss Alex, don't you?* You really have to watch this gal pal. It was her husband who'd been thrown off Mount Olympus, so if it's happily-ever-after that you're gunning for, proceed with caution.

Always listen to your mother, Hestia piped in. She was the goddess of family and domesticity. She deserved a lot of kudos. Not many of the gods practiced what they preached, but Hestia stuck to her guns, and probably listened to her mother. Hence, she remained a virgin.

Dionysus, the Greek deity of wine and ecstasy, raised his glass. *Pffft. Eat, kiss, and be merry!* Pirates once seized him, thinking he was too incapacitated to fight back. Dionysus filled their ship with vines and turned them into dolphins. Moral of the story? Don't mess with a Greek god even when he's drunk. Also, he gave the kind of advice you could really get on board with.

Back on earth, I was still clinging to Alex and still confused as hell. On one hand, my insides were clamoring for his touch. On the other, was the legacy I was supposed to fulfill. Was it fair to write Nikos off, based on one night in Mykonos? He'd brushed me off to cater to Olympia Aravani, but celebrities expected him to drop everything when they pulled into his club. He'd messaged me a few times since then, updating me on the situation. If that brawl hadn't broken out—a brawl I'd initiated—Nikos would be on board and who knows where things would be heading between us? Would I ever be able to look Dolly in the eye if I wrote it off before it even began?

Alex took my silence for my admission. That it really was Nikos I was interested in. He let go of me, all signs of arousal tamed.

"You should head back inside," he said.

I felt his eyes on me as he followed me out of the pool. Drying myself off, I turned to find him in his usual spot, gazing at distant lights.

"Are you coming in?" I asked.

"In a bit." His towel was slung low around his hips, highlighting the V-shaped line below his abs. He wasn't giving me the cold shoulder or sulking. Alex was too self-assured for that. He enjoyed his own company, the same way I did. That's why he came up here every night—to think and dream.

I want to be one of those lights—somewhere by the water, where people can eat and share and connect. I want to be a link in a story that is as old as time.

Alex had a dream. He had talent and drive and ambition. Every night, under the light of the moon, he cast his net toward the heavens to catch the stars.

CHAPTER EIGHTEEN

WHEN I TIPTOED INTO THE GALLEY THE NEXT MORNING, THE first rays of light were just starting to fan out over the horizon. I paused at the door, watching Alex remove something from the oven. Steam rose and condensed on the windowpanes as the aroma of freshly baked bread filled the air. I smiled as he took off his shark mitts and placed them, teeth up, on the counter. He moved between the stove and counter, reaching for milk, scraping seeds off a vanilla bean, wiping his hands before mashing an avocado.

He cooked in an almost meditative state, earbuds in place, turning simple things into sacred rituals. Cracking an egg, grating cheese, boiling water. He picked through a basket of red peppers and held one up to the window, admiring the way the rising sun reflected off its skin.

I see you, he said to me. He saw things people missed, like how a pepper turns bright and beautiful when you hold it to the light, when you take the time to appreciate its wholeness—bruised bits and all. Alex didn't just cook. He poured all his attention into each act, each ingredient. Passion flowed from his heart and through his hands, giving him the magic ability to transform food into emotion. Onions into chocolate. How could it leave anyone immune and unaffected?

I would've stood there watching him all day, if he hadn't noticed me.

"Kalimera, Moti." He unplugged his earbuds and poured me a cup of coffee. "You're up early."

"I won't be around for the rest of the day or tomorrow, so I thought I'd come in early to help." We were midway through the cruise, heading toward Santorini. Isabelle initially chose the picturesque island for the wedding, but Thomas's father was born in Hydra, and he'd insisted they have the wedding there. Not to be outdone, Isabelle arranged for everyone to spend one night in a rented villa in Santorini, so she could still get the dream photos she wanted for her wedding album.

"No swimming lesson tonight." I sipped my coffee and took over the cutting board. "And you'll finally have the cabin to yourself."

"I can finally watch porn in my bed?" Alex looked up from the breakfast cards. He was using a red sharpie to work his way through them.

"Whatever." I flushed at the flashback of Alex's hard chest pressed against mine in the pool. "Just don't use mine for any of your extracurricular activities."

"Well, you'll be happy to know I won't be around either."

"Oh?" For some reason, I had to know exactly where Alex was spending the night, and with whom.

"Since you're all away until tomorrow, Captain Bailey's letting the crew roam wild and free."

"You're staying overnight in Santorini too?"

"No, I'm going here." He pulled out a cookbook from the shelf and flipped it open to reveal a folded piece of parchment paper. Inside was a beautifully pressed white flower—fragile and delicate, looking like it was picked early in the morning, with its petals just reaching out to the sun.

"Folegandros." Alex held it up for me. "It's where I was born—raw and rocky, with cliffs and caves, and an unforgiving terrain. But the flowers still find a way to grow. My mother loved that about them. The white ones were her favorite. We always had bouquets of wildflowers around the house. She picked this on the day she died."

Sunlight filtered through the paper-thin petals as Alex twirled it slowly. It wasn't just a flower—it was a time, a place, a feeling— suspended on a still-green stem. I could almost feel the moment she plucked it, not knowing it might be the last white flower she ever picked. I gazed at it in silence, overcome by its beauty and tragedy. Then, just as reverently as he had retrieved it, Alex placed it back between the parchment paper and returned the book on the shelf.

"Did your mother give you this book?" I ran my fingers over the spine. It was old and thick, the cover stained with use. "Did she teach you how to cook?" Maybe the magic of Alex's food had been passed down from generation to generation, a secret family tradition that—

"Cooking was not my mother's forte." Alex smiled. "In fact, my father and I did everything we could to keep her out of the kitchen."

I chuckled. *Well, there goes that theory.*

"This was my first cookbook." He tapped the cover. "It was a gift from our neighbor. She was a bitter old soul. After my mother died, I spent all my time outside, raising hell. I kept getting into trouble with Mrs. Tavoulari. One day, she was trying to take a nap and threw this book at me from her kitchen window. I was four-teen. I'd never been off the island. I opened the book and suddenly, a whole world was out there—things I'd never seen or tasted or imagined. I spent hours looking over the photos. When I went to return the book, Mrs. Tavoulari told me I could keep it, provided I made something from it every day. She gave me a small blue bowl, told me to fill it, and bring it to her as soon as it was ready. The book was mine as long as I kept that bowl going. So, every day after school, instead of stirring up trouble, I was in the kitchen. She was a smart one—she kept me busy, got her nap, *and* a meal out of it."

"And you learned how to cook."

"This book taught me a lot of things. Cooking wasn't one of

them. Sure, I learned to follow instructions. I learned the basics. But the most important thing I learned is that it's a privilege to cook for someone. What passes through your hands is received by their senses and becomes a part of them. It took me a while to understand that.

"At first, I picked dishes I wanted to eat, or that were easy to make. Then, as I watched Mrs. Tavoulari eat, I wondered about her family. She had no photos on the walls. No one came to visit. It was probably because she was so cranky. No matter what I made, she complained. Too much salt. Not enough salt. Not the right texture. She was annoying as hell." Alex chuckled as he plated a stack of pancakes and topped them with berries and powdered sugar.

"One day, I was sweeping walnut shells off her floor. They were everywhere. She never bothered with a bowl—just pounded them with an old hammer and left the shells lying around. I found a whole bunch of walnuts that had rolled away intact. I took them home and made her a walnut cake. Things started turning around that day. For the first time, Mrs. Tavoulari said nothing. She finished the blue bowl and asked if there was more. I realized I'd been cooking for me the whole time, not her. The more attention I paid to the things she liked, the more she opened up. She started savoring every dish and looking forward to my visits. One evening, she opened the door before I knocked, and she was smiling. Beaming. The dusty curtains were gone, the floor was clean, and a hairdresser had been in to cut her hair. All for a little thought, a little care, and a little love in the kitchen. I've taken this book with me on every charter to remind me of the transformative power of food. And of home."

Alex's magic. It wasn't the kind Ma Anga practiced. His book had no spells or incantations. It was more powerful—a white flower and echoes of walnut shells caught between its pages. Every story has a beginning, and I loved Alex's.

"You're heading home then?" I asked. "Tonight?"

He turned around and glanced at the potatoes I was grating.

"You should soak them in ice water when they're done," he said.

He had a habit of inspecting everything I did and then adding his two cents worth.

These are not uniform, Moti. They won't cook evenly.

Don't touch that! You have lemon on your fingers.

I said dice the tomatoes, not hack them. This is a massacre.

I rolled my eyes, but secretly daydreamed about him issuing other orders.

Lick it, Moti. You know you want to.

"Moti?"

"Huh?" My cheeks flamed as Alex interrupted my Fifty-Shades-Of-Kitchen-Scenarios.

"You want a lick?"

Crap. Did I say that out loud?

I turned around slowly and found him holding the beaters he'd used to whip the frosting. Relieved I wasn't as tuned-out as I'd thought, I jumped on his offering.

"And yes, I'm heading to Folegandros tonight."

"Long way to go?" I swiped the frosting off the metal.

"About an hour from Santorini, on the...uh..." He trailed off as I sucked on my finger.

"On the what?" I stared at him with round eyes and a round mouth. Chef Alexandros was running his own Fifty-Shades-Of-Kitchen-Scenario, and that emboldened me. Making him forget what he was saying made me flush with power. It also made me ridiculously giddy—the high of your crush crushing right back at you. Only, it was more than a crush. I really liked Alex. I liked him inside and out. If I let it, this moment could catch fire. Alex's gaze sweeping over my mouth was like a match striking flammable lips.

"You were saying?" I dropped the beaters into the sink and started washing them.

"Yeah." The apple in Alex's neck bobbed as he cleared his

throat. "Santorini to Folegandros is about an hour on the fast ferry. I told my father I'd have dinner with him tonight. I'm at sea so often, I don't get to see him much." He pulled down the breakfast cards and checked his watch.

As if on cue, Hannah arrived. "Great," she exclaimed, surveying all the trays. "I'll start serving breakfast. The guests are just starting to make their way to…" She paused when she saw me. "Good morning, Moti. What are you doing here?"

I was elbow-deep in grated potatoes. There was no denying I was helping Alex prep the food.

"Chef Alexandros," Captain Bailey entered the galley, holding a slip of paper. "I'm approving the provisions for…"

Now both Captain Bailey and Hannah were staring at me.

"Hannah, you were about to get breakfast going?"

"Yes, Captain Bailey." Hannah looked from Captain Bailey to me to Alex before grabbing two trays. "I'm on it."

Captain Bailey's eyebrows did not resume their normal cruising altitude after Hannah left. "Chef Alexandros? You have one of our guests helping you prepare meals?"

I jumped in before he could answer. "I asked Chef Alexandros for some cooking lessons. Truth be told, I'm a bit of a pain to have around."

True story, considering I'd thrown out the broth he'd been saving yesterday, thinking I was being helpful by cleaning the stockpot.

"Chef Alexandros has been really accommodating. I hope it's not a problem? I'm learning so much and I find it very therapeutic." I grated the rest of the potato I was holding. Therapeutic, my ass. I hated grating anything—my knuckles were in constant fear. But I gave the captain a big smile. If you crinkle your eyes when you smile, you can come across as sincere.

Captain Bailey eyed Alex and me. "Roommates, and now kitchen-mates. How is the situation with your aunt and uncle?"

"Still the same," I said.

She lingered a little longer, then handed Alex the slip of paper she brought. "You're doing a great job, Chef Alexandros. I'll have that letter of recommendation for you at the end of the charter. You shouldn't have any trouble landing the Kiriakis gig."

Then, as she turned to leave, she paused, looked at me, and added, "Just don't mess things up, Chef."

I held my breath as our yacht glided into the harbor. Santorini was a mountain of rocks rising from the sea. Cliffs of striated lava towered around us, a reminder we were sailing into a giant, submerged crater—a dormant but active volcano. From a distance, the ridges appeared capped with snow but were really sprawling villages and towns clinging to the edges of the caldera. Santorini was a study in contrasts—white buildings, blue windows, jagged rocks, and soft domed roofs.

"Come on, come on." Isabelle flapped her list in our faces.

It was Photo Shoot Day for her and Thomas. Teri was in charge of makeup, Fia was taking the pictures, and I was the umbrella-holder. Isabelle's list was of all the spots we had to hit before the sun set. The Three Bells, The Blue Dome, The Cross, The Castle, The Lighthouse, Red Beach, Black Beach, White Beach. Holding Ice-Cream Cones (don't forget to take the rings), Veil Blowing In The Wind (get Teri and Moti to hold), With Donkey (if well behaved and not smelly).

The list went on, all capitalized, which meant it was nonnegotiable. Thomas took it in his stride as he lugged Isabelle's bag of props and outfits out of the cable car that we took to the town of Fira. We skipped the donkey rides that carried tourists up the steep incline. There were at least six hundred steps on the path. I'd be smelly too if I had to go up and down it all day, in the blistering heat.

It didn't take long for Isabelle to deviate from her list. Who could blame her? Perched atop the cliffs, overlooking azure-blue water, every backstreet and arched doorway begged for a click. Swimming pools—the size of bathtubs were squeezed into the most impossible of spaces. We spent so much time off-course, by the time we got to the spots Isabelle really wanted to capture, lines of people waited ahead of us.

While Teri fussed over Isabelle's hair, Thomas crossed out half the locations on the list.

"Half an hour here, which means we'll never get to this. Or this. And if you want to make it to the castle for sunset, we'll have to skip the Red Beach. And the White Beach." He waited until Isabelle agreed, then gave me a wink.

So this was why he was so easygoing. Thomas knew it was pointless to argue with Isabelle. If he let her run wild, she'd eventually hit a wall. And when she did, he'd swoop in to save the day. On the surface it looked like Isabelle was in control, but really, Thomas was steering the ship.

I pulled Isabelle aside when he wasn't looking. "So? Did you take the test?"

She responded with a blank look.

"Are you kidding me? The pregnancy test? Are you pregnant, Isabelle?"

"Oh, that." She grinned. "Turns out, I was just late."

I shot her daggers with my eyes.

"After all the trouble I went through to get you that test, the least you could do is give me a niece or nephew."

Isabelle giggled. "Umbrella, Moti. The sun's hitting my face."

While our white friends were forever chasing a summer glow, Isabelle and I were raised to covet the other end of the spectrum. Our mothers had a heart attack if our brown skin turned a degree darker.

"Who's going to marry you now?" they moaned. "An Indian bride should always be fairer than her groom."

Of course, this wasn't true for Isabelle and Thomas, and as ridiculous as the notion was, Isabelle felt flawed for it. I'm pretty sure she swapped out Thomas's sunscreen for tanning lotion. And his hat kept mysteriously disappearing whenever we were out. If Isabelle couldn't get any fairer, Thomas was just going to have to get darker.

Bake, Thomas, bake.

We were all sweating under the heat of the sun. At Black Beach, the romantic Walk-On-The-Beach Shot turned into a trot because the sand was unbearably hot. Thomas and Isabelle looked like they were treading on burning coals. By the time we got to Oia for the last location on the list—the castle—Isabelle's feet were angry and charred. She kicked off her shoes and rummaged in the bag for her spare pair.

"Dammit. I think I left them on the boat."

Thomas, Teri, Fia, and I clustered around to keep the crowds from trampling her as she searched the suitcase. It was still hours before sunset, but everyone seemed to have the same idea—to head to the castle early and snag a spot before the main event. Matchy-matchy couples thronged by, along with women negotiating cobbled streets in high heels and photography enthusiasts with lenses the size of the Hubble telescope.

"Dammit," Isabelle said again.

"Just go barefoot," Thomas said. At this point, we were all de-corked, de-fizzed, and ready to call it a day.

"But there's donkey poop everywhere. Just call them."

"Call who?"

"The boat. Call Captain Bailey and ask her to send someone over with my shoes."

Which was how I ended up at an ice-cream shop, waiting for Isabelle's shoes, while everyone else went scouting for the perfect location to capture the sunset. I had a newfound respect for married people. Taking wedding photos was hard work and also, the last chance to see what your partner morphed into under extreme pressure.

Tucking the umbrella under my arm, I peered over the flavors in the gelateria. Settling under the awning with my waffle cone, I watched one of the employees write on the outdoor chalkboard marquee: *Stavros is looking for a wife.*

Someone, presumably Stavros's mother, cackled from the street.

A pink scooter sputtered to a stop outside the ice-cream shop. A girl at the next table elbowed her friend and they both stared at the new arrival.

Alex. In off-duty mode. Frayed jeans, a white T-shirt and messy hair, made even messier by his bike ride.

My cheeks burned when he picked me out and dismounted. Suddenly, I was looking at him through teenage eyes, re-living first crushes—the way your heart pauses, then picks up, double-time.

What the hell is going on with me?

It's because he can cook, another voice answered. *What woman can resist an alpha-beta combo?*

"Special delivery." He straddled the bench across from my table and slid Isabelle's shoes toward me.

"Thanks." My skin prickled as his eyes drifted over my bare shoulders. The light was golden, the air still hot and heavy. "Nice ride." I motioned to his bike.

"The only rental I could get at this time of the day. Captain Bailey said to get these here as fast as possible."

"Right." I grabbed the shoe bag from him and stood. "I should get going. Isabelle is waiting on these."

"Wait a minute." His fingers clamped around my wrist. "You're walking around like that?"

I glanced at my bare toes. "I lent Isabelle my shoes."

"So put hers on."

"Isabelle's shoes?" Blasphemy. We wore the same size, but I could never stuff my feet into her designer beauties. "These are part of her bridal trousseau."

"So? It's just for a short stretch." Then his hands were on my foot, cupping the heel as he slid the shoes on.

Prince Charming, with the glass slipper.

I smiled at my Target feet in Jimmy Choo heels. Sparkly rose-gold stilettos that looked damn fine with my blue off-shoulder top and cream linen shorts.

"Alex, I can't walk in these."

He looked up at me, then down at the spiky shoes. "No?"

I slid them off, along with my fifteen seconds of crystal-encrusted glory.

"Fine. You stay here. I'll go." Alex put the shoes back in their bag. "Where do I find them?"

His kindness snuck past my defenses and disarmed me.

"Moti?" He waited, T-shirt stretched tight across broad shoulders, one hand on a pink handlebar.

"You won't need the bike. They're over there." I pointed toward the castle.

"Okay. I'll be right back with your shoes."

I nodded and sat back down. Why did he have to be so nice to me? I needed Alex to be annoying, irritating, overbearing.

He returned with my sandals dangling from his fingers. Flat, comfy, and non-sparkly.

We watched the trail of tourists making their way to the hilltop spot. Couples, couples, everywhere.

"Are sunsets in Santorini really that beautiful?" I asked.

"Not if you head up there now. All you'll get are glimpses from behind a line of shutterbugs. But yes, they're beautiful. Vivid. Electric. Not something anyone can really describe."

"Are you staying for it?"

He shook his head. "I have a ferry to catch."

"Well, I better get going." I grabbed the umbrella and stood. "Did Isabelle and Thomas find a good spot?"

"They're up front. If you use your elbows, you just might get through."

"Right." I chuckled and headed for the street. "Enjoy your time off, Alex."

I heard the revving of the engine behind me as he got on the scooter. Then his voice called over the crowd. "Hey, Moti!"

I turned and caught his eye across the street.

"You ever get time off?" he asked.

Time off? What was he talking about? I was on vacation.

"Hop on." He gestured to the empty spot behind him.

"What?"

"If you want to see the sunset, hop on."

"But…" I glanced toward the castle.

"Away from the crowds."

"Don't you have a ferry to catch?" We were volleying back and forth over the stream of people.

"I do."

We both had things to do, places to be, and yet…

I took a step toward him. Then another. "I should go find Isabelle."

He waited, blue smoke spewing from a pink scooter.

"Is this thing safe?" I poked the cracked leather seat.

He didn't answer.

"No helmet?" I handed him my umbrella. He reached into the cargo basket and slid it into his backpack.

"I can't just take off." I hoisted one leg over the saddle.

"They'll worry…"

My words trailed away as the scooter took off with a lurch.

I shrieked and grabbed Alex tight.

CHAPTER NINETEEN

"**W**HERE ARE WE GOING?" I YELLED, MY HAIR FLAPPING IN the wind.

"Imerovigli."

"Where?"

"Another ten minutes and we'll be there."

Ten more minutes.

I clung tighter.

My first motorbike ride was nothing like the high-powered thrill I'd expected. The scooter struggled and sputtered to keep up with traffic. We got honks and dirty looks as cars and trucks whizzed by. Each time, I prayed we wouldn't get nudged off the narrow winding road. It clung to steep cliffs, with guardrails at only the most dangerous spots. I squeezed my eyes as a bus carrying a shitload of sunset-chasers whooshed by us around a blind curve.

"Spectacular, isn't it?" Alex tilted his head toward the jagged coastline.

Spectacular, my ass. Spectacularly dangerous. The sheer drop, the cobalt sea, the sun low in the caldera.

With my arms snaked tight around his waist, I pressed my cheek between Alex's shoulder blades. It was a nice spot. Warm and solid. It kept the wind from my face. Through the thin fabric of his T-shirt, his muscles felt indecently firm and toned.

Not fair, considering he's around food all day.

The tighter I held on to him, the more his stupid abs got on my nerves. Good. He was being annoying again.

"Better," I muttered, feeling his core flex as he navigated a hairpin turn.

"What did you say?"

My voice rose over the drone of the engine. "I said this better be worth it."

"It already is. Look how much you're enjoying snuggling up to me."

I let go when we entered a quaint little village and we parked the scooter. Alex strapped his backpack on, and we wound our way through the side streets.

Imerovigli. White houses spilling down the edge of a submerged volcano. Panoramic views at every turn.

"Skaros Rock." Alex pointed to a square-topped rock jutting out into the sea, high above the water.

"Is that where we're heading?" A path headed toward the looming rock—hundreds of rocky steps descending, then ascending to the peak.

"We don't have time to make it all the way there, but I know a place where the view is just as spectacular."

Everything around us was starting to take on a pastel hue as we followed the trail toward Skaros Rock. The contrast of red and black cliffs against the shimmering blue of the Aegean Sea was indescribable.

"Here." Alex veered off the path and followed a dirt trail to a rocky overhang. We sat there, at the rim of the caldera, our legs swinging over the edge. Before us was a spectacular, unobstructed view of the bay.

"Ready?" he asked, slipping his backpack off.

"For what?"

He grinned. One flash of his dimple and I knew I was in trouble.

He pushed himself off the rock and landed on the ledge below. "Come on." He held his arms out, waiting for me to jump.

"No way." I threw his backpack at him instead. "I'm fine up

here." I couldn't even *see* the ledge, just his cocky face looking up at me. Behind him was a dizzy drop to the sea. Water, water, everywhere. The thought of plummeting into its dark depths and never coming back up terrified me.

"Moti?" Alex tilted his head. Fear has a face, a look, a desperate energy that's hard to hide.

"You'll think I'm silly, but when I was born, a fortune-teller told my mother I'd die in the water."

He clued in and glanced at the waves crashing below us. "It doesn't matter what I think." His eyes flickered for a moment. "Is that what *you* think is going to happen?"

I shrugged. You accept a lot of things as a kid. You accept the things your parents tell you. They're your first point of contact with the world. You trust them. You base your worth on them. Parts of you remain hardwired when you grow up. Even when you know better, you still feel it.

"Hey." Alex grasped my hand, pulling me back from my thoughts. "I think what you're doing is incredibly brave."

"Clinging to this rock?"

"Learning to swim. Despite being so afraid of the water. Why didn't you tell me?"

I shrugged and gazed into the horizon.

"Trust me?"

He'd asked me once before—in the pool, and he'd lost. He was asking again. He took a step back and raised his arms.

"I promise I'll catch you."

His words bounced against the rocks and echoed in my ears.

I'll catch you...

You...

You...

The wind paused and the waves stopped crashing below. My heart stilled at what I saw in his eyes:

Me...

Me...

Me...

When you've been looked over your whole life, it's startling to find yourself in someone's eyes, to be held in their vision, the same way they hold sunsets and beautiful things.

"Jump," he said.

I closed my eyes and jumped.

My breath escaped as he caught me. Clasped tightly in his arms with my feet dangling off the ground, I forgot about the sun, the sky, the sea. I forgot we were perched on a ledge, high off the volcanic cliffs.

He let me down slowly, but when my feet touched the ground, he held onto me. I wound my arms around his neck. His body tightened, pupils dilating. A spark of electricity shot through me. I traced his jawline with my nose, the stubble scratching my skin like pinpricks—up, up to the corner of his mouth. There I paused, nerves pulsing, overwhelmed by the feeling swelling in my heart.

He lifted my chin and ran his thumb over my lip. "Tell me you're not thinking about Nikos."

"Nikos who?" The sun made his skin glow from within. He made me breathless, and I paused at the marvel of it.

"My egg timer, she takes," he said. "But this?" His lips shadowed over mine, close enough to send sparks flying. "This kiss that's been dying to be claimed...she stalls." His voice was husky, eyes half-closed. "Christ, Moti, I want to taste you so bad, I feel like I'm going to fucking explode—"

I pressed my lips to his. Softly.

An exploration. A proclamation.

We like you, they said. *A whole friggin' lot. We like the way you taste. The way you feel. The way you fit.*

His lips curved when I stepped away—as if he heard the silent exchange. His eyes remained shut, savoring the moment. Then his arms snaked out and dragged me back against him. "I'm not done with you yet."

"Oh my God." I gasped as my body came in full contact with him. "You really *are* ready to explode."

He looked at me quizzically and then chuckled. "Sorry, is it poking you? It's kind of squished between us." He kept his eyes on mine as he reached between our bodies.

No. Tell me he's not pulling it out.

But Alex *was* pulling it out. It was unbelievably hard. And long. It went up. And up. Past my navel, past my ribs. Holy hell. Alex was housing a one-eyed Greek monster in his pants.

I stepped back, steeling myself for a sight of Mr. Cyclops.

Alex was solemn as he held the umbrella up, its capped end pointing toward me. It had been sticking out from the backpack. How it ended up between us, I didn't know, except that it might have been dislodged when I threw the backpack over. The metal shaft was sheathed in fabric and curved into a wooden handle at the other end.

I tried to keep a straight face. He did the same. Our gazes held until I cracked.

"I thought…" I couldn't stop laughing. "I thought…"

"I know what you thought, and I'm completely flattered." He grinned and tossed the umbrella aside. "Now, where were we?" He pulled me in, his heated gaze dropping to my mouth. "I believe we were doing something with our lips."

His head bent. Laughter faded as molten need flared up inside me. His lips were hot, rough, tender, demanding. Everything in me surged toward him with a surprising intensity. Nerve endings lit up like hundreds of hot spots.

"Moti." Alex's voice was thick as he nuzzled his way to the soft spot beneath my ear. He pushed a strand of hair away from my neck. I gasped as he kissed the pulse there, the feel of his stubble raw and delicious against my skin. "Look." He nudged me around and pointed to the sky.

The sun was a big, red ball, setting against charred, volcanic islets in the bay. White homes perched like sea gulls on the cliffs, watching the wide-screen panorama. A sailboat broke the shimmering reflection of the sky, floating over the blood-orange sea.

"Okay. Enough of that." Alex turned me around and went back in for a kiss.

I laughed and pushed him away.

"Fucking Santorini sunsets. How's a guy supposed to compete?" His grin was playful as he unrolled a towel from his backpack.

"Where are you going with that?" My lips were hot and inflamed from his kisses. I wanted more.

"In here." He ducked into a cavern—the remains of a house carved out of the stone. Cave houses were common in the area. This one looked like it had been built and abandoned a long time ago.

Spreading the towel on the ground, Alex patted the spot beside him. It was dark inside, which accentuated the colors bursting in the sky. Viewing the sunset through the circular entrance of the cave house was like looking into a kaleidoscope of changing light and color. Golden hues turned to violet as the sun tilted deeper into the sea. It retreated slowly, getting smaller and smaller, until it was a glittering dot where all the colors met. A white haze settled in the thin line where the sea met the sky. My hand inched toward Alex's as we held our breath, waiting for the inevitable darkness to erase the boundary. Our fingers touched, tip to tip. Then his hand claimed mine.

If hands made sounds, mine would have purred. It was happy. Perfectly content, even though the man holding it was missing an extra thumb. In fact, it was a very bad hand for feeling so right in Alex's warm grip. It was a hand in need of obedience training. It reached out and traced the fading sliver of light along Alex's cheekbone. His breath caught and his eyes turned to mine, a wild flickering in their depths. When his lips grazed soft kisses across my palm, my entire body hummed in response.

This man. His touch. His taste. His gaze.

He watched the play of emotions across my face as his tongue blazed a wet trail along my palm. Nothing soft or chaste about his kiss now. I felt it all the way between the junction of my thighs.

Fuck. The gloves are off. We aren't on the boat. He's not crew. I'm not client. Alex isn't holding back anymore.

It would be so easy to get swept away, to give in to the wild heat that burned for his touch.

He tiptoed two fingers up my arm, leaving a trail of goose bumps. Up, up, past my shoulders, my neck, my jaw.

"So many thoughts." He tapped the center of my forehead softly. "What's going on in there?"

"You won't understand."

"You've decided? Without giving me a chance?"

Our eyes appraised each other: his strong and steady, mine scanning for all the imprecise, nameless things that guide hearts.

"Sometimes," I said. "I think if I do the wrong thing, my mother will die." It was a loaded confession, absurd even, but saying it out loud made it easier to breathe. Saying it made the chains around my chest loosen their hold.

Alex tilted his head. "Explain."

I broke away from him and stared at the indigo sky. "You already know part of the story. The lady who interpreted my natal chart told Dolly my true love would have three thumbs. She said I'd meet him by the water, but I'd also die in the water. And if I married someone other than my true love, my mother would die within seven days."

Alex didn't respond, but at least he wasn't laughing at me. I could feel him putting together pieces of the puzzle. "That's an awfully big responsibility to be walking around with." He wrapped his arm around me, and I rested my head on his shoulder. We watched the lights come on, one by one, on the distant shore. "And you've been carrying it with you since you were born?"

My eyes welled up with unshed emotions, but I blinked them back. The moment was too pretty to be blurred. I wanted to remember it exactly like it was. Sharp and colored. The sea. The sky. The man sitting beside me.

Most people would've tried to make me see how ridiculous Ma Anga's prediction was. Hell, I'd tried to reason myself out of it too. But Alex seemed to understand. Our fears aren't always logical. They just *are*.

"It makes sense now." His voice rumbled through his chest, where my cheek had claimed a spot. "What your grandmother said, about your mother only allowing you to be with someone with three thumbs. Is that what's stopping you from being with me? Is that why you're going after Nikos? What do *you* want, Moti?"

In my heart, I knew. I wanted Alex. Undeniably, irrefutably Alex. "It's easy here. Removed from everything." I gestured to the colors darkening outside the cavern, the villages sparkling with warm, silver lights.

"But Nikos is the easier choice." His fingers stroked my hair.

I almost wished he'd try to sway me, but the truth is no one can battle your demons for you. Your doubts and fears are your own to feed or to slay.

Being with Alex meant turning my back on Dolly. What if choosing Alex over Nikos—a summer fling over a long-ordained sign—led to more? What if a seemingly innocuous path, step by step, ended up leading to Dolly's death?

"See that light over there?" Alex pointed to an island in the distance, its dark outline reflected in the water. "That one's mine. My place by the sea. Fresh fish, tomatoes as sweet as candy apples, string lights on the patio, little tables under gnarled trees." He sat back, leaning on his hands. "Yep. Totally claiming that one."

"I want that one." I pointed to a star. "It would take Dolly forever to get there."

We laughed, and I thought, once again, how much I liked the little groove in his cheek.

"What I wouldn't give to have a moment with my mother." He looked at the sky, as if he might find her among the stars, pinned to the heavens like a sparkling memory.

I wrapped my arms around my knees and rested my chin on them. I wanted the kind of relationship with Dolly that Alex had had with his mother. I wanted to remember her with a smile after she was gone, not regret. If someone tells you they don't care what their mother thinks of them, they're lying—if not to you, then to themselves. Deep down, we all want to be loved by the woman who gave us life. Doesn't matter if you're six or sixty.

"What was your mother's name?" I asked.

"Frida," he said. "She was from Denmark. My grandfather fled there at the time of the Greek junta. My parents met in Copenhagen and returned to Greece after things settled down."

I was half listening, half thinking how I wanted to kiss him again. His fiery mouth, his slow, wet, coaxing tongue.

"Alex?" He was already looking at me, so I don't know why I said it. "Thank you." I tucked an unruly strand of hair behind his ear. He raised a brow. That fucking brow. He was probably trying to figure out the conflicting signals—the push-pull vibes I was transmitting. "Thank you for this…" I gestured around us—a cavern in the cliffs, an enchanted sunset, an evening gift-wrapped with sparkly stars. "I'm sorry you didn't get to see your father tonight."

"I can still take the last ferry out," he said. "Come with me. It's not Santorini, but it's beautiful in a wild, untamed way. One road, one taxi. Bare, rugged, intimate."

The way his voice dropped at the end sent a thousand brazen images flashing before my eyes. His weight on my body, lips crushing mine, our fingers entwined. My toes curled. I wanted it. I wanted it so badly, my cheeks flushed with the intensity of it.

And then what? Another voice piped in. *Get back on the boat and fail at the one thing that would make things right between you and Dolly?*

Nikos was the litmus test. A living, breathing, quantifiable yard-stick Dolly was measuring me by—my love, my loyalty, my worth as a daughter. It wasn't like I never rebelled. It was *my* life after all. I lost my virginity to Vijay Khanna in his uncle's motel. A creaky bed, a musty carpet, the smell of stale cigarettes. Afterward, he brought me ice from the ice machine. I'd wrapped it in a towel and held it against myself. My defiance melted into a wet rag with streaks of blood between my legs. Sex felt hollow and empty, like all my attempts at love and romance. I didn't know exactly how my relationship with Dolly affected my relationship with men. All I knew is I needed her on board before I could be happy.

"I should get back," I said. "Isabelle will be looking for me."

Alex's eyes searched mine, looking for reasons, motivations, the things that bent me. Then he stood and held his hand out.

"I'll take you back to Oia and head to the ferry from there." He helped me up, and we gathered our things.

The ride back should've been different. People on pink motorbikes should be happy. Cotton-candy happy. But Alex was quiet and I was confused. Being sad *and* horny is so confusing. To top it off, I was sad *because* I was horny. If you've ever said no to someone whose kisses sizzle on your lips like butter in a hot pan, because it's the sensible thing to do, you know the feeling. You might pat yourself on the back, but you also want to bitch-slap the part of you that denied you the experience.

I wrapped my arms around Alex and sulked the whole way to Oia.

When he stopped outside the ice-cream shop, I un-smooshed my face from his back and got off the bike. Stray dogs, up from their daytime naps, came around to say hello. The crowds had dispersed, streaming into cafes and tavernas. I had a moment of panic as I looked around.

"You think they'll still be there?" I glanced at the castle.

"Can't hurt to check." Alex parked the scooter, and we made our way to the spot where he last saw them. It was empty, except for a few couples lingering in the dark.

"Oh no. They're probably searching for me." My phone didn't work in Greece—at least not to call or text. If Isabelle had contacted Dolly, the whole situation would be blown way out of control by now. My shoulders drooped with the weight of what I'd done.

"I should've never taken off like that. They're probably worried sick, looking for me. The last thing Isabelle and Thomas need is—" I paused as I thought of Thomas. "Hey, can I use your phone?" Thomas had a local number. Alex had a local number. Greece calling Greece. Problem solved.

I pulled up Thomas's number from my contact list and dialed it on Alex's phone, cringing as it rang.

"Hello?" Thomas picked up on the first ring, no doubt in red-flag mode.

"Thomas, it's me. Moti."

"Moti. Oh my God." He must have put his hand over the phone, because his next words were muffled, probably alerting everyone it was me. A frantic back-and-forth ensued while I clutched the phone and repeated to myself:

You're such a shithead, Moti.

"Moti." Thomas came back on the line. "I'm so sorry. We stopped for drinks and completely forgot about you. Are you still at the ice-cream shop?"

Mother. Fucker.

They hadn't even noticed I was missing. Isabelle wasn't wringing her hands. Dolly wasn't calling the police. No one was looking for me, or waiting, or worrying. I wasn't anywhere on their stage, although I'd given them spotlight roles on mine.

"Everything okay?" asked Alex.

I nodded and felt something growing inside me. "Thomas, can you put Isabelle on the line?"

A slight pause as the phone changed hands.

"Moti!" Isabelle sounded breathless. Music and laughter streamed through from her end. "We'll be there in a few minutes. Wait till you see the photos Fia got. I'll have Thomas set up a slideshow tonight. There's a theater in the villa. We can all kick back and—"

"I'm not going to the villa tonight." Now two things growing inside of me—two round, firm things.

Isabelle was silent. Maybe even shocked I'd cut her off.

"Isabelle." I smiled into the phone. This is what growing a pair of balls felt like. I liked the sensation very much. "I need you to cover for me. I'm not going to the villa tonight. I'm going to Folegandros."

Alex's head shot up. And then a slow, lazy smile that made my cheeks flush.

"Folegandros?" Isabelle repeated. "Is that...what? A nightclub?"

"It's an island—not too far from here. I'll be back before we depart tomorrow."

"What? No. You can't—"

"It's not up for debate, Isabelle. I'm calling in those favors. I'm going to Folegandros with Alex, and I need you to cover for me."

"Alex? Chef Alexandros? You're with *him*?"

I could picture her making wild gestures to Thomas. "But Moti—"

"First grade. Katy Sterling. I took a punch for you in the playground."

"Yeah, but—"

"Third grade. Biology project. You tracked sand through the house, and I took the heat for it."

"I was already in trouble with—"

"Fifth grade. Mateo Martin. I sang twenty minutes straight so Rachel Auntie wouldn't hear you talking on the phone with him."

"Yeah, well. That was probably more painful for her than for you."

"Ninth grade. The exchange student. I guarded the chemistry lab door while you made out."

"He was hot, wasn't he?"

"Prom night. When Mrs. Arora caught you smoking weed with—"

"Okay, okay. I get it. I owe you. Big time. I'll figure something out."

"Thank you." My lips curved as Alex high-fived me. "I'll meet you back on the boat tomorrow." I was about to hang up when she spoke again.

"Hey, Moti!" She waited until I brought the phone back to my ear. "Are you going to...you know? With Alex."

"Shut up." I slid my eyes to him, hoping he hadn't heard.

"He's yummy. Tell me you're at least going to—"

"Bye, Isabelle." I hung up and returned the phone to Alex.

"So?" He put it away and looked at me. "Folegandros?"

The way he said it reminded me of his kiss, abuzz with promises. The night was warm, but a delicious shudder shot through me. Free. Alone. Alive. With Alex.

"Yes," I replied. "Folegandros."

CHAPTER TWENTY

W E RETURNED THE MOTORBIKE ALEX RENTED IN SANTORINI AND took the ferry to Folegandros. I expected it to be quiet, but the port was deserted—not a soul in sight.

I looked at my watch and then at the chalkboard sign again. The bus was late. Insanely late.

"All the schedules are in GMT." Alex stretched out on the bench beside me.

I tapped my watch. "I'm synced to the right time zone."

"GMT, meaning Greek Maybe Time," Alex said. "The bus will get here when it gets here."

I tapped my foot like a thumper rabbit. When you're used to everything running by the clock, delays irritate you.

"Stop that. You're breaking my nerves." Alex quieted my foot with his.

"Breaking your nerves? How dramatic."

He chuckled. "It's a direct translation of a Greek phrase. Something doesn't just annoy you, it breaks your nerves. We're never just busy, we're running without arriving. Something isn't messy, it's a brothel. When you're angry with someone, you say you're going to eat them. Ask someone about the bus right now and he'll shrug and tell you there are flowers and bees around his dick."

"What's that supposed to mean?"

"It means he doesn't care. Everything is *siga-siga* here. Slowly, slowly. I guess you could call it a philosophy, a way of life. Live in the minute. Forget about the rest of the clock face." He covered my watch with his hand and grinned.

Nothing siga-siga about the way my heart quickened at his touch.

"Alexandros!" Headlights flared in our faces as a rusty pickup truck pulled up beside us.

Loud voices. Warm greetings. Then Alex was throwing his backpack in the bed of the truck.

"Come on," he said. "He'll give us a ride to town."

"What? With them?" I pointed to the two roosters eyeing us from wire cages.

"There's a goat in the front, if you'd rather sit with him. He's a mean one though. Yiannis just saved him from the butcher. His owner said he's an inconsiderate, head-butting jerk."

Yiannis shouted something in Greek and they both laughed.

"Yiannis says the timing is perfect," explained Alex, as I climbed into the truck. "His mother-in-law is visiting. Nothing like a head-butting jerk and a couple of early morning alarm clocks to send her packing back to Crete."

The roosters pecked at Alex through the wire mesh when he settled next to them. "Okay, okay." He inched away. "Alarm cocks. That better?" Yiannis guffawed from the front seat while the roosters appeared temporarily pacified.

It was a bumpy ride to Chora, the main town of Folegrandros. Huddled atop a jagged cliff, its narrow lanes were closed to motor vehicles, so we said goodbye to Yiannis and his menagerie. We followed the sound of music down the alleyways until we got to the center, where it seemed the whole town was gathered. Three large squares, tables crammed into every nook and cranny. Food and wine flowed along with the buzz of conversation.

Someone called out to Alex, but before we could make out who, another man engulfed him in a hug.

"What's going on?" Alex said.

"Dimitra's son is off to do his military service. She's throwing a party."

"Pantelis? But I thought she didn't want him to go."

"She doesn't, but you know how it is. This is her way of making sure everyone remembers she wanted nothing to do with it." He paused when his eyes fell on me. "You brought a friend?" He grinned and smacked Alex on the back. "About time. Come. Eat."

He crammed two more chairs around an already-crammed table.

"*Yamas.*" He toasted, raising his glass in welcome.

"*Yamas!*" Everyone guzzled their drinks, like they'd been waiting for an excuse to pour more wine.

"Alexandreee!" A high-pitched wail assailed my ears.

"Dimitra." Alex stood as a pink-cheeked woman came running toward him.

"They are taking my boy." She flung her arms around him.

"Only for a few months. He'll be back before you know it. And look how happy he is." He gestured toward her son, who grinned from the sidelines.

"Of course, Pantelis is happy. He is nineteen and happy to get away from his mother. Look at this face." She cupped her son's chin and pressed his cheeks until his lips pursed. "Some girl will steal his heart and he'll never come back to me. Ftou, ftou, ftou." She spit on the ground three times to ward off evil spirits. "Come with me." She grabbed Alex's arm. "I made all the food myself." She exchanged a sly look with the rest of the table. "I must get him a plate, yes?"

Pantelis tried to get Alex's attention, but the rest of the table cheered her on. "*Yamas!*"

"I'll be right back with something to eat," Alex said before Dimitra swept him away.

He wasn't gone long when a sun-grizzled man with a shock of gray hair took his seat.

"You came with Alexandros?" He gave me a leathery handshake when I nodded. "I am Vasilis."

"Moti," I replied.

"Good, good."

Nothing good about the way he stared at my hair. He reached out to touch it, but I leaned away.

Okayyyy. Creepy old dude.

"Don't be afraid. I just need a little snip." He pulled out a pair of scissors from his jacket.

Oh hell, no. I looked around the table, thinking that perhaps no one noticed Edward Scissorhands beside me, but they were all watching. And smiling.

"Yamas!" They saluted me.

Shit. Now I was getting serious cult-like vibes.

Vasilis snipped the air with his scissors, as if testing the blades, and stood.

Where the hell is Alex? My eyes darted around. *How can he leave me with the Folegandros Fetish Society? Wait. Is he in on it? Did he lure me here as some kind of offering? What better offering to bring to an island than someone who can't swim, right?*

My fingers tightened around a fork. One step closer and I was going to stick it in Vasilis' jugular.

"Mpampa!" Alex dropped two plates on the table and rendered Vasilis scissor-less. A string of curses followed between the two. If hand gestures had been punches, they would have knocked each other out. And then, just as fiercely as they'd clashed, they were laughing.

"Moti, this is my father, Vasilis. Sorry he came at you with his scissors. He's a barber, but he thinks he's a doctor. Give him a lock of your hair and he'll give you a full medical report. If you're getting enough sleep. If you have enough iron…"

"If you have a good womb for Alexandros' children," Vasilis said.

"He's had a go at everyone on the island," Alex said, unfazed. "Every time he sees someone new, out come his scissors."

That would explain why everyone was smiling at me. Sympathy-smiling. They'd all endured his antics.

"Yes?" Vasilis approached me once again.

"Mpampa!"

"Bah." Vasilis was clearly disappointed at having fathered someone who didn't indulge his whims. "You, eat," he said to me, absolving me of the responsibility. If his own son didn't support him, how could he expect a stranger to do so? He lit a cigarette and sighed, contemplating his misfortune.

"We should listen to him." Alex grinned and pushed a plate toward me—tomatoes cut into flowers, fresh goat's cheese, pasta topped with red sauce, string beans, grilled lamb. On another platter was a pile of assorted bread and some pies with a wonderful, smoky aroma. "Let's eat."

Dimitra watched as Alex and I dug in. "Good?"

Alex took a few bites and squinted. No answer.

"Good?" Dimitra turned to me.

The pasta was sweet. Maybe it was the sauce. I switched to the lamb. Delicious, but also sweet. Puzzled but wanting to say something nice, I reached for the bread, dunked it in olive oil, and tried again.

"It's…" It tasted like cake, coated with olive oil. "It's different."

The buzz of conversation around the table stopped. Vasilis held his cigarette away, mid-puff. Everyone's eyes fell on me. In the still, quiet seconds, a bead of sweat formed on my forehead. It hung there a few mortifying beats, then slid slowly down my skin.

"It's different." Dimitra said. "Did you hear? She said it's different!"

I wasn't prepared for the hoots of laughter and clapping that broke out.

Dimitra came around and kissed me heartily on both cheeks.

"You have shared in my pain. My son is leaving tomorrow. Without him, every day for the next nine months will feel like this for me. Like something is not right, like something is different. I want everyone to feel it with me, so today, I used sugar instead of salt in every dish. You will all remember when Dimitra protested mandatory military service!" She beamed around the table.

"Yamas!" Glasses clinked as everyone cheered.

"You must finish." Dimitra looked at my plate and Alex's. "And then, you must dance." She led everyone else to the circle gathering in the center of the square—an outer circle of men and an inner circle of women, holding hands and alternating slow steps with fast steps. They pushed Pantelis to the middle, where he improvised with his arms wide open.

"Welcome to my home." Alex raised a string bean from his plate. I raised one from mine and we ate Dimitra's soggy, sugary protest.

"It's beautiful." I didn't think such places still existed, places where you could walk into a town square and find yourself caught up in a celebration. "And everyone is so warm and sweet—"

Alex swooped in for a kiss. "Warm and sweet." His lips hummed against mine. "So, tell me, when you agreed to come here with me, what exactly was going through your mind? Were you hoping, as I was, to explore this thing between us? This madness that leaves me breathless every time I look at you. Do you think about us lying naked next to each other, Moti? Does it do to you what it does to me?"

I hadn't thought about anything but playing hooky for the night, but my thighs clenched at Alex's words, as surely as if his hand slid between them. My eyes must've given me away, because Alex let his breath out in a slow exhale.

"Come on." He grabbed my hand. "Let's get out of here."

My heart was beating hard and fast when Dimitra intercepted us.

"Dance with us," she yelled over the music. I lost sight of Alex as she pulled me into the circle of women. I moved cluelessly at first, going one way when everyone went another. After a while, I caught on. Two steps to the right, one step forward, then back with a bounce. And repeat. The woman to my right gave me an encouraging nod. Maybe she was just happy I wasn't stomping on her foot anymore. Either way, we laughed and moved in unison.

I glanced over my shoulder as Alex passed by in the outer circle. The dance turned into a game. Eyes-on-eyes—our gazes meeting and holding, before we lost sight of each other again.

And then he was gone. I searched one way, then the other. No Alex.

I was about to excuse myself when someone pulled me away from the circle.

"Gotcha." Alex grinned as we stood together, a little breathless, a little giddy, like two kids playing hide and seek.

I didn't know any of the music playing, but I will always remember the track that came on as Alex held my hand—something about belonging together. My heart synced to the drumbeat, loud and thunderous, as people milled around us. In the silence between the beats, there was only Alex and me, and the sweet, sharp fire flaring between us.

Someone jostled me closer to him, sending my hair across my face. It didn't help that my lips were sticky with the sugary dinner we just had. Alex brushed the hair off my lips—strand by strand— his gaze both soft and heated. Just when I thought he was about to claim them, he smiled, like he'd uncovered something unexpected and enchanting. The little bubble that had been rising inside me burst through the surface with a pop of joy. Our smiles connected. And then we were breaking through the circle, running away from the crowd, hand in hand.

We stopped at the edge of the square, grinning because we couldn't help it. A white path zigzagged up to a commanding church at the top of the hill. Below us, rocky cliffs gave way to moonlit waves. It was the kind of place, the kind of night, that filled you with the thrill of being alive.

"*Tha se sfakso! Tha se pnikso! Tha se skotoso! Tha sou vyalo ta malia! Tha se kano me ta kremmydakia!*" Dimitra ran after her son, Pantelis, with a fork in her hand. He weaved through the tables, laughing and screaming and dodging her attack.

"What is she saying?" I asked.

"That she will butcher him, drown him, kill him, pull his hair out, and cook him with onions." Alex laughed. "He must've done something to piss her off. Or maybe it's because he's leaving tomorrow and she can't stand it." He fell silent as he watched the two of them.

Across the courtyard, Vasilis caught his eye. Father and son shared a look before Vasilis stubbed his cigarette out and walked over.

"Hey." Vasilis patted Alex's cheek. "I miss her too."

Alex nodded. "I miss the way she used to get angry with me."

It dawned on me that they were talking about Alex's mother.

"You know," Vasilis gestured to the plates on the table, "Frida would've messed up the food without even trying."

They laughed and we raised a glass in her memory. I meant to take a sip, but it turned into an embarrassingly wide yawn.

"She is tired." Vasilis laughed. "You must be too, Alex. Why don't you take my car and head home? I'll catch a ride with one of our neighbors."

"Thanks, Mpampa. It's been a long day." Alex took the keys he was holding out. "See you in the morning?"

"Yes." Vasilis pointed to Alex's hair and made a snip-snip gesture. "We do it in the morning." He waved us off and lit another cigarette.

Alex and I took the one road that ran through the length of the island.

"You don't live in the town?" I asked, as terraced farms and thyme-scented hills whizzed by in the dark.

"No. I live there." He pointed to a cluster of lights on a hill. "In Ano Meria. Although I spend so much of my time away, it feels like I live on the water."

I thought of the cabin we shared in the yacht.

Nothing is going to be the same after tonight.

"Moti?" Alex had switched off the engine and was looking at me.

We were parked outside a small stone home, its white walls old and worn, but lovingly looked after.

I got out of the car and followed Alex to the door. A glint in the garden caught my eye, something round and silver. Before I could make it out, Alex pulled me inside.

His kiss was hard, then soft, then hard again, lighting up every inch of me with a sharp, burning need.

Lifting me so my legs wrapped around him, he pushed the door shut and held me up against it, his mouth hot and hungry in the dark. I gasped as his teeth raked my neck, softly biting his way down.

"Alex." I tipped my head, giving him more of my skin, exposing nerves that begged for his lips.

He broke away and gazed into my eyes, his own dark and dilated. I couldn't hide the rise and fall of my chest, the tips of my nipples clamoring for attention through my top.

His hand slid under the hem of my shorts and gripped a curvy ass cheek. Wet heat flared between my legs as he slipped past my panties, kneading the soft, round flesh beneath. My body arched against him, greedy for more.

"God, yes."

He reached for the junction between my thighs and slid his finger inside. His thumb parted my slick folds and found my clit. I opened up to him like a flower to the sun, one leg sliding to the floor while he kept the other around his waist.

Pinned against the door, I gripped his shoulders, giving in to the fiery sensation of his touch. Pleasure came in cascading waves. Building. Building. But the peak eluded me.

If ever there were a time for a mind-blowing orgasm, this was it. I wanted it to rip through me, leave me panting and breathless. But orgasms are strange beasts. Like cats, they don't always come to you when you want them to. At least for me. The only orgasms I'd experienced were self-induced. Still, Alex's touch was a different kind of bliss. My whole body uncoiled, the chase replaced by a sense of molten rapture.

"Feeling more relaxed?" Alex's nuzzled my ear.

"Mmm." All my bones had melted.

"Good. Because I plan on serving a lot more courses tonight." He scooped me up with a panty-dropping grin.

Dear Lord in Heaven. I glanced at the night sky as Alex carried me past the living room.

Thank you.

CHAPTER TWENTY-ONE

I SNUGGLED INTO THE CROOK OF ALEX'S ARM, STRETCHING OUT BESIDE him.

"Alex?"

"I'm listening…"

It was how all our late-night chats started. In the dark. With him on the top bunk and me on the bottom. Except we weren't on the yacht anymore. We were lying side by side on a pile of quilts on his roof, the stars scattered above us like space dust.

He'd carried me into the shower and we'd made out, steam condensing on the glass panels of the stall. Wrapped in towels, we stumbled into bed. The sheets were dusty from his absence, and I ended up making the face you make before you sneeze. Like a naked mole rat squinting at the midday sun. Thankfully, Alex's lips were on my nipple, so he missed it. When he looked up, his bold gaze locked on mine. The moment sizzled with eroticism.

I made the face again.

And the damn sneeze still wouldn't come.

Seriously? There's a man between my breasts—a sexy, chiseled Adonis worshiping my boobs, and I'm staring at him with that face.

The corners of Alex's mouth turned up as he took a strand of my hair and tickled my nose with it. I let out an explosive sneeze.

"Better?" he said, as I stared remorsefully at his sneeze-spattered chest. "I think we need to get you out of here."

Which was how we ended up on the roof. I slipped into his T-shirt, he slipped into a pair of boxers, and we raided the linen closet. Dragging every quilt and pillow we could find upstairs, we made a makeshift bed under the crisscrossing clotheslines. The flat roof had a half-wall around its perimeter, lined with re-purposed containers—olive oil buckets, tins of canned tomatoes, rice buckets, flour buckets, ice-cream containers—all spilling mounds of fragrant herbs and flowers.

"What's your favorite childhood memory?" I asked.

He propped himself up on his elbow and traced my jaw. "You really want to know?"

"I do."

"My favorite memory..." Alex ran his fingers up and down my palm. "My mother, peeling an orange and bringing it to my room while I was studying. She never said a word. She'd come in, put it on my desk, and leave. Sometimes I didn't even know she'd been there until I saw the plate. She had this way of flipping each segment inside out, with the flesh arched out, so I didn't have to bite through the stringy white fibers. Mountains of orange spikes waiting to be scraped off with my teeth. Nothing says love like a plate of cut fruit left silently for you."

Our fingertips touched and held. It felt like a soft, buzzing rope—binding me to him slowly, hypnotically.

"And you?" Alex asked. "What's your favorite childhood memory?"

"Flying a kite." I smiled. "I can't remember where I was, or who with, but I remember the feeling. Running barefoot, looking at it over my shoulder. That feeling of delight when it finally took off. Up, up. Higher than I could ever fly."

My eyes shut as I recalled the tugging of the string in my hand, the way the kite soared and danced in the sky. I lay in Alex's arms, watching the child in me run down the beach, against the endless expanse of the horizon.

I don't know when I drifted off, but the world was blue when I opened my eyes. Blue sky. Alex's blue jeans hanging on the line to dry. A blue bowl next to me, with a note:

Can't believe you conked out on me. Some blueberry yogurt in honor of my blue balls.

I laughed and swirled the spoon in the yogurt. Sitting cross-legged on a sea of quilts, I settled the bowl on my lap and licked the spoon. I could hear the gong of tiny bells and the bleating of goats. In the distance, the sea sparkled with the promise of a new day. A rhythmic, metallic sound came from the garden below. Snip, snip, snip.

I walked to the edge of the roof and looked over. Alex sat on a plastic chair under a trellis of grapevines, getting his hair cut by his father. Shirtless under the sun, his skin took on a warm, bronzed hue. Bare arms, bare chest, bare throat. My cheeks flamed as locks of thick, dark hair collected on the patio stones. I sat on the half-wall circling the roof, observing their ritual.

Every once in a while, Vasilis would stop, take a puff from the cigarette Alex held for him, and step away from his handiwork like a painter assessing his masterpiece. Then the comb would come down and off he'd go with the scissors again.

All through the garden, dozens of CDs were strung, row after row. They dangled over elephant-eared zucchini plants and reflected off buckets spilling the most brilliant red geraniums.

A sudden burst of white light blinded me. I held my hand over my eyes and squinted.

"Kalimera, *asteri mou.*" Alex flashed a CD straight in my face. "Sleep well?"

Sleep? I flushed, only remembering the feel of my nipples swelling like ripe berries in his mouth. Then I double-flushed because Vasilis had caught me in nothing but Alex's T-shirt.

"Kalimera." I waved to them both, tugging the shirt over my knees. "What's with all those?" I gestured to the CDs sparkling in the sun.

Vasilis tugged the string holding them up, making them jingle and jangle like little mirrors. "They keep the birds from eating the vegetables."

"Clever," I said, finishing the last of my yogurt. Then I gasped as he cut a big chunk of Alex's hair. "How much are you taking off?" *Bye, bye, Man-Bun.*

Vasilis shrugged. "I keep going until he says enough. I'm the only one he'll let cut his hair. Since he was a baby. This time he's been away too long. I have been cutting and cutting, and still..." Vasilis lifted Alex's hair to illustrate his point. "This time his hair is like Dimitra's."

I stifled a snicker. Nothing about Alex was like a woman. Not his hair, not his hard, bronzed chest, and certainly not his blue balls.

I folded the quilts and headed to the kitchen. It was a sun-filled room with a window opening to breathtaking views of the windswept hill and beyond it, the Aegean Sea. I could hear the low hum of conversation between Alex and Vasilis as I washed the blue bowl. Its hand-painted markings were time-softened, but still a beautiful shade of cobalt. I held it up, the suds trickling down to my elbows, studying the border—a row of spiny fish following each other around the rim.

"It belonged to Mrs. Tavoulari," Alex said.

I stared. With his locks shorn, his eyes looked bigger—stark and arresting. They settled on the bowl for a few beats, then the corners crinkled as his gaze met mine.

"This was the bowl in your story," I said. "The bowl you brought to her every day."

How many times had it gone back and forth between them, filled with whatever he'd made from her recipe book?

"It was like an ongoing conversation." Alex hugged me from behind, his arms sliding down mine. Our fingers entwined, soapy and wet, around the bowl.

"That's..."

It was all I could manage. Alex was making love to my fingers, his hands over mine, clasping them and then letting go, sliding his fingers in and out of the spaces between them. He nudged my hair aside, exposing my neck to stubbled kisses. The sun filtered through the window, warming my skin, lighting up the smattering of hairs on Alex's arm. A slow, golden moment passed. A *siga-siga* moment. Soapsuds, warm water, goose bumps. The hard muscles of his legs spooning me as my head fell back and I relaxed into the thick heat of his body.

We both jumped apart as Vasilis walked into the kitchen. Alex grabbed a washcloth and started wiping his hands. I was pretty sure it was a ruse to hide his erection.

"Where do you want these?" The Squasher of Siga-Siga Moments dropped a basket full of freshly plucked herbs and veggies on the counter. Plump, bright lemons, sweet onions, green-topped carrots. Dark bits of earth still clung to the leaves of a cabbage.

Alex threw the washcloth aside and snapped at him in Greek. Vasilis' response was just as terse. Back and forth, they argued, sharp gestures punctuating their speech. Finally, Alex nudged his father through the door and shut it behind him. I watched Vasilis through the window, waving wildly at the grapevines, as if seeking their intervention.

"How could you lock your father out of his own home? If I pulled something like that with Dolly, she'd... I don't even know how she'd react."

"It's not his home. His lives over there. See?"

Vasilis had taken the cobbled pathway through the garden and was letting himself into the house next door. He caught us looking at him and pointed to his watch. "What time?" he shouted across the vines.

"I'll come get you," Alex shouted back.

"Fine." He dragged a wooden chair out onto the porch and plopped himself on it. "I'll wait right here."

A staring contest ensued, each willing the other to back down. Finally, Vasilis harrumphed and angled his chair away.

"What was that about?" I asked.

"Lunch."

"Lunch? It sounded like you were having a major argument."

"Well, lunch *is* major. Especially this one. Every time I visit, Mpampa gives me a haircut and afterward, I make him lunch. He putters around while I cook, and we catch up. He looks forward to it, whether I'm gone a few weeks or a few months."

"And this time you shut him out." Their whole exchange fell into place. "Because of me."

"No. Because of *me*." Alex growled and gathered me in his arms. "Because I want you so bad, it hurts." He set me on the counter, my legs dangling over the edge as he wedged himself between them. "I can't cook. I can't think. I'm mad with pent-up desire for you." He cupped my head with one hand, pinning me with his hungry gaze, while the other pushed my panties aside. "I think this is where we left off."

His finger curved into my ready wetness. "This time, I don't intend to stop until you come around my fingers. Or my mouth. Or my cock. Take your pick." His breath was ragged as he eased me onto my back.

Pulling my panties down, he slid me to the edge of the counter, his lips circling my clit. The bold swipe of his tongue sent me spinning to new heights of pleasure. I arched into him, my fingers tugging his freshly cut hair. Pleasure came in cascading waves. First a budding ripple, then as he built me up with short little licks, it bloomed. And bloomed. My thighs quivered. Sensation after sensation rocketed through me. Teeth clenched, toes curled, my body gave a surprised jerk and exploded.

"Mmm. Lunch never tasted so good." Alex left a trail of soft kisses on my thigh.

I had no coherent reply. I was too busy collecting all the astounded parts of me that had just shattered into a million blissful pieces.

"Hello? Earth calling Moti." He grinned with the satisfaction of a man who knows he's turned your bones to jelly, face glistening with victory.

I was sprawled on his counter, panties bunched around my ankles, with no rush to cover up.

What the hell's gotten into you, Moti?

Nothing yet, the newly liberated part of me replied. *But hopefully Alex will.*

I propped myself up, admiring the contours of his arms, his shoulders, his chest. His grin disappeared when I reached for his boxers. My fingers stole under his waistband and closed around his hard flesh. He watched, still as a statue, as I stroked him, the blunt head of his erection straining over his boxers.

"Enough teasing." He whisked me off the counter and carried me to the bedroom.

He must've made up the bed while I was sleeping, because the sheets were crisp and fresh.

"Not so fast." I pushed him off, even though I was already imagining each thrust, each wild, pounding thrill of his possession. I knew Alex's food, and now I wanted a taste of him.

Kicking off my panties, I dipped my head to taste him. His abs clenched, his body rising to meet me. Teasing him with my tongue, I circled his tip, until he knotted his fingers in my hair and slid his shaft between my lips. A long hiss escaped him, like a rod of hot steel doused in water.

Hauling my T-shirt off me, he pinned me under him. I gasped as bare chest met bare chest. He paused for a moment, tearing open a foil package and rolling on a condom. That first thrust, impossibly tight, plunged into me with burning intensity. And then, as if pulling back from frenzied need, Alex stroked my cheek, still buried inside me. Our eyes held, his forehead against mine, a question in his burning gaze: *Are you okay?*

I nodded.

A kiss. Soft and tender. More intimate than the throbbing

pulse where our bodies joined. Another kiss. This one on the corner of my mouth. Drifting up to my jawline. Arms sliding under my shoulders, Alex buried his face in my hair and pulled out almost all the way. I gasped when he plunged back in, hard and deep. My legs locked around him, my body submitting to his rhythm. With each thrust, I stretched and melted around him.

"Alex." Tremors started coursing through my body.

His breath hitched as he sensed my quickening. My head fell back as he re-entered, filling me even deeper. Pleasure burned hot as I felt the cresting, like a wave about to break.

His kiss was rough, pushing me over the razor-sharp edge of pleasure. A wild orgasm rocketed through me. Sensation after sensation of quivering waves.

Holy hell.

Alex's lips swallowed my ragged breath. His thrusts stilled as my body recovered, then picked up again, his own desire rising like a crescendo. He clasped my hips, pulling me into his final thrust. The tendons on his neck stiffened as release rippled through him.

We remained locked, waiting for our hearts to still and our minds to catch up.

I had felt the spark between us, but my senses were spinning from the encounter.

Alex discarded the condom, and we curled up in each other's arms. My body tingled as I settled into his embrace, my head tucked under his chin. His fingers stroked my arm, my neck, my back. His half-lidded eyes lingered over me, as if I were a dream he didn't want to wake up from.

The world was quiet in Alex's stone cottage, just the breeze playing with our limped, tangled legs. The sun crept over our bodies and curtains whispered against the window. I snuggled closer to Alex and dozed off, not wanting this to ever end.

CHAPTER TWENTY-TWO

I TURNED SLEEPILY ON MY BACK AND FOUND ALEX PROPPED UP ON HIS pillow—white sheets, bare skin, and the sharp haircut I was still getting used to. Then, something else clamored for my attention.

Strong male fingers between my thighs. The hot, wet slide of Alex's kiss trailing over my breasts, teasing my nipples. His tongue dipped into my navel and slid lower.

"Alex, we just…" I trailed off as his mouth found my clit.

"That was just the palate cleanser, agapi mou. We still have the second main course… Dessert…" He filled the space between words with a swipe of his tongue. "Mignardise…"

I gripped the sheets and arched into him.

I had no idea what mignardise was, but sex with a master chef definitely had its perks.

Lunch was late. Very late. By the time Alex and I dragged ourselves to the kitchen, Vasilis was nowhere in sight.

"He'll come around." Alex grinned when he saw the empty chair on his porch. "And I know exactly how to make it happen. Open the window." He grabbed a canister from the overhead shelf. "And that one too."

This was Alex in chef mode—fired up and raring to go. It didn't stop him from stealing a kiss when I brushed past him.

"No." He pried the cutting board away from my fingers. "We're not on the yacht." His voice was warm and honey-coated. It begged to be scooped and stored in a glass jar, next to all the herbs and spices lining the shelves. "Today, you're a guest in my home. Actually, in Mrs. Tavoulari's home. I bought it from her during the economic crisis. Everyone was having a hard time making ends meet and she was no exception. It set back my plans to open a restaurant, but it was more important to keep her from losing her home. She died a few years ago, and I decided to hold on to it."

"I'm sorry to hear that. I was hoping to meet her."

"I still have her jar of walnuts." Alex pulled it off the shelf and pried a nut open with his knife. "Now…" He popped a piece into my mouth and patted the stool. "Just sit here and pretend I've left you incapable of doing anything except making heart-eyes at me. Ready? Go."

I laughed as he measured a cup of flour into a mixing bowl.

"Salt. Eggs." He added each ingredient with exaggerated flair. "Hey. Heart-eyes. I don't see heart-eyes."

I propped my elbows on the counter, placed one hand on top of the other, and rested my chin on top. Then I batted my eyelashes and gazed adoringly.

Of course, when I leaned forward, my breasts plopped onto the counter, turning my heart-eyes into a pumped-up case of TOTT: Tits On The Table.

Alex's jaw dropped. Olive oil drizzled down his arm and made a small puddle on the counter.

"Hey." I snapped my fingers, prompting him to pull his eye sockets out of my cleavage.

"Wowzah. You make killer heart-eyes." He looked at the oil can and made its spout nod in agreement. "Killer, dude."

"What are you making?"

"I don't remember. You're distracting me, Heart-Eyes. Go get me some sage from the roof. And a couple of nice, juicy tomatoes."

"I'm banished?" I feigned indignation.

"It's either that or I drag you back to the bedroom. Now, if you were to leave it up to me—"

"I'm going, I'm going." I jumped off the stool. Vasilis would never get lunch at this rate.

Sage grew wild on the island, but Alex grew his herbs on the roof, each pot and bucket lush with something that roused the senses. Rose, honeysuckle, jasmine, eggplant, onions, garlic. The undulating waves of scent changed each time a breeze came in from the sea. I thought of the sterile apartment I shared with Dolly and closed my eyes.

Sometimes you don't know what you're missing until you find it. And when you do, you want to pause and relish it forever.

My time with Alex, my getaway from my *real* life was coming to an end.

Not now. Not yet.

Lingering on the roof, I plucked some tomatoes—warm and sun-ripened. Goats grazed on the sparse greenery below, beautiful and noble, with wide, twisting horns and long beards. The morning haze had cleared, and the sea shimmered with bright shades of blue and turquoise.

I made my way back to the kitchen and found Alex rolling out sheets of pasta with an empty wine bottle.

"Can't find my rolling pin," he said.

I debated telling him about the spot of flour on his nose but decided it belonged there, like the scar on his forearm that looked like a sheet pan burn.

"Something smells good." I peered into the pot on the stove. Shallots were sizzling in butter.

When Alex added the sage, the aroma turned rich and fragrant. He was tossing together a mix of soft white cheese, sun-dried tomatoes, and olives when the door swung open. Vasilis stood at the entrance, sniffing the air.

"I knew it," he said. "Ravioli with sage browned butter.

You're trying to win me over by bribing me with my favorite dish."

Alex didn't confirm or deny it, but there was a twinkle in his eyes. "Here." He handed his father the bowl of filling he'd been mixing. "The sooner we assemble the ravioli, the sooner we get to eat it."

"Yes, but first…" Vasilis put the bowl down and pulled out a corked glass bottle. "The ouzo." He poured some for himself and Alex.

"Yamas!" They toasted, raising their small glasses.

An easy affection flowed between them as they sipped the anise-flavored spirit. I sensed this was a father-son tradition, a warm groove they fell into whenever Alex came home. Drink. Cook. Eat. Repeat. Give each other the freedom to grow, find a reason to come together, and keep coming back for more.

I sighed. Would Dolly and I ever get out of the rigid corners we'd boxed ourselves into and share that kind of fluidity? My life was all about rules.

Don't go in the water.

Don't eat too much.

Don't laugh too loud.

Don't fall in love. With anyone but a three-thumbed man.

"Moti." Alex held out a glass of ouzo. He stood before the window, the streak of flour highlighting his nose. I read once that the afterglow from great sex can rewire your brain, making your partner seem even more attractive. *Something* was making me feel all soft and vulnerable. It was the strangest feeling—free-falling into someone else. Alarm bells started beeping in my head.

Retreat. Retreat.

"I… I'll be right back. Going for a walk."

Alex gave me a puzzled look as I slipped out.

"This is on you," I heard him say to Vasilis. "You creeped her out with your snip-snip last night."

"You think she will agree today? Just a little lock. She won't even miss it—"

The bickering switched to Greek, curt sentences volleying back and forth between them.

Their voices faded as I took the cobbled path to the road, startling a lizard lazing in the sun. A farmer plowing his land stared at me as I passed. Behind him, a lemon tree protected by a circle of stones blossomed under a cloudless sky.

I followed a donkey track and veered toward a one-room church. Wedged between the building and the scorched, sprawling rocks was a small, welcome field of green. A wave of wildflowers rustled in the wind—all except for a patch of white among the blossoms. They were taller, with thick stems and creamy petals that looked like they were reaching out for the sun.

I remembered Alex holding up a pressed white flower.

Folegandros, he said. *It's where I was born—raw and rocky, with cliffs and caves, and an unforgiving terrain. But the flowers still find a way to grow. My mother loved that about them. The white ones were her favorite. We always had bouquets of wildflowers around the house. She picked this on the day she died.*

I sat in the field, wondering if she'd paused to gaze at the sea that day. Let the sun warm her skin.

I picked all the white ones I could find. Sweaty and happy, I headed back to the house, clutching the flowers to my chest.

Alex and Vasilis were cleaning up. The table was set, and the kitchen smelled heavenly.

"There you are." Alex flung a kitchen towel over his shoulder and leaned back against the counter, ankles crossed.

Afterglow hormones were still turning cartwheels in my brain because *damn.* My heart squeezed every time I looked at him—the way his eyes lit up, the half-sweet, half-sexy smile he threw my way.

"I found these." I held the flowers under his nose. The dusting of flour was gone, but his nose was still just as endearing. Ugh.

Alex sneezed. Apparently, I'd shoved the bouquet too far in

his face. Vasilis raised his thick, caterpillar eyebrows. Probably his first time seeing his son receive flowers from a sweaty girl with dirt under her nails. His face cracked into an amused grin.

"White flowers," I said. "Your mom's favorite, Alex."

Whatever remark Vasilis was about to make, it died in his throat. His Adam's apple bobbed as he swallowed the words.

"Thank you," Alex said. Something twisted in his face as he accepted the wilting bouquet. "We haven't had flowers in the house since she passed away. They're beautiful."

"Beautiful." Vasilis nodded and wiped his nose. "I'll go get Frida's favorite vase." He trotted off and returned with an amber glass jar. "It was for honey, but she liked it because it was see-through and she could tell if they needed watering."

Alex arranged the flowers, letting the stems flop where they would. Vasilis made space for them in the center of the table. They stood back, looking at them, then at me, smiling the whole time. I could tell they were hiding something.

"What is it?"

"Nothing." Alex grinned. "We've just missed them, right Mpampa?"

"Yes." Vasilis eyes were gentle when they fell on me. "And now…" He wiped his nose again and sat down. "Let's eat."

Lunch was fresh and ripe and bursting with flavor. An olive oil soaked salad with tomatoes, cucumber, onion, and feta cheese. Crispy fried eggplant topped with creamy tzatziki. Ravioli—tender, translucent, and fat with filling. I held a fork in one hand, and a slice of crusty bread in the other, mopping up the fragrant butter sauce on my plate.

"She eats like one of us," Vasilis said, holding up his own flavor-soaked bread.

I looked up, embarrassed to find them both watching me.

Alex winked at me with a smug grin that made me pause and look down at my plate.

Butter. Bread. Pasta.

All the things I asked him to strike from my meals when I filled out the preference sheet. Not a rice cake or a steamed green bean in sight. Where had my rules gone?

Sometime between midnight snacks, a moonlit pool, and a patch of wildflowers, I stopped fighting food and started making friends with it. Somewhere between the quest for a three-thumbed man, a cabin with no window, and a cloudless day on a rocky island, I fell for the chef.

The irony hit me like a ton of bricks.

Bubbles rising in my chest. The electric surge each time I looked at him. My bones melting at his touch. My heart bursting when he smiled. Eating up all of him—his food, his voice, his words, his body.

Holy Doollally. I'm in love with Alex.

Alex shot me a questioning glance. I shut my mouth and swallowed. I would've been fine if the overwhelming urge to sneeze hadn't gripped me at the same time. Between opposing inputs, my windpipe clenched around the piece of food in my throat.

Oh God. I'm choking. Again.

My hand clutched my neck as I gasped for air.

Alex shot up, his chair grating against the floor. Vasilis caught on a few seconds later.

"I'm okay. I'm good." I sputtered as the spasms faded.

"Slowly. Siga-siga." Vasilis handed me a napkin. "My father had a saying. Bite by bite makes a meal. Moment by moment makes a life. Some of it gets lost in translation, but you get the idea."

I dabbed my eyes and glanced at Alex.

"Pappou was a wise man." He sat back down and regarded me. "You sure you're okay?"

I don't know if I'm ever going to be okay. I've fallen in love with the wrong guy.

But it didn't feel wrong. It felt fantastic—like a little red butterfly perched on my shoulder—rare, flitting, and unexpectedly delightful. There was no endgame with Alex, no rush to the altar, no expectations, no Dolly, no Ma Anga. It made me feel weightless in a way I hadn't felt all my life.

Gravity ceased to exist when I was with him. My feet floated off the ground. My heart soared like it was tied to a hundred yellow balloons. The past blurred, the future evaporated. The place we intersected was all that we had, and it was magical and marvelous.

I smiled at Alex. *Moment by moment, just like your Pappou said.*

CHAPTER TWENTY-THREE

I SAID GOODBYE TO VASILIS AND WAITED AS ALEX GAVE HIM A HUG.

"You're going to take the Kiriakis job next?" Vasilis handed him his backpack.

"You don't take a job on his yacht. You jump on it." Alex grinned. "It's pretty much a done deal. They're just waiting on Captain Bailey's letter of recommendation."

His words faded as I walked over to the chair where Vasilis had cut Alex's hair. The day was starting to get warm, but it was nice and shady by the trellis.

"You will be back? In between?" Vasilis asked.

Something fluttered against my feet as I sat under the grapevines. It was a lock of Alex's hair, thick and dark and still slightly wet. I picked it up before the wind could blow it away.

"I'll be back in a couple of days when this charter is done."

My heart sank a little. Some beginnings had built-in endings. Ours was just a few days away.

I slipped his hair into my pocket, as if it would plug the void that had opened up in my chest.

"Don't forget to water the plants." Alex backed out onto the stone pathway, waving goodbye. "And don't lose the spare key this time."

"*Kalo taxidi.*" Vasilis waved back.

"*Ta leme.*" Alex hoisted his backpack over his shoulder and waited until his father went inside. "Ready to go, Heart-Eyes?" He turned toward me and froze.

Shit. Does Alex have X-ray vision? Can he see the lock of hair I just swiped from his garden? Because how awkward would that be? Not to mention ironic. First his father, and now me, collecting hair samples.

"What is it?"

"The light," he said. "Like stars on your face."

I had no idea what he was talking about, but as he walked up to me, he was touched by the silver flashes from the CDs hanging in the garden. We stood under the grapevines, surrounded by glints of sunlit magic.

"You're so beautiful." His fingers were warm against my face. They smelled of butter and sage. "The world dims around the edges when I look at you, Heart-Eyes."

I swallowed the lump in my throat and rested my cheek on his palm. "I need the recipe."

"For?"

"For what you made this afternoon." I wanted to recreate the moment—the light playing on his skin, the look in his eyes, the way he made me feel like golden honey. "On a cold, gray day when I'm back in Chicago, it'll remind me of today."

"No." His kiss was soft and playful.

"No?" I pulled back. "What do you mean, no?"

"I'm not giving you anything, Heart-Eyes. You crave it, you get your sweet ass to me."

"It's like that, huh?" I swiped his hand away from my butt.

"Don't be like that." His grin was pure mischief. "Not when the whole village is watching."

"What?" I swung around and caught a pair of eyes staring over the garden wall. It was the farmer I'd passed by earlier. "The whole village? It's just a dusty old man."

"Don't be fooled," Alex replied. "He's part of the *Yiayia-Pappou* mafia. Behind every door is an elder, watching all the goings-on in the village—the whos, wheres, and whats. My dignity will be shredded unless you kiss me. Passionately. Like you can't help yourself."

"The Yiayia-Pappou mafia? Like a Grandmother-Grandfather gossip circle?" I waved at the man.

He held something up and called me over.

"For me?" I ignored the tugging on my top as Alex tried to pull me back, still angling for a kiss.

"For you," confirmed the farmer, handing me a bracelet with a little blue bead on it. A black dot was painted on it, resembling an eye. "To protect you from the *mati*. The evil eye. Thank you for pulling out the weeds."

"The weeds?"

"Yes. In my field." He pointed to where I'd picked flowers for Alex.

"You mean the white ones? They're weeds?"

"Yes. They give everyone a runny nose. My wife says thank you too. She sent you a gift from our bees." He handed me a jar filled with honey and set back off for his home.

I turned around to face Alex. "Weeds? I brought a bouquet of weeds home for you and your father?" The look that had passed between them made sense now. Alex sneezing. Vasilis wiping his nose throughout lunch. Hell, I'd almost choked on a sneeze myself. Instead of enlightening me, they'd honored my blunder and placed the weeds in Frida's vase.

"You suck." I wrapped my arms around Alex's neck. "You really, really suck."

In the split second before Alex scooped me up, I felt like I'd float away on a cloud of happiness—breathless with the light, bright quickening in my heart.

"Stay with me, Heart-Eyes," Alex murmured against my lips.

"What?" I blinked.

"When the cruise is over... Stay with me. Extend your trip. Come back to Folegandros with me. If the Kiriakis family hires me, I'll have two weeks before I set sail again. I'd love nothing more than to spend them with you."

"You're crazy."

But my heart surged because he asked.

"You're crazy," I said again, and discovered it's possible to kiss someone senseless while smiling like an idiot the whole time.

We had a few hours to kill before taking the ferry back to Santorini, so we hit a nearby beach. Cutting through a ravine, one of the few places on the island with trees, we followed a footpath down to the water. A small pebbled beach revealed itself like a hidden treasure at the end. With the cliff behind us forming a protective cove, the water was calm and clear, a sheet of turquoise glass.

"No one's here," I said, as Alex rolled out a towel on the rocks. It seemed like a crime to have such a picturesque place all to ourselves. "What's going on over there?" I shaded my eyes and pointed to a group of people across the bay. They were mostly hidden from view, but the canary yellow bulldozer was hard to ignore.

"They're building a hotel on that side. They've been at it forever. They keep starting and stopping. Permits. Finance. Building materials. They seem to be dealing with a new obstacle every time I come home."

"It'll be spectacular when it's done though. Imagine a room right there, by the water."

"Speaking of water…" Alex held out his hand. "You missed your swimming lesson last night. Let's go for a dip."

"What? Out here?" I scoffed at the open sea. A swimming pool was bad enough, but it had boundaries. It didn't swallow up the horizon or make you feel small and completely in awe.

"Such a chicken." His lips grazed mine before he turned to the water, leaving a trail of clothes as he undressed.

I took a mental snapshot of him standing barefoot in his boxers, his body silhouetted against the sky, the perfect shape of his back.

Alex met the sea like it was an old friend, jumping in with a loud whoop. I leaned back on my elbows, my legs stretched out, and tilted my head back. A few clouds passed overhead, dissolving into wispy threads under the heat of the sun. It wasn't long before beads of sweat started collecting between my breasts.

Sitting up, I saw Alex glide like a sleek eel under the water. Shrugging out of my blouse and shorts, I tiptoed to the edge in my underwear. The water was shockingly cold after sitting in the sun, but so clear that I could see my shadow on the rounded pebbles below.

"Come on in," Alex said.

"Cold." I gritted my teeth with each step I took. "Cold. Cold. Cold."

"That's it. I've got you." He met me halfway and enveloped me in his arms.

Truth be told, he was cold as ice, but the feel of his body was infinitely worth it. His hand trailed rivulets of water down my back.

"Your nipples are so puckered up, you could key the side of someone's car with them," he said.

"You lured me in here to insult me?"

"Insult you? My God. I love your nipples. I would totally let you carve your initials on my heart with them…"

I laughed. "But?"

"But we'd have to discuss the font. You know, if it's going to be a permanent thing."

A permanent thing.

"What's wrong?" Alex traced the frown lines between my eyes.

"Nothing." I shook my head. "We both know this can never be a permanent thing."

"Do we?" He cocked his head. "Nothing permanent starts that way. It's something you invite to stay." A glint of challenge flashed in his eyes.

"Alex, I—"

"I know. I've spooked you. Put thoughts in your head that

weren't there before. It's what I do. Give you something to chew on—on the table or off. I think it's time you return the favor." He sunk his teeth into my neck and pretended to take a big bite. "Nope. Not meaty enough."

I squealed as he went for my butt.

Splashing through the water, I laughed as he grabbed me and pulled me back.

"Not cold anymore?" He stroked my arm, shoulder to wrist.

I closed my eyes and tiptoed to give him a kiss. His lips curved and remained curved.

"Why are you smiling?"

"Because I'm happy." He peeked through one eye and laughed. "Because now you're smiling too."

Joy bubbled inside me as he hugged me from behind. We took in the rocks, the sparse greenery, the little cove shimmering in beautiful shades of blue. Resting the back of my head on Alex's shoulder, I looked up at the sky and stretched my arms out. My legs floated up, the tips of my toes peeking through the surface.

"You like this," said Alex, towing me in a gentle zigzag through the water.

"Mm-hm." The sea felt amazing, gliding over my skin. The motion of baby waves was comforting and hypnotic—rising and falling, rising and falling. Like listening to a heartbeat—the ancient, fluid heartbeat of the sea. My body bobbed up and down to its nautical rhythm.

Something warm touched my fingertips. I opened my eyes and saw Alex floating on his back, his fingers reaching for mine. I clasped his hand and shut my eyes again.

Then I did an internal double take. Alex was swimming next to me, which meant...

Holy crap. I'm floating on my own.

As soon as the thought hit me, I panicked. My body tensed. My arms started flailing.

"The more you fight it, the faster you'll go under," Alex said.

"Relax. You're not going to drown, Heart-Eyes. Any time you want, you can just kick off the sea floor."

My feet found solid ground and relief flooded through me. We were still in shallow water. My eyes darted to the shore and our towel spread out on the rocks.

"Don't you dare leave me now." Alex squinted up at me. Water droplets glistened like crystals on his eyelashes. "I know it's hard, but this is it. You give up right now, and you'll be giving up on yourself."

I *knew* what I had to do but making the leap to the other side had my heart hammering hard and fast against my chest.

"Take my hand, Moti. You can do it. You were already doing it. You were floating."

I recalled the gentle rising and falling of my body, the water undulating like a satin sheet around me.

"Come on," Alex said. "Eyes to the sky. Little kicks to get your legs up."

I gave myself up to his voice, letting him guide me. When my body lifted off on a small wave, I filled my lungs with a deep breath, willing myself to stay afloat. The spike of adrenaline in my body leveled out as the water lapped around me.

I was doing it.

I was doing it all on my own.

Not wanting to jinx it, I turned my head slowly and looked up at Alex.

His grin confirmed it.

A joyous sound escaped me and burst into the sky. I shut my mouth quickly, in case that bit of air had been keeping me afloat. Then I laughed again because I was too damn happy to hold anything in.

The groove in Alex's cheek deepened as he threaded his fingers through mine. We turned our faces to the sun and held hands, floating like two starfish in the sparkling waters of the hidden cove. I knew I would never—for as long as I lived—forget this magical afternoon with Alex.

CHAPTER TWENTY-FOUR

I T WAS EARLY EVENING WHEN THE FERRY FROM FOLEGANDROS DROPPED us at Santorini. The port was packed with cruise passengers waiting to board the small boats back to their ships.

"I'll let Eddie know we're here." Alex phoned the deckhand who transported us to and from the yacht.

We stepped from the pathway so he could talk over the noisy chatter of the tourists. I smiled when Alex absently switched sides with me. He was the guy who walked by the side of the road, so he could take the dust or fumes or puddles for you. The thoughtfulness with which he assembled his dishes didn't end when he left the kitchen. It naturally carried over into the rest of his life.

"See that?" someone beside me said. "You see the way she's looking at him? *That's* the look of love."

I swung around and spotted a gray-haired couple grinning at each other. The man was holding a camera and the woman was pointing at me.

"Excuse me?" I shot a quick glance at Alex, grateful he was still engrossed in his call with one hand over his ear.

"You two are so precious," the woman said. "We watched you coming up and I said to Ken, 'Now that couple's going to make it.' We've been making bets while we wait for our ride. It's such a romantic place. Not here, obviously…" She gestured to the throngs of people passing by. "But the island itself. Honeymooners everywhere. I hope we haven't offended you. It's just a game the two of us—"

"We're not married." It was impossible to be offended by their sweetness.

"Ha. You don't need to be married to have a honeymoon glow." She chuckled. "Would you mind taking a quick picture of us, dear?" She squished her cheek against her husband's face after he handed me the camera. "We still have that glow, don't we?"

"You sure do." I laughed as they gave me wide, identical smiles and waited for the click.

"Thank you. I'm Judy, by the way."

"Moti," I replied, handing their camera back.

"Nice to meet you, Moti." Her husband put the lens cap back on and held out his hand. "I'm Ken. We're from Canada. A small town called Hamilton. You?"

"Chicago. Here for a family wedding."

"How wonderful," Judy said. "Although, maybe not. Weddings can be stressful, especially so far from home. Good thing you have someone special to look out for you." She nodded toward Alex.

I thought of the Intro To Orgasms course he'd given me the night before and felt the color rise to my cheeks. *Why yes, he does look out for me.*

Alex hung up, saw my new friends, and gave me an inquiring glance.

"Alex, this is Judy and her husband, Ken, from Canada."

"Nice to meet you," said Alex. "Enjoying your holiday?"

"We're actually on a little detour from our holiday," Ken said. "We're staying in Athens, but Judy's sister and niece got here yesterday, so we thought we'd come see them."

"Speaking of," Judy said. "I think we should start making our way to the dock. Our tender is supposed to get here in a few minutes."

They said goodbye and disappeared into the stream of people on the pier.

"We should get going too. Eddie said he's already on his way." Alex swung his backpack over his shoulder. "You ready?" He picked up a strand of my still-wet hair and gave it a tug.

I wasn't ready, but I followed him to the pick-up spot. Isabelle's umbrella bobbed from his backpack. It took me back to the cave in the cliffs, watching the sun set behind coal-colored islets, the slew of kisses Alex left on my back this morning. A lifetime of memories packed into the flash of a heartbeat. No, I wasn't ready to leave it all behind.

I stepped on something and paused. A key chain with a red and white maple leaf, and the initial S hanging off it. Picking it up, I looked around to see who had left it behind. The back of Alex's head got further and further away from me. Ships crowded the horizon—the Abigail Rose II among them, ready to transport us away. The urge to take, to claim, to keep, overcame me. Clenching my fist, I pressed the silver S tightly into my palm.

S for Stop.

S for Stay.

S for Steal

Alex turned, his eyes searching until they landed on me. He smiled, like he'd found the one face in a sea of faces—a smile lit up by the soft light of the sun. It seeped through every stitch and seam of my heart.

S for Stupid key chain.

My grip loosened, and I started running toward him.

"Come on, Heart-Eyes. Eddie's about to abandon us." Alex grabbed my hand.

"I doubt it." I laughed, as we weaved through the crowd. "If he leaves the chef behind, it'll be peanut butter and jelly sandwiches for everyone."

"Wait a minute. What are these guys doing here?"

The Canadian couple, Ken and Judy, were boarding our boat.

"Hey," Alex called, waving to them with an apologetic look. "I think you're getting on the wrong tender."

"This one's for you?" Ken glanced from Alex to Eddie. "I thought you said—"

"It's for all four of you," said Eddie. "Come on. I'll help you in." He got Ken and Judy seated while Alex and I exchanged a puzzled look.

"Oh my God. Where did you get that?" Judy pointed to the key chain I was holding. "I got one exactly like it for my sister."

"I found it back there." I motioned toward the pier. "Is it yours?" With the red maple leaf of Canada, it had to be.

"Hold on." She peered into her handbag and came up empty-handed. "It *is* mine. Thank you. I wanted Sandy to have a little something to remind her of home."

S for Sandy, I thought.

Captain Sandy Bailey.

"She's always on the go," continued Judy. "My niece too. So this is the charter she was talking about. Remember, Ken? She said it was a cruise for a wedding party. Imagine running into the two of you, from the same group." Judy seemed delighted by the coincidence.

Ken nodded, his eyes twinkling with approval as we took off for the yacht.

"Will you be staying for dinner?" Alex asked.

"Oh no. We'd never crash one of Sandy's charters," Ken said. "We're just popping in for a quick hello. Maybe a cup of tea."

"There she is." Judy waved as we approached the yacht. "Hey. Sandy!"

Captain Bailey waved back from the platform, her smile faltering when her eyes fell on Alex and me.

Crap. I let go of Alex's hand. She'd already warned him once, and that was before anything happened between us.

Ken was the first to get off.

"Sandy, it's been a while."

"So fancy," said Judy, as Captain Bailey welcomed them onboard. "And so much bigger than I imagined. I always pictured you behind the wheel, but this is something else."

"I'll take you for a tour in a bit," the Captain said. "But first let's catch up. I asked Hannah to set a small table for us. You'll find her one level up. Elevator's through there. I'll join you in a sec."

"So good to see you." Judy hugged her sister and started heading inside. Then she paused and turned to Alex and me. "Be sure to look us up if you're ever in our corner of the world. Here's our business card. We'd love to know if our wager turned out."

"Indeed," Ken said. "You know, Sandy, we're betting on these two lovebirds. We didn't realize they were your guests when we saw them on the pier. A happy little coincidence."

"It was lovely meeting you." Judy waved goodbye as she followed Ken to the elevator. "We'll see you upstairs, Sandy."

Captain Bailey didn't acknowledge her sister's parting remark. She was too busy pinning Alex and me with a scathing look. "Lovebirds?"

Crap. And double crap. "Captain Bailey, I—"

"I don't want to know," she said. "What I *do* know is the rest of the passengers are already on board. You need to get started on dinner, Chef Alexandros."

"Yes, Captain." But he stood rooted by my side.

"Is there something else you'd like to discuss?" A warning in her tone.

Alex glanced at me.

Go, Alex. She's giving you an out. Just take it and go.

"No, Captain," he said.

Captain Bailey didn't speak until it was just the two of us on deck. "I don't know exactly what's going on between the two of you, but that man is the best damn chef I've ever had on board. You'll leave, maybe without ever looking back, but you'll be leaving a mark on his career if you don't stop this right here, right now. It would be a shame to withhold the letter of recommendation his next employer is waiting on, so I urge you to steer clear of Chef Alexandros. Am I making myself clear?"

"I—"

"It's my fault," she said. "I had a feeling something was up when I saw you in the galley with him. I should've stepped in earlier. I'm going to have a word with your aunt. If things are still unresolved between her and your uncle, she can have my room, and I'll bunk with Chef Alexandros. I'd like you to clear your things from the crew quarters and return to your assigned cabin right away."

"Yes, Captain Bailey." I would've agreed to anything. The last thing I wanted was Alex to get into trouble because of me. In the span of a few minutes, I'd gone from feeling like I'd grown wings overnight, to a sinking, twisted despair.

I entered the lobby, my shoulders sagging, where I was assailed by two different female voices from two different directions.

"Moti!"

"Moti!"

Rachel Auntie reached me first.

"You're back. Shame on Isabelle for sending you away on your own. I hope you didn't have too much trouble finding it."

"Finding what?"

"You know…" Isabelle slipped her arm through the crook of my elbow and gave me a little nudge. "The stuff I asked you to get for me."

It took a moment to process what the two of them were talking about—the excuse Isabelle used to explain my absence.

"Oh. Yes, of course. I had to look all over for it, but—"

"Well, let's see it," Rachel Auntie said. "Let's see what Isabelle needed so badly for the wedding."

"It's uh…" I glanced at Isabelle, but she'd done her part. It was up to me to come up with something. My eyes darted around, looking for something to magically materialize out of thin air. Now Naani, Joseph Uncle, and Fia all stopped what they were doing and stared curiously.

"It's in here somewhere…" I fumbled in my handbag.

Isabelle grinned. "Come on. Hand it over."

Bitch. I threw her a venomous look, but she only grinned

wider. She was enjoying our role-reversal. I was the one sweating in the hot seat for a change.

"Ah." My fingers closed around the glass jar the farmer gave me as a thank you for pulling weeds from his field. "Here you go."

Isabelle looked dumbfounded, but she recovered quickly. "Honey. And not just any honey. A special kind of honey from a special colony of bees found only in Folegandros. They say bathing in this on your wedding day ensures sweetness and bliss in your marriage forever."

Isabelle was the best bullshitter ever. I couldn't have been more proud.

Naani, Joseph Uncle, and Fia went back to what they were doing. Rachel Auntie took a sniff of the honey. "Hmmph. Looks like any other type of honey."

"But it's not. Thank you, Moti, you're the best." Isabelle gave me a hug, but added in my ear, "I need details of exactly what you got up to with Chef Alexandros, or…" She made a slicing gesture across my neck.

"Moti!" Dolly entered the lobby and headed straight for me, arms outstretched. "My darling. My sweet, sweet *beti*." She deposited two big kisses on my cheeks before pulling me into her bosom for a hug.

Well. This is new.

My arms went around her awkwardly. We were never affectionate with each other.

"Did you see?" She beamed around the room. "All these arrived for you."

Big bouquets of flowers—on the side tables, lining the windows, on the entertainment unit. The lobby was overflowing with them.

"These must be for the wedding," I said.

"No, they're—"

"Hold on. My phone's going crazy." Now connected to the Wi-Fi, it was pinging with notifications. I scrolled through them.

Nikos.

Nikos.

Nikos.

"The flowers are from Nikos." I looked up at Dolly. "He's managed to sort things out with his nightclub. He'll be here tomorrow."

"That's what I've been trying to tell you. More flowers are in the cabin. Come on, I've been waiting to show you."

She grabbed me by the hand and whirled me around. We ran straight into Alex as the elevator doors opened and he stepped out.

He could tell right away that something was up. Dolly was positively glowing with delight. "Hannah is busy with Captain Bailey's guests," he said, "so I thought I'd see if anyone has any special requests for dinner."

"We're fine." Dolly waved him away. "Ask the others." As we waited for the doors to close, she saw him take in the flowers. "Have you ever seen so many? All for my Moti. From Nikos."

His head shot around, the question in his eyes unanswered as the doors slid shut and obscured him from my view.

"It says he wants to make up for our last date. He's arranged a private lunch for us tomorrow." I put the card back in its envelope and moved the bouquet aside.

"I know what it says. I already read it." Dolly flitted around the cabin. "I had to know the minute they started bringing them in. I'd given up, you know. Two more nights until the wedding. It's not as if you got to spend much time with Nikos, but whatever you did, it worked. Oh, Moti." She fell on me again, hugging me like her life depended on it.

To be fair, she believed it did. If Ma Anga was right, me

getting together with Nikos was Dolly's lifeline and she was grabbing on to it with both hands.

"Did you message him back? Did he say what time?"

"Ma…" I extracted myself from her arms. "I can't."

"Can't what?" She looked puzzled. "I know you're nervous, *beti*, but it will pass. *Chalo*, what are you going to wear? It's too bad you can't fit into any of Isabelle's clothes. You know the dress she wore when—"

"Did you hear what I said? I'm not meeting Nikos for lunch. I'm going to message him right now."

"Have you lost your mind?" Dolly snatched my phone away. "What's gotten into you?"

I struggled for a moment. How could I explain to her the fresh imprint of Alex's kisses? The way his words, his touch, his smile sank into my soul?

The chef's gotten into me, Ma. Literally.

"What are you smiling about?" Dolly was starting to lose her patience. "Moti, what is going on with you?"

Normally, I would have dodged, avoided, or diverted any kind of conflict with Dolly, but I pressed on. "I can't see Nikos because I'm seeing someone else."

"Someone else?" She scoffed. "How is that even possible? Nikos was all you could think about when we left Chicago. You're just getting cold feet. A chance like this, with a man like that—it's not something that happens every day. You need to snap out of it or you'll regret it for the rest of your life. Now, let's go down to your room and pick out something to wow Nikos. I think—"

"For Christ's sake, I'm not ten years old. I don't need you to dress me. And I'm not sleeping there anymore. Captain Bailey asked me to move back here with you."

"She did? But Rachel and Joseph still haven't made up. I'm so tired of all their drama, tired of listening to Rachel go on and on about…" She paused and sat next to me. "You know what?

Who cares? This is more important. You're finally living up to all the dreams I have for you." She drew me to her side, stroking my hair with a smile. "My beautiful *beti*. You've made me so happy. I can't even begin to tell you how proud I am of you."

I blinked back the sudden tears threatening to spill over. All my life I'd tried to win Dolly over. I tried to be smarter, leaner, neater, quicker. To mold myself into what she wanted me to be. Most of the time, the voice in my head wasn't even mine. It was Dolly's. But Dolly herself always remained unreachable. Until now.

"Ma..." I took her hands and held them on either side of my face. "Do you see me?"

For a second, as I looked into my mother's eyes, we connected. Then I saw the panic, the shutters coming down, the walls coming up and I was on the other side again. You'd think it would get easier, but it cut just as deep every time.

"It's not about me, is it?" I let go with a sad smile. "It's about what I do to make you happy."

"Of course not." She stood up in an instant. "I only want what's best for you. You and Nikos are meant to be. I don't understand why you can't just—"

"Fine." It was pointless fighting Dolly on it. She'd hold it over my head for eternity. If anything happened to her, I'd always have the niggling doubt that I could have prevented it. "I'll do it. I'll meet Nikos for lunch tomorrow, but after that, I'm done. No more living with the weight of Ma Anga's predictions. Promise me, Ma."

"Okay, okay. You've come this far, no? You think it's just coincidence?" She handed my phone back. "Ask him what time." She peered over my shoulder while I got in touch with Nikos.

"Noon," I said when he messaged back. "He's arranged for someone to take me ashore, and then we'll return together."

"How romantic. I'm so excited for you!"

I bit my tongue. Nothing was going to happen between Nikos

and me. In fact, damn him and his three thumbs. Why'd he have to go and make a big show by sending me a gazillion flowers?

"I'll go get my things from the crew quarters." I tossed my phone aside and stood.

"I'll be right here." Dolly hummed as she went from bouquet to bouquet, fluffing up the flowers.

Walking into the hallway, I noticed something reflecting the pot-lights on the thickly carpeted floor. I picked up a pair of silver keys held together by a generic key ring. They were smaller than the cabin keys, with no tags or markings. My fingers tingled as I held them. A pair of orphan keys. They could belong to any door. They could unlock any possibility. I felt a momentary rush of invincibility and the uneasiness in my bones dissolved. After being caught off-guard by Captain Bailey, Dolly, and Nikos, I clutched the keys, feeling strangely empowered.

I had just pocketed them when Teri stepped out of the suite next to the elevator. Her eyes were red and puffy, like she'd been crying a long time. She blinked when she saw me. Then she ducked back inside and shut the door.

"Teri?" I knocked softly. "Are you okay?"

"Fine," came her muffled reply. "I just got some shampoo in my eyes."

"Can I get you anything?" I waited a few seconds. "Teri?"

I stood outside her door a couple of minutes before I heard the water running. She'd either stepped into the shower again or was trying to get rid of me.

I took the elevator to the crew quarters and slipped inside Alex's cabin. Relief engulfed me in the small, windowless chamber. It was quiet down here, away from everyone's issues and emotions and agendas. But it was time to get back to reality.

I retrieved the clear plastic bag stashed under my bed and added the keys to my collection of knickknacks: The Three of Spades, a ping-pong ball, a champagne glass, an hourglass with yellow sand...

I dug into my pocket. There was one more memento.

It was a lock of Alex's hair, from his hair cut with Vasilis. It was dry now, dark as a raven's wing.

A sharp rap on the door. "Hello? Anyone there?"

"Just a minute." I slipped Alex's hair into the bag and sealed it shut again. Then I kicked it under the bed and opened the door.

It was Hannah, and like Teri, her eyes were red and puffy, like she'd been crying a long time.

What the hell?

"I'm glad I caught you," she said. "Captain Bailey asked me to see if your bags were ready to bring up."

"It's just one bag. I don't need any help with it. Are you okay?"

"Oh, this?" Hannah pointed to her face. "It's nothing. Just a slight allergic reaction to all the flowers that came for you."

"You're allergic to flowers?"

"Something about these ones. I helped carry them inside, so I must be."

"I'm so sorry."

"Don't worry about it." She sniffed. "I'll be fine. Are you sure you'll manage on your own?"

"Yes, thanks." I started to shut the door but paused. "Hey, did Captain Bailey speak to Rachel Auntie about the accommodations or is she still with Ken and Judy?"

"They left a little while ago. Your aunt will use the Captain's suite, and Captain Bailey will bunk here with Chef Alexandros. It's just for tonight and tomorrow, then everyone will disembark in Hydra, so don't feel too bad about it."

If Captain Bailey had shared her concerns about Alex and me with Hannah, the Chief Steward was giving no indication.

"If there's nothing else, I'll get going." She gave me a small nod, still red-eyed and red-nosed, and took off.

I gathered my things and zipped up my bag.

But I couldn't leave.

The question in Alex's eyes haunted me. I couldn't leave without letting him know how I felt. I grabbed a notepad and started scribbling.

Captain Bailey asked me to stay away from you.

I don't want you to get into any more trouble, so if I avoid you, it's not because of Nikos or his flowers.

I'm meeting him tomorrow. It sucks, but it can't be avoided.

I need you to know that.

I need you to know I've never been happier than the time I spent with you.

I drew three heart-eye emojis and slipped the note under his pillow.

My eyes swept over the room and I saw Alex dropping his clothes that first night before he realized I was in the room—his hair tumbling around his shoulders, his naked silhouette outlined against the bathroom light.

Alex, dangling my bra on his finger. *I get in the shower and your bra bitch-slaps me in the face.*

His jaw hanging open, watching me gyrate against the frame of the bathroom door.

I could hear our voices in the dark.

Alex?

I'm listening…

I stood in silence for a few minutes, soaking in the echoes.

Then I clicked the door shut and left.

CHAPTER TWENTY-FIVE

I T WAS MUCH COOLER IN THE GUEST SUITE THAN THE CREW'S QUARTERS and I reached for another blanket. Dolly snored softly beside me. I stared at the ceiling, wishing I was looking at the bottom of Alex's bunk bed. Too restless to sleep, I tiptoed out of the room and clicked the door shut.

The hallways were empty, the lights dimmed. When the elevator doors glided open on the main deck, I stepped out, not expecting to run into a plate of cheese and olives.

"Whoops, look out," Thomas said.

"I'm so sorry!" I intercepted a runaway olive with my foot. "Midnight snack attack?"

"Yeah." He laughed. "Just wiped out the snacking station." He flashed the other plate he was holding, proud of his midnight foraging.

"You mean the kitchen?"

"The snacking station," he repeated, declining the olive I'd rescued. "You know, the small room off the main salon." He got into the elevator and hit the button with his elbow. "Isabelle and I are having a party in the jacuzzi."

"Have fun." I tossed the olive into the receptacle by the elevator as the doors closed.

Ugh. Offering a billionaire an olive that had rolled off the floor.

To his credit, Thomas was sweet and down-to-earth. Plus, he tipped me off to the snacking station. I rounded the main salon and found a small room off the corridor. Thickly carpeted with plush seats, it looked like a mini-movie theater, except the main attraction was the buffet table, topped with all kinds of platters. Most had already been picked over. Apparently, everyone was onto this smorgasbord of munchies. I'd missed orientation on the first day and Alex had kept me out of the loop with his private midnight snacks. Our little game. A silent conversation.

My feet started making their way to the galley. Tonight, separated from him, I needed to know we were okay, that he got the note I left him and understood why I had agreed to meet Nikos.

Please be there.

Please be there.

My throat clenched at the thought of finding nothing but an empty counter, nothing but Alex's silence. But there was a small plate waiting in the same spot he always left it. I wasn't hungry for what it held. I was hungry for what it meant. Always steady, always strong. Alex was the one thing I could always count on. My throat clenched even tighter as I reached for the note:

The stars weren't the same without you tonight.
They told me tomorrow is a terrible day for a picnic.
Absolutely, frissin' awful.
But you do what you have to, and I'll do the same.

Lifting the dome off the plate, I found a single star-shaped cookie. It reminded me of all the nights we watched the stars on the sky deck. Sleeping under their twinkling canopy on Alex's roof. Watching them come alive, one by one, after the sunset in Santorini. Holding hands and floating like stars on the water.

I picked up the little star. It wasn't a cookie at all, but a piece of baklava Alex had cut into a star—a five-pointed, multi-layered slice of sticky-sweet heaven.

I saved the note and pulled up a stool. Then I lined up another one next to it. Breaking the baklava in half, I toasted my invisible companion.

"To men who pluck stars instead of flowers." I bit through the buttery layers and honeyed walnuts and smiled.

We sat together as I finished my half of the treat, my legs swinging off the stool as I licked the last crumbs from my fingers. I covered the rest and turned off the light.

Climbing back into bed, I drifted off, smiling at the thought of Alex finding half a squished-up, crumbly star in the morning.

CHAPTER TWENTY-SIX

"T IE IT UP HIGHER. LIKE THIS." ISABELLE DEMONSTRATED WITH her sarong. "Not you, Naani."

"Sure." Naani tossed aside the sheer fabric she was experimenting with. "No one wants to see *my* legs. Just wait until I get back from the thermal springs. You won't recognize these beauties." She patted her veined calves. "Hippocrates himself wrote about the rejuvenating powers of the Lakkos baths."

"A few hours marinating in the hot springs of Milos isn't going to give you Tina Turner gams, Naani." Isabelle fixed the knot on my sarong and stepped back. "And what's with the sudden urge to turn back time? I don't know how you managed to convince us to spend our last day on the yacht *off* the yacht."

"I just want to know what the hype is all about. You'll thank me when your skin is glowing on your wedding day."

"As long as I'm not smelling like a boiled egg from all the sulfur in the water." Isabelle tilted her head and appraised me.

"Look at you." Naani's eyes met mine in the mirror. "An overnight tryst with the chef. A private picnic on the beach with the millionaire. *Vah re vah.*"

"You *know* why I'm going." I made a face. "And Isabelle, you can stop fussing around. I'm not wearing this." I untied the sarong from my waist and slipped on the white Indian-style kaftan lying on my bed. It swirled around my ankles, its breezy folds covering my arms and legs.

"Saving it all for Alex," Isabelle whispered to Naani, but loud enough for me to hear.

"The chef has left his mark." Naani wagged her finger at me.

"Really? He did?" Isabelle tugged the kaftan away from my body and peered down my back. "Where?"

"I don't know about those kinds of marks." Naani said, chuckling. "But in here for sure." She patted her heart.

"You two are impossible," I said, but I couldn't help smiling as I grabbed my sunglasses and hat.

"Moti *beta*, hurry up." Dolly waltzed into the suite. "They're all set to..." She trailed off when she saw me. "How beautiful you look. *Meri pyari si gudiya*. Hold on one minute." She went into the bathroom and returned with a small pot of *kajal*—the traditional, velvety black eyeliner. Rubbing her index finger over the surface, she applied a small dot on the side of my forehead. "There. Now you are not so perfect. No jealous, evil eye will fall on you."

"I'm already wearing this." I dangled the bracelet the farmer in Folegandros had given me, with the eye-shaped blue bead.

"Double protection from Nikos's lustful eyes. Indian *and* Greek magic. One can deflect his right eye, the other, his left." Naani made cross-eyes at me.

Dolly ignored her and kissed me on both cheeks. "Have fun. I'll be waiting right here when you get back."

"You're not going to the hot springs with everyone else?" I asked.

"No. I want to hear about everything the moment you return."

"Ma..." Something about the way she was looking at me—*really* looking, stopped me. Moments of connection with Dolly were like rare pearls. The last thing I wanted was to squelch the light shining in her eyes. I was the one who'd put it there. Maybe I was wrong to let her go on spinning happily-ever-after scenarios with Nikos and me, but I wanted to find a gentler way to let her down. And when I did, I hoped she would still look at me the same way.

"What is it?" she asked.

"Nothing. I better be off." I grabbed my handbag and paused. "Bye, Naani. Bye, Isabelle."

And then, as I turned to go, I heard Dolly say, "Love you, *beta*." My footsteps faltered at her words.

Dammit. A lump the size of a golf ball lodged in my throat. I was such a liar for playing along with the whole Nikos thing. I told Dolly there was someone else, but she only heard the things she wanted to hear.

"I love you too." The words flew out of my mouth like they'd been waiting, fully formed, for the right moment to squeeze through.

Dolly smiled, and for those few seconds, we were as open and perfect as we'd ever get—me pretending to be the daughter she wanted, and her loving me for it.

I skipped the elevator and took the stairs, looking for Eddie. I found him readying the tender for our trip ashore, to the spot where Nikos had picked out.

"All set?"

"Almost. Just waiting for—" He broke off and grinned at someone behind me. "Perfect timing."

I glanced over my shoulder and saw Alex and Hannah carrying coolers into the boat. My heart went off on a wild gallop at the sight of Alex.

His arms glistened in the sun as he handed one of the coolers to Eddie.

"One picnic lunch, ready to go."

I cringed. Nikos had asked Alex to prepare lunch for us, and of course, Alex was obliged to follow instructions.

His eyes twinkled when they met mine. "Enjoy your afternoon."

He was way too upbeat for my liking. *Your confidence in us is great, Alex, but a little pathos would be nice, considering I'm heading off to some remote cove, to be alone with your biggest nemesis—a three thumbed man.* I adjusted my floppy hat so he was no longer in my line of sight.

"Hey," he called softly.

When I ignored him, he tapped my shoulder.

"Heart-Eyes."

"What?" I snapped.

"Thank you for my morning star."

"Half star."

"I missed you last night. Captain Bailey snores like a horse."

"Good." My face broke into a reluctant smile. "I hope you didn't get any sleep."

"I didn't, because I was thinking about you. I should've been planning today's menu. It's the grand finale dinner, and I have no idea what I'm going to serve."

"You thrive under pressure," I said, trying to disguise the heaviness in my chest. The grand finale dinner. Tomorrow, I'd be saying goodbye to Alex. More than anything, I wanted to spend the day with him—in the galley, pretending to help, listening to his favorite tunes and watching him put together the final meal.

"Alex?" Eddie said. "We need to get going."

Alex's expression filled with pathos then. *I really, really don't want you to go*, it told me, even as he nodded and got off the boat.

"Be sure to try the pastitsio," he called. "In fact, try a little of everything."

He stayed on the platform, watching us drift away. His smile was pure gold, like a kid who'd left a hidden surprise.

I smiled back, watching him as he got smaller and smaller.

The yacht was still on the horizon when Eddie steered into a quiet inlet and cut the engine.

"We're here already?" I asked. We were on a narrow sandy beach, squeezed between the cliffs and the sea. The water was a startling cobalt blue, warm and clear and shallow.

"Captain Sandy decided to anchor the yacht close by, so we didn't have to backtrack to pick you up," Eddie said, unloading the coolers onto the beach.

In the shadow of the cliffs, a table and two chairs were beautifully set with sparkling plates, wine glasses, and silverware. A canopy of white sheets, held up by tall pieces of wood, fluttered over a blanket by the beach. Cushions and pillows lay scattered over it. A couple of loungers faced the sun, with drink tables lodged firmly in the sand beside them. Ice buckets, towels, water bottles—everything meticulously laid out for a picture-perfect beach picnic.

"Did Nikos do all this?"

"Eddie and I were here earlier today, setting up," Hannah said.

Of course. All Nikos had to do was snap his fingers and everything fell into place.

"Are you all right?" I asked. Hannah seemed to have recovered from her allergies, but she wasn't her usual bubbly self.

"I'm fine." Her smile didn't quite reach her eyes. She probably had a ton of things to look after on the yacht, and here she was, laying out chocolate-dipped strawberries.

"Here comes Nikos." Eddie pointed to the water-taxi approaching the inlet.

I shaded my eyes and squinted into the horizon.

It was Nikos all right—shirt unbuttoned and flapping in the wind, his buffed-up muscles unmistakable as he waved at us.

"Glikia mou." Arms outstretched, he engulfed me in a big hug. "How I've missed you."

I turned my head, so his lips landed on my cheek.

"So coy." He laughed. "I love it."

Hannah signaled Eddie. "That's our cue to leave."

"I just need another minute," Eddie said. He was setting up a pair of speakers between the crevices in the cliffs.

"Take your time, Eddie. No rush." Nikos led me to the table and held out the chair before seating himself. "I'm thinking it would be nice to have Hannah serve lunch before you leave."

"I've laid everything out exactly as you requested," Hannah said. "Captain Bailey is expecting us back—"

Nikos cut her off with a dismissive gesture. "Captain Bailey can wait. My date deserves to be waited on like royalty. I think we'll start with champagne."

Hannah wavered for a second. Then her professional demeanor kicked in. "Of course."

"Nikos." I leaned across the table. "We don't really need Hannah and Eddie to—"

"Shhh." Nikos put his finger on my lips. "I promised to make it up to you. So, let me."

Hannah uncorked the champagne with an expert pop and filled our glasses.

Nikos took a sip and shook his head. "Nope. Not cold enough. I don't think you put enough ice in that ice bucket. How long has this been sitting out here?"

"We just took it out of the—"

"I shouldn't have to tell you how to do your job. Is it too much to ask—"

"Stop being such a jerk, Nikos," a voice piped up.

My eyes flew to Hannah.

She stared at me.

I stared at her.

I was the one talking. "Let's go, Hannah. I don't care to be in the company of someone who treats people so poorly." I got up, but Nikos grabbed my wrist.

"Hey. Hey. I'm sorry." He looked from me to Hannah. "I'm sorry, Hannah. She's right for calling me out. I've been a complete asshole to you."

There was no doubting his sincerity. He was like a spoiled kid, throwing his weight around and needing to be reminded of his limits.

Hannah nodded, her chin quivering. "I have to go," she said. "Eddie has to get the other passengers to the hot springs. You two should stay. Please stay. Don't let me spoil your afternoon."

"Hannah," Nikos said, but she spun on her heel and headed for the boat.

Nikos turned to the deckhand, but he was already on his way to check on her.

"Moti?"

Moti with a hard T. I'd corrected him the first time he said my name, and he'd never attempted it again until today.

"Moti, please sit down." He looked so dejected I almost felt sorry for him.

"Thank you," he said, when I sat.

"Don't thank me yet. I'm only staying because I need to clear some things up."

"Fine." He let out a tired, frustrated sigh. "My day can't possibly get any worse. My plan totally backfired."

"You guys okay if we take off?" Eddie called to us from the boat. "Captain Bailey just radioed us in."

"Go." Nikos raised the glass of champagne that started it all. "Cheers." He downed it as Eddie started the boat.

"The cell phone signal isn't strong here," Eddie called over the drone of the engine. "Use the flag when you want to come in." He pointed to the green flag lying on the ground beside us. "Stick it upright in the sand. We'll keep an eye out for it on the yacht."

"Got it," said Nikos, watching as the tender took off, leaving a trail of foam in the water. "Well…" He poured himself another glass of champagne. "It's just you and me."

"About that, I haven't been completely honest with you."

"Oh?"

"Everything was fine in the beginning. I was completely smitten with you. At least, the idea of you. It meant a way out for me, but…"

I took a deep breath. *Forgive me, Dolly. I'm about to destroy whatever future you've envisioned for Nikos and me.*

"I've fallen for someone else," I said. "Madly. Completely. Unexpectedly. The only reason I agreed to meet you today is because my mother wanted me to. Now I can tell her I did as she asked, but it didn't work out. I'm sorry for using you to get her off my back. I have no intentions of pursuing anything with you."

A furrow formed between Nikos's grape-green eyes. "You used me?"

"I know. I feel terrible about the flowers and the—"

"Let me get this straight. *You...*" He pointed my way. "Used *me.*" He pointed at himself.

I kept my eyes on his extra thumb, the magical digit I had pursued all my life, only to push it away. I deserved whatever his bruised ego was about to unleash on me.

Nikos slapped his thigh and roared with laughter. "Well, I'll be damned. That's just..." He trailed off, chuckling. "That's a first for me, but you know what? I deserve it. That's karma for you."

"How's that?"

"It doesn't matter. I applaud your honesty."

"There's something else."

"By all means." He leaned forward. Intrigued? Entertained? "Don't let me stop you."

"The incident at your club? The one you had to stay back for?"

"Yes?"

"I started it."

Nikos blinked. "I'm sorry?"

"I started the brawl that landed you in trouble. If you go over the security footage, you'll see."

"I have people who analyze things like that for me. I'm sure they know exactly what happened. It's a nightclub. We're used to containing these kinds of situations. The reason everything blew up that night wasn't you. It was Olympia Aravani. Once the paparazzi got a hold of that little bit of information..." Nikos held his hands up and shrugged. "But if you're truly remorseful, there *is* something you can do for me."

He chuckled when he caught the look I threw him. "Nothing questionable. Believe it or not, I've learned a few lessons today. All that aside, I've been meaning to conquer one of these cliffs for years. Would you mind taking a picture of me diving off that one there?" He pointed to its flat-topped summit. "One for the record, then we can head back to the yacht. What do you say?"

"Sure." Heading back sounded good. Even though Captain Bailey was keeping an eye on Alex and me, I just wanted to be where he was.

"It'll take me about ten, maybe fifteen minutes to get to the top."

"You want me to go with you?"

"You'll capture the perspective better from here. Take as many shots as you can before I hit the water. Use the burst mode for that." He demonstrated the camera function on his phone.

"Got it."

"Great." Nikos shrugged his shirt off and left it dangling on the chair. "Ten minutes. And then look for me up there."

I found a spot on the rocks, where I could get a clear shot of him. It sloped gently into the sea, so I dipped my toes in the water while I waited.

Apart from the glint of glass on the distant yacht, it felt like I had the whole island to myself. Milos was a multiplicity of colors. The gods had thrown all the colors on a canvas that had exploded from the sea. Luminous bone-white rock, frozen in giant swirls like folds of whipped cream. Red volcanic cliffs, dark rocks rising starkly out of the water, sheltered coves colored green and blue by mineral deposits and tiny beaches made by lava flow.

"Ready?" The echo of Nikos's voice bounced off the stones around me.

I stood and gave him a thumbs-up. *Holy shit. That's a long way to drop.*

But Nikos wasn't fazed. Arching his body like a rainbow, he launched off the cliff and dove gracefully into the water.

Click. Click. Click. Click. I captured all of it, including the few seconds before impact, when his body straightened into an arrow parting the water. He disappeared a few moments and emerged with a victorious whoop. I took a few more shots while he swam and headed back to the table.

As I reached across for some water, my eyes fell on the glass-domed dish labeled Pastitsio.

Be sure to try the pastitsio, Alex had said.

I helped myself to a wedge, thinking it looked a lot like lasagna.

It tasted like lasagna too. Luscious layers of meat, pasta, and tomato sauce baked to a creamy goodness with what tasted like bechamel sauce. There was something else, something sweet. Cinnamon? Nutmeg? Yes. But as that first bite melted in my mouth, the aftertaste was overwhelmingly candy-like. Yuck.

What the hell, Alex? What kind of dish is this?

I took a sip of water to wash it down and went for one of the appetizers instead. It was topped with feta cheese—something I was familiar with, so I knew what to expect.

I ended up spitting it into my napkin. It tasted like it had been soaked in sugar water.

I sampled the dips, the fritters, the salad, the bruschetta.

Sweet. Sweet. Sweet. And more sweet.

By the time I got to the stuffed grape leaves, I was laughing.

Just as Dimitra protested her son's departure by switching the salt for sugar, Alex was protesting my picnic with Nikos.

Shading my eyes, I walked to the water and smiled at the hazy outline of the yacht, hearing his protest loud and clear.

Beyond the narrow arm of rocks that separated us, Nikos was still swimming. The water was much shallower where I stood. And warmer too. I lay my kaftan on the sand, weighting it with a couple of pebbles. My hands were darker. I loved my masala-chai skin tone, but the deeper, dusky shade was a reminder of my afternoon with Alex. In spite of all the childhood drillings to stay out of the sun, my legs, my back, my whole body belonged in it. I wasn't too dark, too short, too fat, too anything.

I held my arms up to the sun and twirled, humming as I let

the water kiss my feet. Scooping up some sand, I let it wash away in the gentle lap of the next wave, like cool lava receding from my fingers. I sat cross-legged on the beach with the sun on my back and the sea before me.

It was a perfectly rare, perfectly beautiful day.

And then, to make it even better, I spotted a starfish.

"Hey there, little fellow." I waded into the water to get a better look.

The small starfish was purple, its spindly arms reaching for deeper waters. I gathered it in my hands and took a few steps into the sea.

"You'll be safer here." I was about to let it go when I noticed a barnacle-covered rock jutting into the water. I thought the darker color below the water's surface was from patches of lichen, but as I approached, I realized dozens of purple starfish were feeding off the barnacles.

"Is this where you want to go?" I tried to get my little starfish to the rock, but the mass of seaweed around the rock made it impossible to see where I was stepping. I followed the rock around and found a clearing at its craggy tip.

"Whoa." I steadied myself as the sea pulled at my legs in a sudden rush. I was in a lot deeper than I'd realized. Settling the starfish down, I started making my way back.

The next rush of water dragged the sand beneath my feet away with it. Suddenly, I was neck-deep in water, and clinging to the rock. A wave of panic swept over me.

I can do this. Alex taught me how. I searched for the yacht and held it steady in my vision. *I can—*

The next powerful surge swept me off my feet. I gasped, my nails scraping the edges of the rock, my feet searching for a seabed no longer there.

Fuck. I was caught up in a current. I could feel the sea pause around me as it gathered force, the brief reprieve ringing like alarm bells in my ears. When it came for me again, my heart was pumping furiously in my chest. I latched on to the barnacles, oblivious to the razor-sharp edges shredding my skin. Every muscle in my body—my arms, my feet, my shoulders, my chest—clamored to hold on to the last solid thing within my reach.

The rock slipped from my grasp, millimeter by millimeter, and then all at once.

I'd imagined drowning many times, in many different scenarios. I pictured my arms and legs flailing frantically. Yelling for help. Splashing. Thrashing.

My drowning was quiet, my movements restrained by the current. Everything happened under the surface. One minute, my head bobbed above the water and the next, it was gone.

I was gone.

My hair floated like tangled seaweed around me. A stream of bubbles escaped from my nostrils, rising a strange angle. The current dragged me through the water like a fisherman reeling in his catch. My lungs were on fire, every cell in my body screaming for air.

When the pull slackened, as the sea stopped to take a breath, my arms and legs kicked desperately to get to the surface, but the harder I clawed, the deeper I sank.

Alex's words came back to me.

The more you fight it, the faster you'll go under.

Eyes to the sky. Little kicks to get your legs up.

I looked up, but the light was starting to dim. Black blotches seeped along the edges of my vision. I couldn't tell whether the hammering rush in my ears was the water or my heart about to explode. I couldn't hold my breath much longer. My lungs were going to inhale. Air or water—it didn't matter. As I struggled to keep myself from breathing, darkness held out its arms.

Like a babe being cradled in her mother's embrace, I let its cloak fall around me.

Flashes of recollection spiked through my mind, little beeps of activity in the flat line that the sea was compressing me into.

Naani rubbing Vicks VapoRub on my feet. *In the morning, you'll be all better.*

Running after my father as he rolled his suitcase to the car. *Don't go. Please. Don't leave.*

Moti, Moti, Moti. The incessant chanting of the kids when I'd gone back for another slice of birthday cake. *Fatty, fatty, fatty.*

Prem Prakash Pyarelal. Who was he? I couldn't remember.

My memories slowly seeped into the water like indigo ink from purple starfish.

Come on. Hand it over. Isabelle grinning, as I fumbled in my bag for something. For what?

Love you, beta, Dolly said. *Finally* said.

Dolly had said to stay away from the water.

As the sea rushed into my lungs, one final memory floated up from the darkness.

Don't you dare leave me now, Alex said, water droplets glistening like little crystals on his eyelashes. *I know it's hard, but this is it. You give up right now and you'll be giving up on yourself.*

My eyes flew open, my chest convulsing as my lungs fought to expel the water.

Take my hand, Moti. You can do it. You were already doing it. You were floating.

I reached my arms up through the darkness.

No, I told it, even as the sea flooded into my lungs. *Not now. Not yet.*

Something propelled me upward. The dying person's abnormal surge of well-being. A brief burst of energy before death. Perhaps the black dot that Dolly marked me with. Or the bracelet I wore to ward off the evil eye. Someone's prayer. Or my own will to survive.

This is not how my story ends.

The first breath was like fire scorching my airways. Air and water collided in my throat, my nostrils, my lungs. I gagged and went under again. The current wrapped around my body like a python ready to devour its prey. I felt its grip around my chest, squeezing out the air I'd managed to steal.

When the water closed around me again, I knew it had me.

As the world dimmed around the edges, everything fell silent.

Like a bubble rising to the surface, one final thought:

Alex?

I'm listening…

I've never been happier than the time I spent with you.

ALEX

CHAPTER TWENTY-SEVEN

S HE TOLD ME SHE WAS GOING TO DIE IN THE WATER. IT WAS WRITTEN in the stars the day she was born. I dismissed it, the same way I dismissed anything that defied logic. I should've listened.

I couldn't explain why the hair on the back of my neck stood when she was around. Or how, when she smiled, my heart felt like it had been hit with a million jolts of electricity. There was no logical reason to explain why pieces of me were dying alongside her still, limp body, and yet it was as real as the air I was breathing. Air that she was not.

I should've fucking listened.

The kicker was that I'd watched Moti go in the water. I told Eddie I'd keep an eye out for the flag, signaling a pick-up request, but really I was stalking their goddamn picnic. I picked up the binoculars a hundred times. I had a clear view from the galley and at one point, I saw her sitting on the rocks. Maybe the glint from the binoculars caught her eye or maybe it was my imagination, but I could've sworn she looked directly at me.

The next time I checked, she was wading into the water. God, she was beautiful, in her striped swimsuit, with droplets of water dancing on her skin. The thought of saying goodbye sat like an undigested lump in my stomach.

Panic started to set in a few moments later. Why the hell was she going in deeper? And where the hell was Nikos? The second I saw her clutching onto the rock, I knew she was in trouble.

I bolted for the tender, pushing Dolly out of the way as I swarmed the deck.

"Excuse me?" she exclaimed.

Fuck. Eddie had taken the faster boat to drop everyone off at the hot springs.

"Sound the alarm," I yelled, as I launched the rubber dinghy. "Tell Captain Bailey to get her eyes on the shore." I pointed to the picnic spot.

"What's going—"

"It's Moti." I revved the engine, peering through the binoculars once again. No trace of her. I let out a curse, eyeballing how long it would take me to get to her. Nikos spotted me coming in and swam up to meet me. He manned the boat, searching the surface, while I dove beneath, where I'd last spotted her. The current was powerful even for a seasoned swimmer like me. Despair grew heavier as the seconds ticked by. Within three minutes of submersion, most people are unconscious. Within five minutes, the brain begins to suffer from a lack of oxygen. Within ten minutes...

I wasn't looking for blood, but that's how I found her—a darker tinge against the water. It was gone the next instant, folded into the sea's massive, greedy palm. Diving under the surface again, I made a slow, wide circle, eyes wide open.

Once again, I came up empty-handed.

She's here. I know it. I can feel her.

I took another breath and plunged beneath the water again.

I spotted her dark tresses first, fanning out under me through blue shafts of light. A flat fish with gold eyes darted away as I swam toward her, my heart pounding hard and fast against my ribs. She floated vertically, suspended in a slow-motion matrix. Ribbons of blood rose from her arm, curling upward like smoke from a snuffed-out candle.

Her stillness felt like hell to me.

I undid the rope around my waist and tied it around her.

I got you. I got you, Heart-Eyes.

The alarm bells in my head got louder when I brought her up. Her body was slack, her lips a fatal shade of blue.

"Over here," I yelled.

Nikos gunned the motor, and we got her on the boat.

Come on, baby. Come back to me. I urged between chest compressions and mouth-to-mouth resuscitation.

Water and tears dripped down my face as I pushed—one hand on top of the other—on her breastbone.

If I hadn't taught you to float, you wouldn't have gone in the water. You would've stayed away.

I'm sorry, Heart-Eyes. I'm so fucking sorry.

My arms grew numb from pushing on her breastbone, my heart frozen from the shock of her cold, clammy skin. Her expressionless face. Her lifeless form.

Come on. Breathe, baby, breathe.

My compressions became more forceful. It didn't matter if I hurt her, bruised her, broke her ribs. None of it would matter if I didn't get her to expel the water.

I felt a slight contraction of her diaphragm, followed by the sweet, glorious sound of her coughing. Choking. Gagging. Moti's hand wrapped around her throat as she thrashed on the bright yellow floor of the dinghy. I convulsed over her writhing body—laughing, crying, the relief unbearable even though she was struggling to breathe. She was back. And she was alive. Nothing else mattered.

I wrapped a blanket around her shaking body.

I didn't let go when the onboard medic rushed to our side.

Or when the medic cleared Moti, contingent on twenty-four hours of monitoring.

Or when the doctor from Milos—the one I insisted Captain Bailey call for a second opinion—confirmed the prognosis.

Moti was going to be all right.

We tucked her into the big bed in the captain's suite. She slept, and I kept watch.

When she jerked in her sleep, her body stiff with panic, I rubbed circles on her chest. I held her hand, careful to keep the pressure off the bandages covering her scraped skin.

"It's okay. You're okay." I soothed the lines on her brow. "I got you, Heart-Eyes."

I didn't hear Hannah walk into the suite until she rested her hand on my shoulder.

"I'm sorry, Chef. We have a boat full of people who haven't had anything to eat. I prepared some snacks and Captain Bailey's pushed the dinner hour back, but she's requesting you get back to the galley."

Fuck Captain Bailey.

I knew Hannah was right. Moti was exhausted, but she was in the clear. I glanced at Dolly, who was keeping vigil on the other side of the bed. She gave me a nod. *I'll look after her.*

It took every ounce of willpower to step away. I dropped a kiss on Moti's forehead.

"I'll be back."

I didn't care if her mother was watching. Or if Hannah or Captain Bailey or the entire world was watching.

"You need any help?" Hannah asked, following me to the galley.

I shook my head. I had twenty-four more hours on the clock. Twenty-four hours left in this charter. I was still an employee, contractually bound to fulfill my obligations of feeding everyone on the yacht. The frustration of being dragged away from Moti made me want to punch holes in the wall. It was the same seething burn in my chest that followed my mother's death.

Except Moti is alive. So why am I so freaking angry?

Because I almost lost her without telling her how much she means to me.

The edges of my heart curled up in flames, the unspoken words flaring like dry kindling in my throat.

I'd asked Moti to stay for another two weeks, when I really wanted her to stay forever. I was chasing a dream that kept me from home most of the year. In a couple of years, I'd have enough capital saved to open a restaurant. I'd have a base. I could commit to the kind of relationship Moti deserved.

Her near-drowning jolted everything to the forefront. All the things I thought I had time for were clamoring to be seen and heard *now*.

I took a deep breath, willing myself to calm the hell down. If there was one thing I'd learned in the kitchen, it was that food was more than the sum of its ingredients. Food absorbed the subtlest of nuances—the way it was sliced and stirred, the way it hit the pan. If you paid attention, food told you all kinds of secrets, like whether the oregano was gathered in the spring before it bloomed or in the summer, after it had been dried by the sun. Food told you if it was hastily thrown together or allowed to breathe and simmer. It spoke to you about care. Or neglect. Most of the time though, food slipped right through—because no one was listening—to be absorbed by all the things already simmering inside us.

I kept an eye on the clock as I cooked. Captain Bailey would join the main table for the farewell dinner. Moti's grandmother opted out of her early meal and would also be present. Moti was confined to bed rest, so a tray would be delivered to her suite. I cross-checked my notes and worked my way through the passenger list quickly and meticulously.

I finished garnishing the plates and was checking on the crew's dinner when Hannah stepped into the galley.

"Right on time," I said.

"Am I?"

I turned around, shark mitts over my hands, and froze.

Moti had never looked more fragile. Or more alive. Her hair was still gunky from the sea, the strands clumped around her face.

"You look like the first time I saw you," I said. "Like a wave crashed on top of you."

A dry laugh escaped her.

"Yeah, well. That was a roadside puddle and some idiot on a motorbike. This time, the whole sea crashed on top of me."

My heart caught in my throat. "Are you okay?"

Her eyes followed mine to her bandaged arm. "I'm fine. Just scraped myself holding on to the barnacles."

"Christ, Heart-Eyes."

My entire being screamed to take her into my arms. I took a step toward her, but she held up her hand.

"Let me finish. You saved me. I don't just mean in the water today. You saved me in here." Her hand went to her chest. "You believed in me. You told me I could do it. And I did, Alex. I came back up. I made it to the surface. If it wasn't for that one breath before I went under again, I wouldn't be here."

"You saved yourself. You—"

"I'm not done yet."

I waited, but she just stared at me. She looked tired, but her eyes gleamed with a new luminosity.

Then she rushed into my arms, lifting her perfectly sculpted lips to mine. No kiss had tasted sweeter, no moment righter.

"I love you, Alex," she said, pulling back and gazing at me with her liquid brown eyes.

I was wrong. *This* kiss was sweeter, *this* moment righter.

Her body melted into mine as I held her, my hands still encased in shark mitts.

Dear God, I never want to let her go.

Something swelled in my chest, so big that I couldn't contain it anymore. "Moti, I—"

"I thought you were advised to stay in bed." Captain Bailey's words cut me off. "Moti, shouldn't you be resting?"

I felt Moti's spine stiffen, like someone had taken a whip to her back. She ignored Captain Bailey and kissed me again—a soft nuzzle on the cheek. When she let go and turned around, I realized Captain Bailey wasn't alone. She was accompanied by David, the onboard security officer.

Security's involved because Moti disregarded the doctor's advice? I bristled at the ridiculousness.

"You're right, Captain Bailey," Moti said. "I should be resting. I've done exactly what was expected of me for most of my life, and you know what? My life almost ended today. So I'm here, thanking the man who saved me. In case you're still looking for something to say about Alex in your letter, how about *that*? And for the record..." She reached for my hand but ended up coming away with the shark mitt, which she waved in Captain Bailey's face. "This man has been nothing but honorable. Anyone would be lucky to have him on their team. I'm not just talking about the magic he creates in the kitchen, I'm talking about who he is—heart and soul. I'll happily take a bite out of anyone who stands in his way."

She slipped on the shark mitt and chomped her way past Captain Bailey and David, holding it at eye-level like a sock puppet, its red mouth trained on them.

Damn, I thought as she walked out the door. *Moti 1 went down and Moti 2 emerged—spunky, spirited, and ferocious.*

I hid a smile when her head popped in again. The rest of her body followed as she tiptoed back inside and slid the mitt across the counter.

"You might...need that."

Okay, maybe not so ferocious. Moti 2 still had to master the art of the grand exit.

Captain Bailey and David exchanged a look when she was gone. Then they turned their gazes on me.

"What?" I said.

"Does this belong to you?" Captain Bailey held out a clear, zippered bag. "It was found in your cabin."

I recognized Moti's little stash of knickknacks. There was a new addition, something dark and distinct.

"May I?" I took the bag from Captain Bailey and examined it. The world stopped on its axis when I saw what it was.

A lock of my hair.

A strange warmth flooded my limbs—a buzzing, liquid feeling

I'd never known before.

She'd stolen a piece of me and squirreled it away for when we had to say goodbye.

How the hell am I going to let her go when my heart is brimming over?

"Well?" Captain Bailey prodded.

I wanted to shield Moti from the entire world, to keep her safe and happy and carefree. Explaining her impulses to Captain Bailey was one thing, but to her family? I knew how much it would embarrass her to own up to her need to take random objects.

I already saw the way Dolly made her feel—like she wasn't good enough. I'd witnessed her jump to her cousin's bidding. She was a comma among the characters of her family—unnoticed and overlooked. Hell if I was going to stand aside and let her take the fall for a bunch of souvenirs.

Taking the blame might ruin my chances of landing the Kiriakis gig, but I wasn't going to give them any ammunition against Moti. I was already in trouble for breaking Captain Bailey's cardinal rule: Thou shalt not hook up with the guests.

"It's mine," I said.

"Are you sure, Chef Alexandros?"

"Yes." I handed the bag back.

Captain Bailey sighed and gave the security officer a nod. "Chef Alexandros, you are relieved of your duties effective immediately."

"Please come with me," David said. "You'll be placed in confinement until we arrive at the next port, at which point, you may request a lawyer."

MOTI

CHAPTER TWENTY-EIGHT

THE DINING ROOM WAS FILLED WITH ANTICIPATION WHEN I WALKED in.

In contrast to our first night around the table, all the empty, unexplored days had been filled and we were coming together with our lines and edges redrawn by the experience.

"Moti." Nikos rose from his seat and led me to the table. "How are you feeling?"

"Come sit next to me, *beta*." Naani patted the empty chair beside her.

"What are you doing here?" Dolly got out of her chair. "You should be in bed. Come, I'll take you back."

"I'm fine," I replied, shaking her hand off my elbow and settling down beside Naani. "I'd much rather be around everyone, and I don't want to miss the farewell dinner."

Every time I closed my eyes, I woke up with my heart hammering, clawing at the bedsheets like I was trying to rip breathing holes through a layer of cellophane. My accident had also dampened everyone's spirits. They'd all stopped in to check on me. The last thing I wanted to do was weigh down Thomas and Isabelle's wedding celebrations.

"It wouldn't be the same without you," Isabelle said. She looked stunning in a floor-length blush gown.

Everyone was dressed in formal attire for the last night on the yacht. I did a double take when I saw Captain Bailey. She was still in her uniform, but her hair was down and her face softened with makeup. She sat at the head of the table with George on one side, and Joseph Uncle on the other. My eyes went around the rest of the table, chair by chair: Kassia, Rachel Auntie, Fia, Teri, Dolly, Isabelle, Thomas, Nikos, Naani.

And me.

Thirteen of us gathered for the farewell dinner.

Hannah arrived with our food. Her manner was cheerful and professional when she set Nikos's dinner in front of him. No sign of their earlier altercation.

"I'm glad you decided to join us, Moti," she said. Then she turned to the steward who was assisting her. "Cancel the room service for Cabin Five and bring it to the table. It's the special meal on the counter."

The steward left to get my dinner and Hannah stepped back to introduce the first course.

"Given the events of the day..." She shot a quick look at Captain Bailey. "Chef Alexandros could not prepare the menu he originally planned for tonight. The good news is he still put together something special. The bad news is it's just one course, followed by dessert. I hope you enjoy."

"It looks delicious," George said, admiring his artfully assembled plate. "What is it?"

"To be honest," Hannah said, "Chef Alexandros didn't say, but all special requests have been accommodated, so you can dig in with no reservations."

"A mystery dish on the last night," Joseph Uncle said. "How intriguing. Chef Alexandros is a hero for saving our Moti *and* whipping up a meal for us."

"To Chef Alexandros." Isabelle and Thomas raised their glasses. The rest of us followed.

"A light meal for you." Hannah took the tray from her assistant and served me a bowl of what the doctor had ordered.

"Thank you." I wasn't hungry, but the aroma beckoned like genie hands rising from the broth.

As always, the table went quiet while we ate, each of us

immersed in our own experience. It was never just a meal. It was emotions, memories, textures, flavors—crisscrossed together, like a net woven in Alex's kitchen to capture our senses.

With each spoonful of broth, my belly turned warmer and warmer—at first a pleasant, glowing sensation, and then, as I continued, the heat churned higher and higher. All the hidden, burning things inside me came clamoring to the surface, gasping for air.

Ma Anga was right. I died in the water. I recalled the moment its icy tentacles slid into the back of my throat, the explosion of air bubbles, the pain erupting like hot lava and seeping into every fissure in my body. The darkness had been a relief. How long I stayed there, I didn't know. What I *did* know was that I wasn't the only one jump-started back to life. Anguish. Desire. Frustration. Elation. They had risen like titans along with me. With each mouthful, they grew bigger and bigger, until my stomach felt like a cauldron about to spill over.

I wasn't the only one reacting to my dinner. Beside me, Naani reached for her water and dabbed her napkin on her forehead. Fia hand-fanned herself. Nikos shrugged out of his jacket and loosened his tie. Like wildfire, the chemical reaction spread around the table, even though we weren't eating the same thing.

"I have some unfortunate news."

All heads turned to Captain Bailey, who looked surprised at her own voice.

"I planned on telling you later because I didn't want to ruin dinner, but I can't seem to keep it in any longer. Mr. and Mrs. Gonsalves came to me earlier today." She gestured toward Joseph Uncle and Rachel Auntie. "Mrs. Gonsalves wanted to get into the safety deposit box in their suite, but she couldn't find her key. We issue two sets per cabin and both had been in her possession. All the wedding jewelry was in their safety deposit box, so they were understandably distraught."

Distraught was an understatement. No Indian wedding was complete without lots of gold. Many families started saving decades in advance. Back in the days when all the property went to sons, people shared their wealth with daughters in the form of gold. The tradition also had its roots in the dowry system which, although illegal now, still influenced the well-being of the bride and her status in her new family. Gold for the in-laws, gold for the groom. Hair accessories, nose rings, earrings, bracelets, and necklaces for the bride. I knew for a fact Rachel Auntie and Joseph Uncle had stockpiled a sizable stash for the day Isabelle got married.

"Security began a thorough search of the premises, starting with the lowest deck," Captain Bailey said. "The keys were found, and nothing was missing from the safety deposit box. Unfortunately, it was found in a crew member's cabin. Chef Alexandros has admitted to its possession. He'll be turned over to the authorities at the next port."

The silence that followed was jarred by a ring tone.

"Sorry." Thomas's father silenced his phone.

I stared at my plate, shocked by the news. Why in the world would Alex take the keys to Rachel Auntie's safety deposit box?

The silence stretched out as Hannah collected our plates and brought out dessert.

"Galaktoboureko, a creamy custard pie," she said. "And for you, some fruit, Moti."

I blinked at the five orange segments before me. Flipped inside out, they were arranged like a starfish on the plate.

My mind flashed back to lying on a pile of quilts next to Alex, the stars glittering above us on his rooftop.

What's your favorite childhood memory?

My mother, peeling an orange and bringing it to my room while I was studying. She never said a word. She'd come in, put it on my desk, and leave. Sometimes I didn't even know she'd been there until I saw the plate. She had this way of flipping each segment inside out, with the flesh arched out, so I didn't have to bite through the stringy white fibers. Mountains of orange spikes waiting to be scraped off with my teeth.

Nothing says love like a plate of cut fruit left silently for you.

I gasped like I'd been splashed in the face with cold water. The keys I found in the hallway, the ones I stashed away under the bunk bed in Alex's cabin, along with all the other stuff I stole—they were the reason he was in trouble. I took Rachel Auntie's safety deposit box keys and Alex took the fall for me.

Everything bubbling inside me spilled over, like someone flipped the release valve on a pressure cooker. Words vented out in a jet stream of admissions.

"I steal things," I said. "Things I don't think anyone will miss. I've been doing it for as long as I can remember." I glanced at Joseph Uncle and George. "I took the playing card that messed up your game. I took a champagne glass from Naani's suite. A ping-pong ball. Coffee stirrers. An hourglass. A lock of hair." I fixed my gaze on Captain Bailey. "I took the safety deposit keys. Not Alex. I didn't know what they were for, but I know you found them in a zipped plastic bag under the bunk bed. I know because I hid it. I'm a thief."

I faced my family with my secret. What should've mortified me, felt cathartic. "I'm the culprit. And my name is not Mo-tee," I said to the rest of them. "It's Mo-*thi*."

Once again, the silence was interrupted by George's phone. Before he could reach for it, Kassia tossed her napkin over it.

"I want a divorce," she said. "I've had it with all these phone calls. I'm sick of you skulking off to answer them. I know you're having an affair. I've ignored it for months, but enough is enough. As soon as the wedding is done, I'm leaving you. It's over, George."

Thomas's father stared at her, his jaw slack. His phone kept ringing.

"You can't divorce me," he said when it finally stopped. "We're Greek Orthodox. We stick together for life. Do you really think I'm having an affair?" He held his hands up. "Like one woman isn't hard enough to handle." Laughter started like a newly sprung leak from his chest. It sounded like relief, like a dam bursting open. "I'm not having an affair, Kassia. We're going bankrupt. All of this…" He flashed his arms around. "One last hoorah. They'll be swooping in as soon as we get home."

From across the table, someone gasped.

Isabelle.

Before she could compose herself, Nikos piped in.

"I love you," he declared, his eyes smoldering with intensity as he gazed at me.

What the hell?

"The flowers, the picnic, the whole thing with Moti… It was all for you."

Wait a minute. I swung around. He wasn't gazing at me.

"I was trying to make you jealous, Hannah," he said.

Another gasp. This time, from Captain Bailey.

I was caught off-guard myself, although it made sense in retrospect.

You used me? He laughed when I confessed about using him to get Dolly off my back. He'd used me too—to get to Hannah.

He ignored Captain Bailey's reaction and forged on. "I wasn't ready to commit then, but I am now. I've gone about it the wrong way, but if you let me, I'll spend the rest of my life making up for it."

Our eyes bounced from Nikos to Hannah.

"You've been awful to me," she said.

"I know."

"Mean."

"I know."

"You don't deserve my love."

Nikos hung his head, misery settling on his shoulders. "I know."

"But you have it anyway. You've had it all along."

"What?" Captain Bailey said as Nikos's eyes lit up.

"I know it's against the rules," Hannah said. "I know you told me to never fall for one of the passengers, but it happened. Nikos and I met last summer, on another charter. I'm sorry, Mom. I know you met my father on a yacht just like this, and I know it was so much more for you than it was for him. That's why you're so adamant about the rules. But I love Nikos. I love him, Mom."

Mom.

Now all eyes bounced between Hannah and Captain Bailey.

My mind flashed back to Ken and Judy, the Canadian couple Alex and I had run into in Santorini.

Judy's sister and niece got here yesterday, so we thought we'd come and see them.

Their niece. Captain Bailey's daughter. Hannah.

She didn't have allergies to the flowers Nikos sent me. She'd been crying.

And now I knew why the captain was so determined to keep Alex and me apart. It wasn't just the rules. It was more personal.

"You have no idea how happy you've made me." Nikos stood and went around to Hannah. "No more of this." He took the pitcher of water from her hand and placed it on the table. "I mean, unless you want to," he added when he noticed her expression.

"I'm still on duty, Nikos." Then, when his face fell, she softened and threw her arms around him. "Oh, what the hell."

As we watched, captivated by the intensity of their kiss, the next person succumbed to the spell that had been cast on the table—a spell that was making us all spill our guts out.

"I like to play dead."

Our eyes swung to Dolly. She was standing, as if trying to make herself bigger than her secret.

"For those few minutes when everyone is fussing around me, it feels like I matter, like I'm worth something. Because I sure as hell don't feel worthy of much. Truth is, I'm a coward. A fake. I've been faking it all my life. The only time anything felt real was when I was with you, Fia." She raked in a deep breath, her bosom puffing out like her heart had just been released from its shackles.

"I'm sorry I didn't fight for us, Fia," she said. "The day we decided to tell our families, I failed you. And I failed myself. I didn't have the courage to stand up to my father, so I married the man he picked out for me and left you behind. I tried to make it work with Moti's father. I really did." Her eyes met mine for a brief second, an apology cocooning the shock of her revelation, before she went on.

"But you were always there. I hated you, Fia. If I'd never met you, if you hadn't been so sure and unapologetic about who you were, I would've never fallen for you. Our friendship would've been just that. But seeing you again... I feel exactly the way I did all those years ago. I love you, Fia. I always have, always will."

Dolly. And Fia.

What happened between you and my mother? Was it a guy?

It was most definitely a guy, Fia said.

Was he worth it?

I don't know. You should ask Dolly.

I wasn't the only one reeling from Dolly's confession. Naani, Rachel Auntie, Joseph Uncle, Isabelle were all staring at her with their mouths open. She'd kept it from all of us.

Finally, Fia spoke. "I didn't push you into the water."

"No, you didn't."

"Then why did you accuse me of something so ludicrous?"

"Because I wanted to punish you."

"For what? What did I ever do to you?"

"You make me feel things I don't want to feel. Don't you see? I didn't choose this. I wanted to make different choices. Easier choices. And you just... You just... You won't let me be. I convinced myself you were a mistake. I was young and curious, and I got carried away. But I've been running from the truth the whole time and I'm so exhausted. I love you, Fia. I'm ready to tell the whole world because that's my truth and I can't hide it anymore."

Fia remained stone-faced. An ancient, fortified castle. Immutable. Unbreachable. Then the lights turned on, one by one, like a welcoming home for a lost loved one. "Well, it's about time you came to your fucking senses."

Dolly made a sound, like the one that had escaped me when I realized I was floating on my own. "Fia, I—"

"You hurt me, Dolly. You hurt me really bad. I don't know if we can ever go back to the way things used to be. I need to process things. And I need to know you're not doing this because your horoscope said it was a good day to come clean, or your tarot reader told you to go for it, or some psychic hotline re—"

"I turned to those things because I was afraid to make my own decisions. It was easier to transfer the responsibility. But no more, I promise. I'm not afraid anymore."

As Dolly and Fia faced each other across the table, it felt like a wave had crashed and we were all swirling in the ebb. But I was wrong. The tide was still coming in. I caught a whiff of Vicks VapoRub as Naani adjusted her shawl and spoke.

"I'm moving back to India after the wedding," she said. "To be with my first love. I found Prem Prakash Pyarelal on the internet. We're both widowed now and want to spend the rest of our lives together."

My mind reeled with her revelation. All this time, Naani hadn't just been surfing the web on her phone. She'd been chatting with a man halfway across the world.

He fed me eggplant fritters, she told me. *The secret looks, the butterflies in my stomach, the half-empty bottle of perfume he slipped into my hands.*

"Dear God." Rachel Auntie slammed her palms on the table. Naani stiffened beside me. I sensed a mother-daughter showdown, but Rachel Auntie turned to Joseph Uncle instead.

"The whole world is pairing up, and here we are, sleeping in separate cabins. Enough is enough, Joseph. You're such a stubborn, stubborn man. Can't you see I'm miserable without you? You could sell popcorn or porn and it wouldn't make any difference to me. It's time to stop sulking. I've given you enough space to brood. You are loved, Joseph. I couldn't ask for a better man to go through the ups and downs of life. If you stopped feeling sorry for yourself long enough, you'd see that."

Before Joseph Uncle could respond, Isabelle jumped in.

"I'm sorry, Dad," she said. "I'm sorry if I made you feel I'm ashamed of what you do. You and Mom have treated me like a princess all my life. I've picked up more from the two of you than you might have wanted me to. Appearances have always been so important. Even when things are falling apart, you put your best face forward. I was painting my own faces on you, what I wanted everyone to see. All the while, I've been hiding my own truth from you." She took a deep breath and gripped Thomas's hand on the table. "I've converted to Greek Orthodox. Because I love this man. I love him more than whatever labels I was born with. He's strong and honest and sincere. No matter what surprises life throws our way, I know we can get through it together."

She glanced at George. This was Isabelle, accepting Thomas without his family's fortune, without the lifestyle she envisioned for them.

I could feel the speculation lift off the table—the weigh-ins that hover in the background whenever someone marries into money.

She smiled at Thomas. "Through thick and thin, baby."

The moment stretched out as Thomas averted his gaze. "Isabelle..."

Her smile disappeared at the tone of his voice. The air went still as she waited for him to continue.

"I knew," he said, so softly that I almost didn't hear. "I knew we were filing for bankruptcy."

Her hand fell away from his clasp slowly, fingers curling inward like a burned leaf. "You knew? You knew, and you kept it from me?"

"I was going to tell you after the wedding. I wanted to give you the kind of day you've always dreamed of, the kind that we planned to have all along. I couldn't take that away from you. The spark in your eyes when you look at me, like all your dreams are coming true—I never want to see it extinguished."

Everything funneled down to the two people who had brought us together that evening. We'd all fallen, one by one, like dominoes, and we watched as they teetered, the silence between them wobbling back and forth.

Then the one person I forgot about spoke up.

"I can't do this anymore," said Teri. "I was supposed to be the one getting married this month." She paused, feeling the weight of our stares. "I'm not married. I got a restraining order from my fiancé instead of this ring. I took it anyway." She flashed it before us. "I had to get out of there. When I saw the ad for a job on a luxury yacht, I doctored my resume up a bit. I figured the bride would want a married woman who's been through it all, right?" She glanced at Isabelle. "I'm sorry I lied. I can't be your maid of honor when everything reminds me of the wedding dress hanging in my own closet. I've made a mess of things. I need to head back home and sort things out. I quit."

Isabelle's gaze remained on her, steady and unwavering. She nodded, either at Teri's resignation or whatever dialogue was running through her head.

"It's okay," she finally said. "I won't be needing a maid of honor after all." Pushing her chair back, she stood and looked around the table. "The wedding is off."

CHAPTER TWENTY-NINE

THE WEDDING TOOK PLACE ON THE ISLAND OF HYDRA, IN THE SAME church where Thomas's father was baptized. Joseph Uncle didn't walk Isabelle down the aisle. In the Greek Orthodox tradition, the father accompanies the bride to the entrance of the church and the groom takes over from there. Hydra was a non-motorized island, so Joseph Uncle walked Isabelle all the way to church, through bougainvillea-drenched streets with no names.

Rachel Auntie and Dolly flanked Naani as she zigzagged her way up the stone-paved paths. I followed behind, while Fia ran up ahead, taking pictures of the bridal procession. A pair of minstrels led the way—one with a violin and the other with a lute. Turquoise views of the port glittered between stone walls. Salt-white houses rose from the hills ringing the amphitheater-shaped harbor. It was a bright, brilliant day for a wedding that almost wasn't.

"Ready?" Joseph Uncle paused as the church came into view. Thomas stood at the gate, holding a bouquet of flowers for Isabelle. "One last chance to reconsider."

"You're the best dad ever." Isabelle kissed him on the cheek. "I haven't been the easiest daughter, but you're still looking out for me. I wish Thomas didn't keep things from me, but I know in my heart his intentions were good. He really loves me, Dad. I can't keep rejecting his apologies. I can't imagine my life without him. We still have a lot of things to figure out, and I hope we do it as gracefully as you and Mom did over the years. You can let go now, Dad. I'll be all right."

Joseph Uncle nodded, too choked up for words as he handed

her over to Thomas. Rachel Auntie slipped her hand in his, and we followed them through the gates of the small, whitewashed church. Inside, ornate gold frescoes glowed in stark contrast to the simplicity of the exterior. The smell of burning candles hung heavy the air.

Isabelle and Thomas held hands as the priest recited prayers and placed twin crowns, connected by a ribbon, on their heads. The ceremony was somber, until the priest said something about how the wife should fear her husband. Isabelle stomped on Thomas's foot with a laugh. The small congregation cheered her on even as Thomas tried to playfully pin down her rebel foot.

"*Na Zisete!*" the guests exclaimed, after the priest invoked blessings and removed the crowns.

I handed out small bags of *koufeta*—sugar-coated almonds packed in odd numbers to signify the indivisible bond of marriage.

"If you slip this under your pillow tonight, you'll dream of the person you're going to marry," a guest informed me.

"I don't plan on sleeping tonight," I said. "I'll be up celebrating all night."

Truth was, the only person I reached for when I closed my eyes was Alex.

Nikos appeared by my side. With Teri gone, we were paired up once again as the best man and the maid of honor.

"Ready to go?" he asked.

"Lead the way." I smiled. We'd played each other in our own way, but something had solidified between us. Something had solidified between every person who'd been at the table on the final night. That last dinner had been a confessional booth—the thirteen of us, offering up our sins.

Under the rain of rice and rose petals, I looked at the faces of everyone present, one by one. Naani frowning at her phone, busy messaging PPP (my new name for her boyfriend as Prem Prakash Pyarelal was a mouthful). Beside her, Dolly laughed as Fia crouched on the steps—lens up, shoulders hunched—trying to capture the rice storm and protect her gear at the same time. George's phone rang in the chaotic swirl of pink and white. He looked at the screen and slid the phone back into his pocket. Kassia reached for his hand and squeezed.

I didn't know what awaited Thomas's parents when the creditors caught up to them, but the look they shared was of two people wanting to shut the world out for another day. Standing next to them, Joseph Uncle and Rachel Auntie beamed as Isabelle and Thomas turned to wave goodbye. From driving their baby girl home from the hospital to being bystanders at her wedding, they'd never stood together with more love and respect for the other.

Nikos and I walked Isabelle and Thomas through the church gates, to the narrow street outside.

"Congratulations, Mrs. Papadakis." I hugged Isabelle, feeling a rush of emotions for my cousin. Childhood memories. The games we made up. The pranks we played.

"You." She stepped back and held my hands. "It was meant to be you all along. I'm sorry about Teri. I can't imagine sharing my wedding day with anyone else by my side."

"You might change your mind." I picked the rice grains off her hair. "We still have the reception to get through."

"You're not going to topple off the stage again, Moti. I made sure there is no stage."

"You underestimate my propensity for disaster."

We laughed as Fia took candid shots of us.

"Isabelle?" Thomas nudged her toward the handsome horse waiting for her. "We need to get going."

"On that?" She wrinkled her nose. "I know the island has no cars, but I'm not leaving on a smelly donkey."

"It's a horse, and not just any horse. A bridal horse. Look how he's decorated with pretty flowers. He's even got a white cloth over his saddle. You ride, and I get to lead you through the streets and show off my new wife."

"No."

"Isab—"

"Uh-uh."

"Fine." Thomas handed her the bridle rope. "I'll ride. I'll be damned if we're going to let a single penny go to waste from now on."

"Fine."

They clip-clopped down the hill with Nikos and me trailing behind. The camera clicked as Fia captured the moment: Thomas on a bridal horse and Isabelle with a bouquet in one hand and the leash to her husband's horse in the other, pausing every few steps to dislodge her heel from the cobblestoned streets.

As people grinned and stopped to congratulate them, my eyes fell on the cobalt-colored harbor. Somewhere among the water taxis, the fishermen's boats and the line-up of stylish yachts, Captain Bailey was disbanding the crew of the Abigail Rose II.

The morning we anchored in Hydra, I'd taken Alex's phone and entered my details in it.

"What are you doing?" he asked.

"You said nothing permanent starts that way. It's something you invite to stay." I handed the phone back to him. "I'm inviting you to stay."

"This is lame," he said, scowling at the screen.

"Not exactly the reaction I hoped for."

"You know what I mean." He trapped me against the counter and nibbled on my ear. "Stay with me. The cruise is done, but we don't have to say goodbye just yet."

"I'm not saying goodbye, Alex. I'm only just saying hello to myself." Once the truth had bubbled up to the surface, I couldn't stop it. "I want to move out of the apartment I share with Dolly, get a place of my own. I want to take swimming lessons. I want to chase my dreams while you chase yours. And when the time is right, I want us to chase new dreams together."

Taking it slow was right for both of us. Alex had his letter of recommendation, the job on the Kiriakis charter, and a ferry to catch out of Hydra. Two weeks in Folegandros and he'd be off again, finally earning enough to save up for his dream restaurant on the water. But as I watched the ferries depart, knowing that Alex would be on one of them tonight, I wanted nothing more than to kick off my shoes, run all the way to the harbor and straight into his arms.

CHAPTER THIRTY

T HE WEDDING CEREMONY HAD BEEN A SOLEMN AFFAIR, BUT THE reception was the exact opposite. Held outdoors on a terrace hanging over the sea, it blazed with lights and music and merriment. No speeches or toasts, just eating and dancing and more eating.

Isabelle and Thomas had two first dances—the first to an Indian Bollywood tune and the second to Greek music. Everyone cheered and threw money as they danced. From the corner of my eye, I saw George slide his foot out from under the table and pull one of the bills toward him. Then he snagged another. On his third attempt, he jolted upright as if he'd been pinched hard by Kassia. They bent their heads together in a heated conversation while the guests took turns leading Isabelle and Thomas in circle dances.

"Moti," Rachel Auntie said, coming up to me.

"You don't think…" She looked at me with a familiar expression and then we both looked at Dolly. She was standing behind Naani's chair, deep in conversation with Fia.

We laughed. The chances of Dolly playing dead were slim, especially when she confessed to faking it all along.

Just then, Naani stood, her eyes wide and round. She clutched her chest and stumbled backward. Her chair fell back and hit the floor.

Rachel Auntie and I rushed to her side as Dolly and Fia caught her and lowered her to the ground. Naani was pale and she kept moving her lips, but no sound emerged.

"Naani," I said.

Her ashen face turned my way.

"Puh…" She pointed feebly toward something.

"*Paani?* You want water?"

I stood and reached for the jug of water on the table at the same time as Nikos. The first time I set eyes on his miniature extra thumb, I'd been getting water for Naani.

"Here." Nikos poured a glass. "Is she okay?"

My stomach lurched at the thought of losing her. I held the water to her lips, but she shook her head.

"Puh…" she said, attempting to get up this time.

"What is she trying to say?" Rachel Auntie cried. "You think she's had a stroke?"

"What's going on?" Isabelle joined the circle of chaos and clutched my arm. "What's wrong with Naani?"

An elderly man nudged his way through the crowd, calling, "Rosa? Rosa Rodrigues?"

Isabelle and I exchanged a look. How did he know her name?

He tried to kneel beside her, but the creak of old bones got in the way.

"Puh…" Naani whispered.

"Yes, sweetheart. It's me. I wanted to surprise you, but maybe it wasn't such a good idea. I couldn't put off seeing you any longer. Greece is closer to India than Chicago. So I thought, why not? I'm sorry if I startled you."

Puh… Puh… Puh.

PPP.

Prem Prakash Pyarelal.

Naani's first love. In the flesh.

We got her on a chair and let her catch her breath. "It really *is* you," she said. "I thought I was seeing things. You weren't replying to my messages. I thought something was wrong."

"You thought I'd croaked and my ghost had come to say goodbye?" He chuckled. "I was on the plane, *jaanu.*" He sat beside her and took her hand in his. "My God, it's good to see you."

Naani took in his bare, mottled scalp, the bright line of his dentures, his shiny suit. "It's good to see you too, *pyare*."

"There you are." One of the hostesses caught up with Naani's boyfriend. "So sorry," she said to Isabelle. "He slipped through when we weren't looking. Sir, please follow me out." Her tone was more pleading than authoritative. I wouldn't want to call security on a geriatric wedding crasher either. At least not without giving him some cake.

"It's all right," Isabelle said. "He can stay."

"Thank God." Dolly plopped on a chair after the hostess retreated. "You gave us such a scare," she said to Naani.

"*Saara drama kya tum pe hee chhod deh? Yeh to boori baat hain, na?*" Can't let you shoulder all the drama, can we? That would be unfair, right?

"*Abh jao tum sab,*" Naani went on. "*Niklo yahaan se. Tamaasha khatm.*"

Now leave us. All of you. Show is over.

We took the hint and dispersed, giving Naani some time alone with her *pyare*.

"You know, Moti," Nikos said. "The best man hasn't been fulfilling his duties tonight."

"Oh?"

"He hasn't asked the maid of honor to dance." He held out his hand. "Would she do me the honor?"

I smiled. "She would."

We'd barely joined Isabelle and Thomas on the dance floor when Nikos froze.

"You okay?" Thomas reached out to his friend.

Nikos gawked, his eyes fixed on something beyond Thomas's shoulder.

I swung around to see what had captured his attention.

Hannah.

She looked stunning in a fitted black dress, but it was the power-wattage of her smile that lit her up as she greeted Nikos, who continued staring at her.

"Thomas invited me," she said. "Mom's here, too." Captain Bailey waved as Hannah pointed her out.

"You mean she's okay? With this?" Nikos gestured between himself and Hannah.

"Don't know." Hannah shrugged, grinning. "But she came, so..."

"Well, let's go say hello. Excuse us. Moti? I promise to make it up to you."

I laughed. "Please, not another beach picnic. Go, good luck."

I danced with Isabelle and Thomas in a circle of well-wishers—twisting, turning, holding hands with people I'd never met before. Stars and string lights twinkled as the night bound us in a sparkling feeling of togetherness. It was bright and brilliant—an echo of another night among spinning strangers in Folegandros, when my eyes had played hide and seek with Alex.

I dropped out of the circle and lined up at the henna station.

"What kind of design would you like?" the lady asked.

"A star, on my wrist, please. But can you make it look like the letter A?" It was customary for the bride to hide her groom's initial in the intricate pattern of her henna. Dolly and Rachel Auntie told us if the groom didn't find it on the wedding night, he'd be dominated by his wife for the rest of their marriage. Isabelle and I smirked every time we heard the story. We knew it really meant no sex for him that night.

I waited for my henna-tattooed star to dry in a quiet corner of the deck. Bits of conversation drifted my way.

George stood by the bar, talking to Joseph Uncle. The ring-tube of underwear Joseph Uncle had intended for Isabelle and Thomas (the one he told her to get rid of after his gift-giving fiasco with her in-laws), hung like a wreath between them. Isabelle asked for it to be displayed at the reception. Joseph Uncle's chest swelled the moment he saw it.

"I think I can make it work," George said. "How soon can we set it up?"

"Give me a couple of weeks. I'll send you the catalog as soon I get back. Pick the ones you want and—"

"What do I know about underwear? Just ship me some of your best sellers. The movers and shakers, you know?" George wiggled his hips.

Oh God. Thomas's father is getting into the underwear business with Joseph Uncle.

"With my contacts and your experience, we'll conquer the islands." George held up his glass.

"To thongs and bikinis," Joseph Uncle said, as they clinked their drinks.

Um, my cue to exit.

I took the stairs leading down to the water. Leaving my shoes on the last step, I strolled down the narrow beach. The sand was damp and cool under my feet, the air crisp as it came in from the sea.

Something flashed in my face as I watched silver-tipped waves shimmer under the night sky. It disappeared when I turned toward it. My eyes went back to the water and the fleet of lights gliding over the horizon—a ferry leaving the port. Maybe Alex was on it. Maybe he'd left already.

It happened again—a soft glare on my face that disappeared before I could figure out where it came from. A passing boat? A strobe over the dance floor?

I turned my attention to the star on my wrist. It didn't look much like an A, but each of its five points stood for a month. Five months before I saw Alex again. We were going to make it work. And what better place to meet up than the CIA? The Culinary Institute of America's New York Campus. I smiled, thinking about how I was leaving Greece with so much more than I'd arrived with—so different from what I'd expected, and yet infinitely better.

When the annoying glint flashed over my eyes again, I swung

around to catch it. Every muscle in my body stilled. Then, a grin stretched across my face, so wide that I could feel it in my cheeks.

Alex. He stood by the stairs, angling a CD so the light reflected onto my face. I flew into his arms with a delighted whoop.

"What are you doing here?"

"I came to say goodbye." He scooped me up, his arms encircling my waist.

"We already said goodbye." I laughed as he nuzzled my neck.

"Isabelle invited me." His breath stirred goose bumps on my skin. "Plus, I wanted to give you something." He lay the CD down on the stairs and picked up a white cardboard box that was propped up next to my shoes.

"What is it?" I asked. It looked like a small takeout container.

"A final treat before I leave."

Music stopped blaring from the speakers. There was loud cheering, followed by a slow, smooth ballad.

"It's Isabelle and Thomas's last dance," I said.

The air between us grew tight. Alex lay the box back down on the steps and took me in his arms. It was our last dance too.

Our eyes held as we shuffled to the tune, the sand gritty between my toes. No fancy moves, no spins or turns—just Alex's lips brushing against my forehead, my chin on his shoulder, the swaying of our feet.

"Hey." Alex cupped my jaw, his thumb caressing my cheek. "It's a crime to be sad on a beautiful night like this."

"Not sad," I said. "Just quietly drinking you in. The night. The stars. The way you smell. The way you feel."

Left. Right. Left. Right. In time with the crashing and receding of the waves.

"Did anyone tell you how beautiful you look tonight?"

"You like me in a *salwar khameez*?" I wore the traditional combo of a long tunic and closely fitted pants, both in a deep shade of sapphire. My *dupatta* cascaded off one shoulder, the silver embroidery glittering against the blue.

The music stopped, but we ignored the clapping, the muffled voices, the creaking of the planks above us.

"I'm a terrible maid of honor for sneaking off," I said.

"You should be fired."

We laughed and continued swaying.

"I don't want tonight to end." I wrapped my arms around his neck.

"It doesn't have to." His lips stopped a hair's breadth from mine. "Change your mind." A soft kiss. "Come with me." Another brush of his lips.

"I thought we decided to take this slow."

"You decided. I just want to throw you over my shoulder and take you home."

"Five months." I chuckled as his teeth tugged at my ear lobe like they wanted to drag me away. "I'll see you in five months. You're going to be away for three of them anyway."

"I'm not away now." His lips parted mine in a slow, drugging kiss.

My mouth was still burning when he pulled away.

"I have to get going, Heart-Eyes."

I nodded, the lump in my throat getting bigger as he straightened my *duppata*.

"See me off?" He grabbed the backpack he'd left lying on the sand and reclaimed the box from the steps.

I put on my shoes and followed him up the stairs to the street level. The music had stopped, but the guests lingered on the terrace in the back. The street was quiet, the cobblestones reflecting the golden glow of streetlamps.

"Don't wait too long to open this." Alex handed me the take-out container.

"Okay." I kept my eyes on it. "Alex, I—"

"No. Don't say it. You just…" He swallowed and took a step back. "You just stand there and make heart-eyes at me, okay?"

I squeezed my eyes shut and nodded. When I opened them

again, he was walking down the street, his backpack bouncing with each step. He stopped a few streetlamps away and turned around.

"What?" I called out.

"Just checking," he said.

I laughed in spite of the distance growing between us. Of course, I was still making heart-eyes, eating up the way the light fell on his hair, the outline of his shoulders, his long, easy strides. I watched him get smaller and smaller, until he was almost beyond the curve of the hill. He turned around again and waved, walking backward, step by step, until he disappeared from view.

For a moment, the whole island went quiet. The night was emptier, and the air rushed away from me toward the shadows that Alex had melted into.

"Go." Someone slid something cool and solid into my hand. It was the handle to my suitcase.

I turned to find Dolly by my side.

"Go, *beta*," she said. "If you leave now, you can still catch him."

I stared at her. "Wha—"

"I haven't always been a good mother, have I? I built a wall and kept you on the other side. It's not that I didn't love you. I just never loved myself enough to let anyone in. But you… You always tried to break through, always tried to meet every expectation. You offered up your love, but it only reminded me of the choices I made.

"I did exactly what was expected of me, too. I walked the path my father laid out for me, even though it meant denying my truth. I was suffering, and I pulled you into the same cycle with me. It's time to break free, *beta*." She nudged the suitcase toward me. "*Ja*. Do it for both of us."

"But—"

"No buts. I asked Isabelle to invite Alex tonight. My God, the way he was watching over you while you slept. Like nothing else existed. We were all scared to cross him. *Maineh phaisala karliya*. I've decided. He is the one for you."

"He is?"

"*Haan*. Like I'd let you marry anyone else."

"But you always said it has to be someone with three thumbs."

"Of course it has to be someone with three thumbs. I'll die if you marry anyone else, or have you forgotten that part? But Alex already has three thumbs, *na*?"

"What are you talking about?"

"Look." She pointed behind us.

Naani was standing there, giving me a thumbs-up. "One," she said.

Beside her was Rachel Auntie, doing the same. "Two."

"Three." Dolly raised her own and stood beside them, all three thumbs in a row.

Three soul sisters passing on the baton, cheering me to take it and run as fast as I could toward my own happiness.

I looked toward the harbor. "I don't know if I'll make it in time."

"Over there." Rachel Auntie pointed to the bridal horse. "Quickly now."

The horse's handler, who had dozed off under the tree, opened his eyes as if alerted by a sixth sense. He blinked, unaccustomed to three generations of women stampeding toward him.

"I need your horse." I threw the strap of my evening bag across my body. "I have to get to the port."

"No, no." He grabbed the reins. "This horse must wait here for the bride."

"Listen, young man." Naani wagged her finger at him as Rachel Auntie and Dolly leveraged my butt, hoisting me onto the saddle. "This is an emergency."

"Emergency?"

"Yes," Dolly said. "My daughter has a man to catch. Now you either cooperate or you'll have to answer to the mother of the bride."

She shoved Rachel Auntie before him. He didn't look too

convinced, so she added, "The father of the bride too. And wait until the bride and groom hear about this."

"Okay, okay." He conceded. "But I have to go too, so I can bring the horse back."

"Well, go then." Dolly handed him my suitcase.

"Hurry," Naani said, as he led the horse down the street.

"Can't you go any faster?" Rachel Auntie called after.

"This is a show horse," the man said. "Not a racehorse. We'll get there. *Siga-siga.*"

I turned around when we got to the end of the street. Dolly, Naani, and Rachel Auntie stood like three colorful flags waving at me from the top of the hill.

I raised my hand in return and caught sight of the small white box trailing alongside my *duppata*. I'd secured Alex's takeout container to the end of my shawl before mounting the horse. Untying the knot, I opened the cardboard box, expecting to be wowed by one of his special midnight snacks.

Just like all the other times, I found a note, but this time, no snack. I unfolded the paper, holding it up to the streetlamps so I could read.

You said no to potatoes and pasta and bread, but you changed your mind about those.

I'm hoping you'll change your mind about this too.

I frowned. Nothing else was in the box.

No. Wait.

I fished out a ticket for the ferry he was taking out of Hydra. I glanced at the departure time and then at my watch.

"Excuse me, can we go a little faster?" I asked.

"Almost there. You enjoy the ride." He pushed a button and bright lights started blinking around us. His horse wasn't just a bridal horse. It doubled as a carnival of moving lights.

Neon hues bounced off the white-washed homes as we clip-clopped along the street. I glanced at my watch again.

Come on. Come on. I'm going to miss him.

The prolonged blast of a ferry horn spurred me into action. "I'm sorry." I grabbed the reins from the horse handler and gave the horse a little bump with my legs. "I have to go."

"Hey, stop!"

I shot him a contrite look as the horse sped up. "Sorry!"

In my head it was a graceful gallop, the mad dash, the romantic airport scene where the main character is jumping over all the barriers to intercept her love. In reality, it was a bouncy, jarring trot that rattled my bones. I held on for dear life as we approached the terminal.

One of the ferries was sliding out of the dock.

No. No. No. Nooo.

"Wait!" I pulled up, my heart jumping in my chest. "Come back." I waved my arms, trying to catch someone's attention.

I glanced at the clock over the ticket office and then back at the ferry.

Dammit. I just missed him.

Slumping in the saddle, I unclenched my fist and let my crumpled ticket slip away from my hands. The horse shifted under me as I fished my phone out of my evening bag.

Alex, I messaged.

Nothing. I connected to the terminal's Wi-Fi and tried again.

Alex.

I slid awkwardly off the horse and patted him.

My screen lit up: *I'm listening…*

My heart somersaulted with delight.

I stole something, I typed.

Heart-Eyes. Nooo. What?

Look toward the terminal.

My phone was quiet for a few ticks, and then it pinged again.

Is that you? You stole a mini disco?

It's a horse. I chased you down on a freaking horse. I just missed you.

LMAO. Only you.

"There she is." I swung around at the sound of the horse handler's voice. He was leading a small crowd toward me.

I love you, Alex wrote.

I bombarded him with heart-eye emojis. *Gotta go. I'm about to be lynched by a mob.*

I saw Isabelle, Thomas, George, and Kassia trailing behind the man.

My people, I thought. Dolly, Rachel Auntie, Naani, Joseph Uncle and the rest of the wedding party came into view. *I'll live to see another day.*

I handed the horse back to his owner and reclaimed my suitcase. "I'm so sorry for taking off like that."

"You missed the ferry?" Isabelle asked.

"I feel horrible for pulling you away from your reception."

"You didn't. We were on our way to the hotel. This..." She pointed toward the receding lights of the ferry. "You and Alex would've been the perfect ending to our day."

"What now?" Dolly asked.

I shrugged. "It's fine. I'll see him in a few months."

We faced the water together, our faces glowing with fluorescent hues from the disco horse, now being led away.

"Ah, well." Joseph Uncle put his arm around me. "It was a valiant effort, kiddo."

We turned away from the harbor, breaking into little groups. Isabelle and Thomas held hands as they led us back to the hotel. PPP steadied Naani as she zigzagged her way out of the terminal. I walked next to Dolly, a sense of ease settling between us. We weren't exactly strolling arm-in-arm, but a new equilibrium was in place.

My phone pinged.

Hey, Alex typed. *Where are you going? Next ferry is in an hour.*

I looked back at the ferry gliding over the horizon. Alex was probably still tracking the horse's lights across the harbor.

I laughed. "Guys. That wasn't the last ferry out of here."

"I love this part," said Fia. "You know…" She held out her hands like she was unrolling a banner. "But wait, there's more."

I grinned as everyone paused, their eyes on me. It wasn't just me reaching out for something bright and shiny. It was all of us, grabbing on to the skirt tails of life.

"Go get him, Moti." I didn't know who said it first, but then everyone was cheering me on as I ran toward the ticket office, the wheels of my suitcase hitting every bump and ridge along the way. The empty box still tied to the corner of my *duppatta* bounced against my leg as I raced up the window.

"One ticket," I said. "To wherever *that* ferry is going."

My phone pinged with another message from Alex.

You're still going the wrong way.

You're still following the horse I hijacked? I'm at the ticket office.

That's my girl. You just saved me from hijacking this ferry.

I grinned and accepted my ticket. It felt like the beginning of a new adventure.

In the distance, the colorful caravan of the wedding party wound its way back to the hotel. On the horizon, little lights shimmered over the water.

Alex, I typed, filled with a warm glow.

I'm listening…

I found a bench and sat, smiling at the screen, knowing he was doing the same.

EPILOGUE

THE NOTEBOOK HAD A BATTERED BLACK HARDCOVER AND A RED SPINE. Its original stitching barely held the dry, brittle pages together.

"I found it buried at the bottom of my mother's trunk," the woman sitting across from me said. "It's been a few years since she passed away, but I still get the occasional call from her clients. Māi kept notes on all her readings, but no one's ever asked to see them." Her bright, blackbird eyes shone with excitement. "When your *naani* said you were coming all the way from America, I searched everywhere for them."

"I can't believe I'm holding Ma Anga's notebook in my hands," I said.

"I knew I had to meet you the moment your grandmother told me your name. Your mother must have been Māi's biggest fan."

"Dolly certainly took Ma Anga's advice to heart." I paused as the waiter placed small round pieces of bread, wrapped in newspaper, on our table.

"From the gentleman there." He gestured toward the serving hatch separating the kitchen from the rest of the tea shack. Alex grinned back at me, his face peeping through the opening with an expression of pure delight.

"It's crusty on the outside and fluffy on the inside," he called. "You have to dip it in your tea. Go on." He made a dunking gesture. "So good."

"Don't mind him, Shilpa," I said. "He's like this whenever we're on a vacation. Every restaurant we go to, he ends up poking around in the kitchen."

"Well, he's right." Shilpa laughed and picked up her bread. "It's made for soaking up sweet, hot tea." She held one hand under her chin as she bit into it. "Would you like me to translate the entries in the book? They're in Konkani."

"That would be great."

Shilpa wiped her hands and searched the ink-speckled pages. "Ah, here we are. Dolly. You want me to start at the beginning?"

"Just the phone call Dolly made from Chicago after I was born, when she asked Ma Anga to interpret my natal chart."

Shilpa scrolled down the page before moving on to the next one.

"Hm." She frowned, a few pages later. "It's the last entry for Dolly, but…" She pulled out a faded envelope stored between the pages and continued reading. "It says Mãi canceled the session. Her dog died and she was too distraught to give a reading."

"That can't be right," I said. "Dolly repeated their conversation many times, ever since I was a kid, so I'm sure they talked."

"They talked, but just long enough for Mãi to make this entry." Shilpa scanned Ma Anga's writing, line by line. "We didn't have a landline at home back then, so Mãi went to the post office to take Dolly's call. She waited there for three hours because of a mix-up. When the call came, the connection was bad. She stayed on the line long enough to explain the situation. Then she went home."

"That's it?" I couldn't keep the disappointment out of my voice. I was in Goa to visit Naani. It had been three years since she moved to India to be with PPP. Telling her that Alex and I were getting married had been the highlight of my trip, but I also wanted to learn about the event that shaped so many years of my life.

"Not exactly," Shilpa said. "Mãi added it was a hot day. She drank three bottles of cola while waiting for Dolly's call and walked home with a full bladder. The envelope…" She peered inside before handing it to me. "It's the money your mother wired for the reading."

There were a few bills and a handwritten note inside.

"What does it say?" I passed it on to Shilpa.

"It's a reminder she owes Dolly a reading, minus the three Thums Up."

"The three what?"

"Thums Up. It's a cola drink. Māi had three Thums Up at the post office while she waited for Dolly's call."

"Three Thums Up." My ears perked. "Did Ma Anga say anything about the three Thums Up to Dolly?"

Shilpa glanced at the notes. "No, but Māi was meticulous about her bookkeeping, so if she was going to charge Dolly for the Thums Up, she might have."

"It doesn't add up." I sat back. "Even if Dolly misinterpreted part of their conversation."

"Hey." Alex joined us, reclaiming his chair. "What's with that look? Is there more to the reading than you bargained for?"

"The opposite," I said. "There's nothing at all. Not even the part where Ma Anga told Dolly to name me Moti."

"I assumed your mother named you Moti to honor Māi's loss," Shilpa said.

"I'm not sure I follow."

"Here." Shilpa unzipped her wallet and fished out a photograph. "This is Māi."

Ma Anga was a big woman with a big presence that spilled through the two-dimensional border of the photo. Shilpa pointed to the little white ball of fluff in her mother's armpit. "This is her dog, Moti."

"Her dog?" I said. "I was named after Ma Anga's dog?" My brows shot up and disappeared somewhere in my hairline.

"He was Māi's beloved companion through life. The pearl of her heart," Shilpa said.

"He wasn't even a *she*?" My voice was close to shattering the tea glasses. Then again, I just found out I was named after a dead poodle. With a penis.

"I'm sorry you're disappointed." Shilpa sniffed and put the

photograph away. "But let me tell you the story. Māi found Moti by the water, seven days after her mother passed away. He was a stray who'd been adopted by a group of cormorants—fishing birds. He thought he was one of them. He kept diving off the rocks, into the water. He wasn't a good swimmer, but no matter how many times he went under, he paddled back to the rocks and dove in again. Māi brought him home to keep him safe. He got her through the loss of her mother. They remained inseparable until he died. Māi was heartbroken when she lost him. She believed he was her soul mate."

Maybe it wasn't so bad being named after a fluff ball—a confused but venerated little fluff ball.

"Sounds like they were very close," I said. "What happened to him?"

"He drowned," Shilpa said. "We were on a ferry and he just… He jumped off. We think it was the birds diving into the water that set him off."

"Unresolved childhood issues," Alex said. "They'll get you every time." The laughter lurking around the corners of his mouth tipped into a full-blown grin.

"Let's see if I have this right," I said. "Ma Anga meets her canine soul mate, Moti, by the water, seven days after her mother passes away. Moti dies in the water years later. Ma Anga is grieving for him and cancels her long-distance reading with Dolly. She conveys this to Dolly over a bad telephone line. She might've also mentioned drinking the three Thums Up."

"Exactly what Ma Anga said, we'll never know, but Dolly came away with an entirely different message," Alex said. "Like a game of Broken Telephone."

"I wish I could give you more," Shilpa said. "I hope this was helpful. It's a long way for you to come and see me." She put Ma Anga's notebook away and glanced at her watch. "If there's nothing else, I should get going."

She stood and shook our hands.

Alex regarded me across the table after she was gone.

"What?" I asked.

"Nothing." But his mouth twitched like he was dying to say something.

"Spit it out," I said as we left the tea shack and walked under the shady trees to our rental scooter. "You know you want to."

He straddled the seat and leaned in, running his finger along my jaw. "Dude, you were named after a dog who thought he was a bird."

I folded my arms and counted to five. Sure enough, the indent in his cheek deepened into a full-blown dimple. We'd met eight times over the last three years and each time that damned dimple made an appearance, my heart flipped for him all over again.

I mounted the scooter and wrapped my arms around his waist. "Dude, you named your restaurant after a girl, who was named after a dog, who thought he was a bird."

Alex's dream had turned into reality, in the same spot he'd taken me swimming for the first time in Folegandros. A hotel was being constructed across the bay then, but the deal had fallen through. When the property came up for sale, Alex snapped it up and opened his restaurant: Moti On The Water.

The name was a play on its meaning in Hindi—a pearl on the waters of the Aegean Sea.

Now it was about a dead poodle.

Alex's laughter rippled through the air as we took off, along palm-fringed roads and endless rice paddies, the wind in our hair. Goa in the monsoon was gray and lush. Waterfalls trickled down emerald hills as we passed spice farms and sleepy fishing villages.

"Look." Alex pulled over and pointed to the stretch of golden sand by the road. "Are those what I think they are?"

I squinted, but the sun was low in the horizon and directly in my eyes.

"I'll be right back." Alex took off for the beach and returned with a bright, diamond-shaped kite. "Come on. It's not going to fly itself."

I smiled, falling into step beside him. It was exactly the kind of thing Alex did—stop and take a great big bite out of life.

The beach was empty, except for a group of kids, with their eyes trained skyward.

"Did you take one of their kites?" I said.

"I paid good money for it." Grinning, he handed me the spool, climbed on a rock, and held the kite up. "Ready?"

I couldn't remember the last time I'd flown a kite. I took a step back when Alex let go, keeping the line taut between me and the kite. For a moment, it floundered, nose-diving toward the ground. Then the wind caught, and the spool unraveled.

Laughter floated from my throat as the kite soared upward. I pulled back on the line, keeping the tension and letting it climb until it was flying high. Jubilation engulfed me as I watched it turn and pull and dance.

I was connected to the sky, the wind, the soft light filtering through the clouds.

Alex hugged me from behind and I leaned into him, recalling the star-speckled night on his roof.

What's your favorite childhood memory? he asked.

Flying a kite.

"You remembered," I said.

"I'm always listening, Heart-Eyes."

I laughed and kicked off my shoes, my heart soaring as high as the kite.

"Guess what?" I flew barefoot over the sand, letting the string out until the kite was nothing more than a tiny diamond in the sky. "I can swim, and now I can fly."

"You and the poodle you were named after," Alex called, as I ran along the water. "Both freaking delusional."

He charged down the beach after me, our footprints melting into the waves as the sun dipped beyond the seam of the horizon.

THE END

ACKNOWLEDGEMENTS

To all the readers, bloggers, and countless people who make it possible for me to live this dream—thank you for your love, for your energy, and for pushing me to be better with each novel. None of this would be possible without you. All the heart-eyes in the world for you!

Thank you to my smart, witty editor, Suanne Laqueur, who is also an extraordinary writer. Having you edit this book was an honor and a privilege.

Hang Le, you made my cover dreams come true again. You and me forevers, baby!

Elena @elenasbookblog—your input on the Greek aspects of this story were invaluable. Thank you for lending Moti authenticity, and for doing it with so much love and enthusiasm.

Cat Porter, Pauline Digaletos, Kate Steritt—my sincere appreciation for your help in perfecting this book before it went out.

Stacey Blake of Champagne Book Design—you are a gem for going above and beyond the scope of formatting. Eternally grateful for your patience, professionalism, and attention to detail.

Many thanks to Jenn Watson and the entire team at Social Butterfly PR for loving this book and making sure it got out there.

Christine Estevez, thank you for giving Moti a final polish, and for your unwavering support and friendship.

Heather Orgeron, Tracey Jerald, Sydney Parker, and all the early readers—my heartfelt gratitude for taking the time out of your busy schedules and sharing your thoughts.

Soulla Georgiou, in case it's not abundantly clear, I'm grateful for you every single day. Your friendship lights my path.

Nina Gomez, you inspire me with all that you do. Thank you for braving pigeons for me.

To the incredible tribe of women whose paths I've been fortunate enough to cross—Amoa, JoDo, KitKat, Michelle Kannan, Alissa Marino, Miria Ardizzi, Wendy LeGrand... It's impossible to name you individually. You remind me, time and time again, of how blessed I am to be a part of this incredible community. I adore you!

A million thanks to all the ladies of Leylaholics Book Nook. Your kindness carries me from start to finish.

To my husband and son, thank you for understanding when I retreat into my writing cave, and for loving me even when I emerge a zombie. You are my pillars, my sunshine, my resting post.

ALSO BY LEYLAH ATTAR

Mists of the Serengeti

The Paper Swan

53 Letters for My Lover

From His Lips

ABOUT THE AUTHOR

Leylah Attar is an award-winning *New York Times, USA Today*, and *Wall Street Journal* bestselling author of contemporary romance and women's fiction. Her novels draw on a colorful tapestry of influences. Currently residing in Toronto, Leylah writes stories about love—shaken, stirred, and served with a twist.

Connect with Leylah Attar:

WEBSITE: www.leylahattar.com

FACEBOOK: www.facebook.com/leylah.attar

INSTAGRAM: @leylah.attar

TWITTER: @leylahattar

Made in the USA
Columbia, SC
26 February 2021